MEN OF EVIL MIND

BOOKS BY BONNIE CALLAHAN

REMY VS. ROME

ROAD OF STARS AND FLAME

ON PRINCIPLE

MEN OF EVIL MIND

MEN OF EVIL MIND

This book is a work of fiction. Names, characters, places, and incidents are either the product of the author's imagination or are used fictitiously, and any resemblance to actual persons, living dead, business establishments, events, or locales is entirely coincidental.

FIRST EDITION

Cover design by Gia Thompson
GIACREATIVE.CA

ISBN 979-8-9860846-5-7

For Kate, and all the ghosts we carry with us.

I love you.

(And I'm still sorry about your tooth.)

MEN OF EVIL MIND

Ten Years Ago

AT THE ROCKY EDGE of the river, the girl—light brown hair hanging below her ribs and crimped from the braids he'd just watched her undo—pressed a hand to her soft belly. The strings of her pale blue bikini were knotted messily at her back and hips, with one of her earbuds dangling free from her ear. The hint of too-loud pop music floated to where he stood close by, hidden among the trees and dense summer shrubs, though the angry flash of water drowned out most of the sound.

The summer rains had swollen the river, and it battered against its banks in bursts of white. The girl stood on a large flat rock that jutted over the stream, the stone slick with water and glaring in the afternoon sun. The buttery, sweet scent of tanning oil reached him as she sprayed her golden legs.

Stepping into view, he cleared his throat. The girl swung her head up, her deep brown eyes, ingenuous like a cow's, widening and creasing at the corners as her smile spread. He was beside her in a few short steps, the river raging just inches from their feet. He reached for her, his smile mimicking the girl's, and his hand clasped her shoulder.

She peeped in surprise at the firmness of his fingers, and his smile grew broader as hers faded into confusion.

He tightened his fingers against her bare skin, the bones shifting under his touch. She reared away from him, one foot sliding toward the water as it slipped against the stone. Desperately, she reached for his shirt, leaning into the hand that he had seized her with to keep from falling.

In the distance, the sound of a car door slamming shut echoed through the low hills, and they both turned their heads toward the noise. Much closer, a stick cracked among the trees. He hauled the girl into his chest, her feet finding purchase, and ran the back of his fingers up her bare arm as he listened.

There was a rustle, a soft grunt, and he laughed at his good luck when a tusked creature wandered out from the tree line, followed by two striped piglets. The girl laughed, too, until his fingers stilled.

He grinned as he dug his hand into her hair, covering her mouth with the other as he forced her back again with his body, back to the edge of the stone. Her fists felt like bird wings as they beat against his chest, nothing but hollow bones and soft echoes of air. He tilted his head, studying her eyes and the strange ways that fear contorted her pretty features. The sudden angularity of her cheeks and brows, skin stretched tight over her skull in agitation. The gaping hollows of her nostrils.

He wanted to see her mouth—the twist of panic.

He wanted to hear her scream.

He glanced around the riverbank once more, then dropped his hand from her mouth, rubbing his thumb along her plump lips, down her chin, and to her belly. He kept his voice low as he told her why he'd come and what happened to girls like her.

She gaped, stupid and frozen, her mouth whispering his name. She was begging, and the desperation disgusted him.

What a disappointment.

He sighed, releasing his hand from her hair.

A blur of summer-tanned limbs, followed by a splash, the sound dulled by the roiling waves. He shaded his eyes against the sun and saw her water-darkened head bobbing amongst the rapids like a shadow.

He kicked the bottle of tanning spray in after her—satisfied when the girl disappeared at last beneath the swells—and walked away, her pink towel absorbing the sound of his footsteps on the stone.

1

THE TRAIN CAR SMELLS like death. Not in a hyperbolic, someone-took-their-tennies-off-and-it-reeks sort of way, but like actual oily, thick, hot death. The kind of stink that settles, heavy, in your nose and on your skin. The kind that makes you recoil on instinct. That makes some primordial part of your brain scream: *run*.

I just hope the well-groomed businessman I'm sitting beside doesn't think that smell is coming from me.

I know it's not coming from *him*. The first-class Intercity train cabin is pure luxury. Edoardo wanted to send a private car to collect me at the airport since he couldn't make it down from Florence. Much to his chagrin, I jumped in an unmarked cab to Termini instead, hoping to make it in time to catch the 6:15 pm train for Orvieto. Traveling first class was a compromise.

And by compromise, I mean that Edo purchased the ticket and emailed it to me while I was still trying to get my luggage out of the cab. In this case, his generosity was appreciated. I barely made it onto the train without the struggle of fighting with a ticket machine.

The extra wide first-class seat is especially appealing after sitting between two strangers on the thirteen-hour flight to Rome. I'm so exhausted that even the smell of carrion circulating through the vents couldn't keep me from passing out. I set the alarm on my phone and text Matteo to call me if he hasn't heard from me by seven.

After smearing some very minty lip balm on my lips to help temper the stench, I twist my hair into a braid and wrap the scarf from my carry-on around my neck, using it to cover my face before closing my eyes. I'm drifting right on the edge of sleep, gazing over that much-dreamt-of precipice, when someone starts shouting.

I pull the scarf down to my chin, fighting against the impossible weight of my eyelids to see what is happening. A few rows ahead, an older woman lays into the ticket inspector. He gives her the *stai calma* hands, an Italian variant of the calm down gesture, and then opens her window with more pomp than necessary. The wind rushes in hard and warm, smelling even worse than what we've been breathing for the past thirty minutes. Half the train car audibly gags, and the inspector slams the window shut as a chorus of complaints rings through the cabin.

The smell is too much for people wearing fancy suits to take. I agree. No one should be subjected to the smell of putrid flesh against their will.

But I'd also love to squeeze in a little nap.

"Something probably just crawled into the air vents and died," I mumble. The man next to me turns and stares at me like I'm crazy—snuggled up and half asleep while the passengers revolt around us.

"No one should spend this much time so close to death," he says, his accented voice muffled by the hand he's holding over his nose, as if the fetor can't worm its way through his fingers. "It's bad for you."

I shrug—in disagreement, but he doesn't need to know that. I've seen my fair share of death, and not just because I spent the past five years as a nurse in hospice. Being close to death won't hurt you. Not in the way he means.

But in his defense, the smell is really awful.

The echo of my Grandma Miriam's voice plays in my head: *The dead are* always *close, Victoria*. My fingers find the last red string she tied around my wrist and twist it tight against my bones, the strand pressing into my skin.

The man's eyes follow the movement, and I drop my hand, laughing at myself just loud enough to guarantee he will now think I'm completely nuts.

A voice comes over the intercom, asking all passengers to take their seats. The ticket inspector comes through the cabin again, locking the bathroom doors from the outside and telling everyone to remain seated. Someone gets up to follow him into the next train car, demanding information, and we all watch as the passenger bangs on the glass window after discovering that this door, too, has been locked.

Then, within seconds of being caged in, everyone on the train is standing, and the man on the intercom can insist all he wants that we need to get our asses in our assigned seats, but it appears I'm the only one who is going to listen.

We enter a tunnel, and the darkness feels cold despite the warm, early fall weather. I shiver and pull the scarf tighter, watching fluorescent lights blaze to life past the windows. The noise of the engine echoes against the walls and back into the carriage like we've suddenly hit warp speed. Then, for a moment, nothingness as our foul-smelling train slows on the far side of the tunnel and emerges back into the world.

Police lights replace the stark incandescence of the tunnel. The sound of sirens is muted but persistent against the hum of the passengers and the clanking of the wheels. The train comes to a sudden stop, and everyone is thrown forward.

I bet they wish they'd been sitting now.

But instead of calming down, the passengers press their faces against the glass on the left side of the train, sickly blue light streaming over their features.

"Orte," someone says, and I relax again—this is our first and only stop before Orvieto. I'm less than an hour from my home away from home.

That *will be* my home now. For a while, at least, depending on what happens with Edo's job in Florence. Depending on what happens with us, so close after two years of long distance.

I yawn as I stand and join the others at the window across the aisle, surprised by the number of police officers and emergency responders bustling around the platform. The intercom crackles back to life, and I startle.

"All passengers are requested to remain silent and in their seats with their tickets and identification ready for inspection. Please place bags at your feet and keep your hands where they are visible," a woman tells us, first in Italian and then in English.

A current of suspicion, charged and humming and edging at our heels, stalks the passengers back to their seats. I hustle to mine. People peer at each other from the corners of their eyes—some whisper. The man I've been sitting beside gives me an appraising look and shifts ever so slightly toward the far side of his seat like this is all somehow my fault.

I text Matteo that I'm likely going to be late. I apologize for holding his evening hostage, even though that's precisely what the train is doing to me. The man beside me leans in to read my messages, his curiosity overcoming his misgivings. I smile at him because the only thing I have to hide is the illegal edibles I brought on the plane in hopes of catching a few winks.

Two men in uniform board our train car, and despite the polite request made by the woman on the intercom, *no one* remains silent. Their hands are definitely visible, though, as they point and wave and communicate a universal *what the fuck*.

The process of questioning the passengers is slow. The officers work their way from the front of the car to the back, fielding as many questions as they ask. I'm near the middle of the car and find I'm getting increasingly fidgety the closer the men get—the same negative rush that comes from walking out of a store without buying anything or driving with a cop behind you.

My hands shake when I pass the officers my documents, and the shorter of the two narrows his eyes at my face.

"Victoria Jacobs?" he asks, lining my passport photo page up with my real-life face, which seems unfair after so much travel. I tug the scarf loose so he can see me better.

"Yes."

He examines the photo again and nods. "Final destination?"

"Orvieto. I have friends there. But I just flew into Rome today," I tell them, and my voice sounds squeaky and dishonest. Luckily, the new stamp in my passport that corroborates my story does the rest of the speaking for me, and they move on to the man beside me, whose documents they barely glance at.

It is 7:42 pm by the time they tell us our car is cleared, and we are all invited to exit the train.

"But," I stammer to the guy beside me. "How will I get to Orvieto?"

He's on his phone and ignores me as he gathers his things, ready to high-tail it out of the death-infused train car. I let out a long, slow exhale, the dampness collecting in the folds of my scarf and against my skin, and stuff everything back into my backpack. Whatever. I'll take the next train. Or I'll sleep on a bench.

I don't care.

I'm just so tired.

After waiting for the train to empty, I maneuver my luggage and carry-on out of the tight storage space by the bathrooms. I'm hauling the oversized wheely suitcase out the door, wondering if it could double as a bed, when I hear someone call, "Tori!"

I swing my head around and shut my eyes against the frantic, wandering beam of an overpowered police flashlight. My lids are resistant to opening again, caught in the world's longest blink, but the thrill of knowing that when they do, I will see one of my favorite people fills my blood with just enough of a jolt to keep me from falling asleep standing up.

"Matty," I cry out, dropping my belongings and staggering into his arms.

I have known Matteo Graziano practically since I was born—and I spent the better part of twenty years in love with him. Our mothers are best friends, and his sister, Tibi, is my best friend. He was always the off-limits (and, to be fair, uninterested) older brother. Dirty blonde curls and a shy smile. A body that made thirteen-year-old me turn into a stammering, blushing fool. And the kindest heart.

Now, he's kind of my best friend, too. Or at least, I like to think so. He appears to be here to rescue me, after all.

"How are you?" he asks. His golden-brown eyes are dark in the sparse overhead light, but I can feel them on me, hunting for an answer I'm not ready to give.

"Sleepy." I step out of his arms and glance back at the tracks. The officers have flashlights and are searching the undercarriage of the train. "How did you know to come to Orte?"

He reaches down for my carry-on and swings the strap over his shoulder. "I was following your train on the app."

"I feel bad that you drove all the way down here," I say, collecting my scarf from where it's puddled on the concrete. "I could have—"

He raises his eyebrows. "Could have what? Camped out at the station for the night?"

"If I had to."

"Your mother, my mother, Tibi...Edoardo. They would all kill me if I let that happen. Besides, I was looking forward to seeing you." He gives me a gentle nudge before grabbing the handle on my suitcase and pulling the heavy canvas bag off my shoulder. Usually, I'm not one for chivalry, but today is the exception. First, the train ticket from Edo; now Matteo towing all my stuff to the car. Some battles aren't worth fighting.

I follow him down the concrete platform, staying outside the yellow line but close enough to the train to see people inside the illuminated cabins still being questioned. Close enough to see the officers on the tracks.

"Hey," he says, drawing my attention back. He studies my face and then smiles. "You look good, Tor."

I try to disregard the way he can still make my cheeks hot and the fact that he's lying. I wonder what my mom has told them all.

"You don't look too bad yourself," I say, keeping my tone as cheeky as possible. Matteo also happens to be Edoardo's *actual* best friend. "New haircut?"

"Yep." He musses his curls with his free hand. "Just got it cut this morning."

"Let me guess: you have a Hot Young Vintners of Italy calendar shoot coming up," I tease. "I hope you got a good month."

Before he can respond, a woman yells from the tracks near the front of the train, her voice urgent. *"Ho trovato qualcosa." I found something.*

I shudder, knowing all too well that there are a lot of ways death can look. And after this summer, I'm not interested in seeing more.

Three days, the coroner had estimated, from the time of death to the moment I found Grandma Miriam, face up on the ground beside her bed. I was three days late. Four, if you count the call the night before it happened, the rumble of Tums against plastic in the background as she casually mentioned a sour stomach.

It was the first time a dead body ever made me vomit. I quit my job, hoping it would also be the last.

Matteo, who knows why I was eager to leave San Diego, rests a hand on my back and steers me toward the parking lot, where

I take a deep breath of fresh, clean air filled with hints of heat and autumn. Not an inkling of bodily decay.

"Thanks for coming to get me," I tell Matteo through another yawn as he opens the door of his Alfa Romeo for me. Behind him, the blue lights of the police cars dance in the leaves of the chestnut trees that line the parking lot. His face is in shadow, but I still see his mouth widen in a smile.

He pets my head, running a hand down the length of my braid. "Try to rest," he says before shutting the door and leaving me in the perfect, quiet, sweet-smelling darkness of his car.

2

I STRUGGLE TO OPEN my eyes when Matteo shakes my shoulder. "We're here, Tor," I hear him say, his voice distant and dreamlike. I can't even muster a grunt in response.

I passed out as soon as Matteo started the engine in Orte.

Maybe he will let me keep sleeping if I don't move. He can park and leave me, and since this is small-town Italy, I won't have to worry about being abducted or worse. I can just stay right here cuddled up in—my lashes flutter as I survey the soft thing keeping me warm—Matteo's jacket.

The temperature has fallen since we left Orte, and if I'm under his jacket, and he's outside...I finally force my eyes open and see a short-sleeved Matteo rubbing his hands over his bare arms. There's no way all that lean muscle is keeping him warm.

"I already carried up the luggage. Should I take you up next?" Matteo asks, propping a hand on the top of the car door.

I laugh, a dry, tired sound. "Sorry I didn't help," I say as I wiggle out of the car, passing Matteo his jacket when I stand. The car door can only open about a foot and a half, tall tufo walls rising on either side of the sloping, cobblestone street. A light jutting out of the wall up ahead, stretching over the street on an ornate cast iron bracket, bathes everything in hushed gold.

Matteo leads me to a gate set into the wall that opens to a set of stairs. We have to go up one at a time; the stairs are barely a single-person wide, but he stretches his hand behind him for me to cling to. How did Matteo manage my massive luggage? Each step is awkwardly tall, making me feel a little drunk as I try to navigate them without falling on my face, letting Matteo drag me upward.

We land on a small patio. A light by the door has been left on, the half-moon sconce casting an incandescent arc over a bottle of wine and two glasses on a round wooden table. The rest of the apartment's exterior is hard to make out.

"I love it," I say, taking in what I can of my new home. I walk over to the table, grab the bottle, and turn it around to check the label: Graziano Vineyard's award-winning Orvieto Classico vintage. My eyes widen, and I gape at Matteo.

He smiles.

"Did you have this here just waiting for me?"

He comes over and takes the bottle from my hands. "I can put it in the fridge if you're too tired."

I cross my arms. "I will never be too tired for a glass of the best wine in Umbria."

"In *Italy,*" he corrects, with that same shy smile I've always loved. "At least according to *Vino* magazine's Tomasso Delinquente. But it should be chilled."

"Pop it in the freezer while I splash some water on my face."

"Will do. But don't brush your teeth. Mint and grechetto are a disgusting combination."

I run my tongue over my teeth, gritty and gross after hours of travel. "I'll keep these bad boys nasty just for you." I grin at Matteo and then step into my first, very own Italian apartment.

The downstairs is small but functional—exactly what I was looking for. There is a living room with one too many couches, a four-person dining room table, a well-stocked liquor cabinet in the corner, and a tiny kitchen partially hidden behind a yellowing lace curtain. To my right is a winding white marble staircase.

About halfway up the short flight of stairs, I pause. A shallow alcove in the wall bears the home's mandatory portrait of Padre Pio—his gray beard and bald head fading in tones of sepia against an artificial purple background. Tchotchkes are lined up along the edge: origami swans, seashells, a single earring, and behind it all is a painting, crude and unpolished. I bend to take a better look at the artwork: the silhouette of a woman who, despite being painted entirely in black, appears to be screaming, her face contorted, as she walks out of the misty woods. I shiver and keep walking, flipping on all the upstairs lights as soon as I reach them.

Matteo has placed my things in the larger of the two bedrooms. I dig out my deodorant and swipe under each arm, then brush my travel-knotted hair before washing my face in the bathroom. The hall is small and narrow, just like the street below and the stairs up to the apartment. The door to the second bedroom is directly across from the bathroom. The hall light brightens the blue walls and the decorative strip of teddy bear wallpaper that rings the room. I close the door before heading back downstairs.

"What's with the painting on the landing?" I ask, pushing back the lace curtain to join Matteo in the kitchen.

His jaw tightens for a moment, his features hardening as he runs the point of his knife along the casing of the salami and asks, "What painting?"

I laugh. "The really fucking scary one."

He looks over his shoulder, nodding toward the rest of the house. "To be fair, the entire house is filled with pretty questionable art."

"How'd you find this place?" I ask, sidling up beside him at the counter. He's slicing the salami onto a plate. On the label, I read the word *cinghiale*—wild boar. I reach past him for another knife and start cutting a wedge of pecorino.

"A girl I knew grew up here. Her dad rents it out now, usually to study abroad students. He's happy to have a mature adult living here for a while."

"Who is this mature adult you speak of?" I ask, pointing the knife at him. "A roommate you failed to mention?"

"Tor, you've basically been an adult since you were twelve." He looks at me, his expression so thoughtful I'm forced to hip-check him into the refrigerator.

"Grab the bottle, and let's toast to my new adventure." I pick up the plate of charcuterie we've been preparing and head out onto my patio. Matteo arrives a second after me, and we both gaze up into the sky, the stars bright between ribbons of dark clouds.

He glances at me. "I'm glad you're here."

I smile up at him, then set the plate down. "It's nice to be back."

Matteo pulls out a wine opener, slicing the foil along the bottle's lip in one smooth motion. "You know, Mom would love to have you stay with her and Dad if this place doesn't turn out to be the right fit."

I haven't lived with another person since my first year of college; even before that, my parents were away so often that I spent a lot of time alone. I don't plan to impose more on the Graziano family than I already have.

"This place is perfect," I say, ignoring the way the hairs on the back of my neck seem to rise ever so slightly when I peek at the upstairs windows.

"Good." Matteo lifts his full glass, looking at me over the moisture-clouded rim. "Welcome home, *patatina.*"

The nickname makes me laugh. Patatina *can* be a term of endearment, but in this case, it is an almost twenty-year-old joke—at my expense—that the Graziano family will not let die.

All because one time, while spending a week at the beach in Rimini, I offered Tibi my *patatina* when she complained hers was covered in sand. Only I was talking about my potato chip, and she was talking about her lady bits.

I clink my glass against his. He watches me, eyes still and expectant, as I take a deep drink, his own glass still hovering between us.

"Oh my god," I all but moan, wiping a dribble of white wine off my lip. "This is delicious."

"Are you sure you got any in your mouth?" He reaches out a knuckle to swipe a drip from my chin.

I raise my glass again, narrowing my eyes as I tip it against his, and then proceed to run it directly into my front teeth. I whimper.

He bites down on his smile. "Have they outlawed cups in California since I last saw you? You seem out of practice."

"You should probably just hand me the bottle."

He stacks some cheese and salami on a slice of local bread and holds it up for me. "Eat something first?"

I wrap my fingers over his and lean in to take a bite of Matteo's makeshift sandwich, jumping and dropping my hands as a resounding laugh fills the small patio. I stand quickly, scooting my chair farther from Matteo's with my foot as Edo steps into the edges of the light. He is grinning his huge, friendly grin, eyes the brightest blue against his still summer-tan skin. Edo is unconcerned, as always, as he takes in his girlfriend and best friend.

He walks up to me, scooping me into his arms. "Surprise, *amore mio,*" he whispers against my ear—another nickname, this one less creative but just as lovely.

"I didn't think I'd see you until tomorrow," I say, burying my nose into his neck as he lifts me off the ground.

His lips graze my jaw. "You know I couldn't wait that long, Victoria."

I wrap my legs around his waist as he lifts me. When our mouths meet, I am suddenly very awake and not at all hungry.

Edo moved to Orvieto from Genoa with his mom during his last year of high school. His father, another Edoardo Mazza in a long line of men bearing the same name, is a politician. And a duke, or a count, or a marquis. I can never remember which. Edo is, by default, also Italian royalty. But he rarely brings it up, though his look is terribly aristocratic.

Growing up, Matteo was always the heartbreaker of Orvieto, the gorgeous bad boy with a good heart, and like any wise man anticipating a threat, he took Edo, then quiet and reserved, under his wing.

And what a team they made: Matteo with his floppy curls and gold-rimmed glasses, Edo with his black hair, blue eyes, and dimpled cheeks. Two teenage playboys nobody could stay mad at. No young woman in the entire green heart of Italy was safe.

Including me, clearly.

Matteo jiggles his car keys, and we both turn to him, breaking a kiss that leaves me breathless and disoriented.

Edo sets me down and tugs me in close to his side. "Thanks for picking Victoria up for me. They've been keeping me late at the office. I hope it wasn't an inconvenience."

The words cause a flush of unreasonable disappointment at the suggestion that Matteo was only here at the behest of Edo.

Matteo catches my eye. "It was my pleasure," he says, offering a quick, soft smile.

"Here," Edo says, digging a hand into his jacket pocket, "let me pay for your gas."

A look of annoyance flashes across Matteo's face, his lips tight with a suppressed sigh. "That's not necessary. You two enjoy your evening," he says, turning towards the stairs.

"Thanks for the wine," I start to call after him. "It's—" but Edo's hands are already in my hair, and he's backing me into the apartment—and who am I to say no to a good bedding down after five months apart?

3

My dreams are strange, which isn't unusual these days, but I do manage to squeeze in three decent hours of rest before Edo kisses me on the forehead and works the covers out from where I've twisted them between my legs. He pulls the soft blanket up to my shoulders, whispers that he loves me and will return to Orvieto as soon as possible, and tiptoes out of the room.

I smile, snuggling down into the bed. The air beyond the covers is infused with the promise of autumn, and the sheets hold the memory of Edo. Despite the strangeness of the last few months, I feel excited. Maybe, for a little while at least, my purpose in life doesn't have to be predicated on anything more than being here, in a place I love, with people I love.

A familiar chill runs up my spine, like the brush of fingers along my back, a long exhale on bare skin.

The people you love never leave you, I hear my grandma's voice whisper, and I pull the covers over my head, yawning away a shudder. I doze for a couple of hours, lazing amongst the images that rise unbidden to the forefront of my consciousness when I lower my defenses in rest: My twin sister, Alex, the last time I saw her alive—our final goodbye the pained, forced twitch of her index finger. The oily, untouched tea in a chipped San Diego Zoo mug on Grandma Miriam's bedside table.

My mother, renowned psychiatrist and podcast queen Meg Lancaster, constantly reminds me that there are medications that can help with that. She sends me links for Pexeva and Alodorm and Anafranil, with little asides about how this one will do the trick. Then she will call me and start on about how her patient was just like me, and now they are *cured!*

But I don't necessarily want to say goodbye to the things I see, the memories that cling close to the surface, always waiting to emerge in that limbo between consciousness and sleep. In many ways, they are the closest I can get to what I've lost.

When the calls of neighbors up and down the street and the screams of a frustrated child flood the bedroom alongside the blazing sun, I stretch my arms above my head and reconcile myself to wakefulness.

Blinking at the brightness, I pad my way to the open window, shutters thrown wide, and wonder why the hell Edo would unlatch the windows before leaving. But the day promises to be gorgeous. Below, my little patio is a quintessential Italian tableau in the daylight. Two unfinished wine glasses glitter in the sunshine, Matteo's bottle of award-winning Classico between them. The breadbasket, meat and cheese board, and corkscrew—cork still attached—are arranged so perfectly before them, the definition of the shadows on the floral tablecloth so certain, that it looks like a painting. A still life. The perfect Renaissance triangle captured through my window frame.

I leave the windows open and throw on a sweater before wandering downstairs, grabbing the open door to the teddy bear room to shut it as I pass.

On the stairs, my eyes snag again on the painting on the landing. It is the antithesis of the view from my bedroom window and even more off-putting this morning than last night, the details more vivid and menacing. The sky is reminiscent of a mottled bruise, uneven purples and blues filling the background of the small canvas. Everything else is painted in black, rough and so thick that the trees are three-dimensional, extending from the image like embodied shadows.

Not the girl, though. She is flat and faceless. But she is definitely screaming.

I delicately move the painting behind the portrait of Padre Pio.

The art in the living and dining area isn't much better. Art deco giclées cover the walls, all women with sharply angled chins and hooded eyes that follow me, daring me to look away—which I don't hesitate to do—as I head outside to clean up the table.

I grin at the feeling of the cold stone on my socked feet. Vines, spilling over from the other side of the wall, cover the left side of the patio. On the right is a solid golden wall of tufo blocks, the palazzo rising far above my little home.

The low wall at the front of the patio is lined with rectangular terracotta planters, none of which match, all containing a specific something—herbs mostly, with one in the corner filled with blood-red geraniums. Over the edge, it's a sheer drop to the sloping street, not too high, but enough to make me dizzy as I watch a bicyclist pass by. On the other side of the narrow road is another tufo palazzo, a single, brown-shuttered window facing my patio, a line of faded dish towels strung up beneath it.

I take the food inside, and driven by guilt and my otherwise food-less kitchen, I make the questionable choice to put it all in the refrigerator before recorking the wine and taking another small sip of Matteo's Classico from one of the glasses.

It really is delicious. I swallow, and it tastes like summer, safety, and first kisses. It tastes too good—and dangerously easy to drink. I pour the rest down the drain and shift my attention to the living room, crossing my arms as I survey the space from beyond the drawn-back lace curtain of the kitchen.

Having spent most of the past five years in the homes of people who, at least at first, were strangers, I am good at drawing lines between personal and private. I can sense when someone wants to say more or show me more, and I also know when something is none of my damn business.

And *this* is none of my damn business. However, this is also my home for the foreseeable future, and I'm curious. The building is at least six hundred years old. I'm sure it's full of stories.

Ghosts, Grandma Mir's voice huffs. *Full of ghosts.*

I snort, twisting the red string double-knotted on my wrist—for protection, she'd always insisted—as I make my way to the stone fireplace in the back of the room. Dark wood cabinets are built in on either side, with shelves of books stacked above them.

The only ghosts here are the ones I brought with me. And boy, are they loud.

I can almost feel the eyes of the women in the paintings on my back, narrowed and full of judgment, as I pull on a brass handle, jiggling to get the drawer to slide open. It resists, but I work it slowly out, the wood groaning as it drags against the frame.

My phone rings, blaringly loud in the otherwise still space, and I squeak in surprise, jerking the entire drawer right out of the wall. Its contents fall onto the ground, papers and pens spilling in wild piles at my feet. I scramble to stuff it all back in, feeling bad for snooping, and then search for my phone in the cushions of the couch where I tossed it earlier.

"Hi," I answer, sounding slightly out of breath. I'm staring at the woman in the portrait above the couch, her modeled curls and monochromatic green dress. She's staring back.

"Did you sleep well?" Matteo asks. "You still sound a little tired."

That is because I haven't slept well in months, but last night wasn't the worst of it. I tear my eyes from the woman and walk back out onto the patio. "Slept fine, thanks. And thank you for picking me up and bringing me home. And for supplying food and wine. And for finding me a home in the first place. And a job. I guess we still need to talk about that, but—"

"Tori, you don't need to thank me."

"Oh, but I do," I protest. "You made my escape to Italy possible."

"I just made it a little quicker. You would have figured it all out on your own. Besides, you're family. I had no choice," he adds, his voice playful. When I was thirteen and Matteo called me family, I hated it. But now it feels like coming home, like being safe and held in a way I haven't felt so fully since I moved in with my grandma in high school. "And since you don't begin working for a few days, how about I pick you up around noon for lunch with my parents at the vineyard?"

"Yes, please. I can't wait to see them. Will Tibi make it up?"

"She didn't call you?"

If she had, I'm sure I would have heard it. My ringer was five-alarm fire-level loud when it rang. Something about the way he asks makes me tense. "Is everything okay?"

"She broke up with that Irish literary anthropologist guy she was seeing and wasn't sure they'd be done dividing property in time for her to eat with us."

"Dividing property?"

"Intellectual property. They co-wrote a book of poems."

"They were dating for two months."

"Tibi," Matteo says, a shrug in his voice.

"Tibi," I acknowledge.

Tiberia Graziano has always played by her own rules, bowing to conventions and adhering to cultural and social constructs only when it suits her. Tibi is a Tibi-pleaser, the idea of people-pleasing in general completely outrageous to her—a trait I always envied growing up with the weight of my parents' expectations and hopes heavy on my shoulders.

I still want to be Tibi when I grow up.

"See you at noon, then?" he asks.

"I'll be waiting on the street."

"Ciao, *patatina.*"

"Bye, Matty G.," I say, grinning as I aim my thumb over the end call button. I pull it back when I hear his muffled voice still floating out of the receiver. "Wait, what?" I ask.

"The news," he's saying when the phone is back to my ear. "They were talking about your train from Rome."

I grimace. "Oh god, do I want to know?"

"It was nothing too gruesome. A wild boar—massive, they said, male—got stuck up in the train's undercarriage somehow. The carcass had probably been up there a few days, at least."

Gross, but not morbid. "Well, there goes my appetite for *cinghiale.*" I look over my shoulder into the house and decide to throw away last night's leftovers after all.

"No *cinghiale* at lunch today," he promises, repeating that he will see me at noon and telling me to get some rest before hanging up.

I'm looking at my phone after the call closes, chewing my lip as I scroll through the notifications and read the texts Tibi sent an hour ago when I was still in bed. When I check my call log, it's empty. "Weird," I murmur, double-checking the ringer before I glance back at the drawers, then at the women on the walls, and concede a walk might do me good.

4

BEFORE GOING OUT IN public, I decide it is in everyone's best interest that I take a long-overdue shower. Halfway through, I have to pop out of the tiny plastic stall to crack the window open. The steam in the bathroom is dense, almost fog-like, and I can hardly see the shower caddy, hanging inches from my face.

When I get out, the only towel I can find is so small and stiff that it leaves me nearly entirely exposed when I try to wrap it around my body. I pad, dripping a trail of water behind me, into the bedroom to search for a human-sized towel in one of the two mirrored armoires on the back wall. Standing before my reflection with the bed behind me, the sheets well-rumpled from my reunion with Edo, I smile.

I'm not used to being taken care of—never by my parents, and definitely not by a boyfriend—but I'm trying to get better at letting Edo try. Last night, I dutifully accepted the unlimited train pass he bought me to visit him in Florence. I also graciously tried on the coat he purchased from some overpriced store because he knew I wouldn't have anything to keep me sufficiently warm in the chill of the Umbrian winter.

If it were up to Edo, he'd set me up in a perfect apartment—*his* perfect apartment—and have the family staff feed me Aperol spritzes and cheese to my heart's content.

The thought makes me queasy, which is why I insisted on finding and paying for my own apartment—though, as it turned out, Matteo found me the apartment. And why I plan to continue working.

Matteo found me the job, too.

A flutter catches between my belly and my chest, and I take a deep breath. Twins. I'll be nannying two-year-old twins.

I'm always surprised by the things that spark that ache of loss, especially after spending four years as a hospice nurse.

When Matteo told me about the family, he was gentle, hesitant even. "Two girls," he explained when I asked, his voice soft. I blinked away the haziness at the edge of my vision, chuckling at my uncharacteristic sentimentality. Chuckling as I mentally backed away from the mountain of grief I've yet to conquer, the true specter that haunts me.

"I'm in!" I'd declared with feigned enthusiasm. "I can't wait to meet them."

It will be good for you, I reassure myself now. I need a change. Maybe the man on the train was right: a person shouldn't spend too much time close to death.

I have officially had my fill.

After slipping on jeans and a light sweater, I dry my hair, put on some sneakers, and spend five minutes fighting with the gate at the bottom of the stairs. None of the keys on the set Matteo left me seem to open it, so I'm trapped. To my left, at the base of the stairs, is another thick metal door. Now, in the daylight, I see that the patio sits on the roof of whatever this room is—probably a medieval wine or vegetable cellar—but the grating at the top of the door gives dungeon or secret chamber vibes. It's too dark inside to see beyond the bars at the top of the gate and creepy enough to make me feel more frantic about getting out.

After two trips back up to my apartment—I refuse to call Matteo and confess I'm too much of an idiot to get out of my gate—I discover a buzzer on the wall near the top of the stairs. I hit it, and I hear a heavy click; the gate pops open just enough to confirm that I am no longer imprisoned. Before leaving, I test my keys on the exterior lock to make sure I can get it open, and then wander down to Orvieto's Porta Maggiore—an ancient arch a single car wide in the fortified, soaring block wall; the town's old entrance, in use for over a thousand years—and around the side of the hill to the Anello della Rupe, the ring path that circles the base of Orvieto.

To my left is a wall of leafy trees, vines tangled in their limbs and nettle carpeting their feet. The Umbrian forest is not yet ready to succumb to the call of the changing seasons. To my right, rising hundreds of feet into the air, is the flat face of golden volcanic tuff on which Orvieto is built—a gilded island in a sea of rolling green.

I pass a chapel set into the side of the cliff, not much more than a cave carved out from the stone itself, a crucifix sculpted directly into the volcanic rock behind the altar. Not long after, a small path cuts off the main route and leads to the necropolis, the hints of its squared tombs and pinecone-shaped adornments visible through the trees.

This is one reason why I've always loved the town. Time is less linear here, and the past is a distance like any other—twenty yards to the 1500s, half a mile to the world of the Etruscans. Sometimes, if you stand in the right place, you can exist in all the thens and nows simultaneously.

It is a collision of time and space. Orvieto and my heart have that in common.

I've been walking for an hour when I notice how late it's gotten—the bells of the Duomo, Orvieto's massive 13th-century cathedral, clang the hour from up on the hill. Matteo will be at the house in an hour, and when I look around to get my bearings, I realize I've wandered off the main trail into a denser stretch of forest. The birds are loud in the trees, but there's another sound that makes my skin prickle.

Grunting.

I stumble backward, running into a post. Attached is a small, laminated sign that reads: PRESTARE CAUTELA IN ZONA PER I CINGHIALI IN NUCLEI FAMILIARI. LA

SPECIE FEMMINILE PUO ESSERE AGGRESSIVA PER L'UOMO.

My Italian could use some refreshing, but I get the gist. *Be aware of groups of boars in the area. The females can be aggressive towards men.*

Or, more likely, humans in general. I back away quietly and return to the path. Presumably, the females have their piglets to protect from me and jealous male boars.

The scent memory from the train fills my nostrils, then my mind—the thick, putrid stench of decaying flesh—and I take the nearest route off the ring path and up to the hilltop.

When I get home, I still have twenty minutes to spare and decide, before seeing Matteo's parents, that I should change my humidity-dampened top and put on a dash of makeup. Not because I need to impress them, but because I know his mom will worry if I show up with such discernible, deep, dark circles under my eyes.

The gate at the bottom of the stairs doesn't give me any problems, and when I reach the front door, I discover I forgot to lock it, so I don't even have to try to figure out which key fits.

Inside, I bound up the marble steps, only to freeze halfway. A slender, balding man stands at the entrance of the hallway, smiling at me.

"Emma?" he asks, his eyes glassy. He doesn't seem much older than my parents, but I've worked with several dementia patients, and I soften at the vulnerability in his expression, his apparent confusion. I don't know why he's here, but he may not, either.

"No," I shake my head. "Victoria. Tori Jacobs." I explain that I'm Matteo Graziano's friend and am renting the house.

He smiles. *"Certo. Scusami,"* he says, laughing at himself. His face and his eyes clear. "Welcome, I am Claudio. Claudio Mancini, your landlord."

We shake hands, and he apologizes for startling me. He just wanted to make sure that the gas heaters were ready to go. It's supposed to get cold soon. He shows me how to turn the heat on and directs me to a drawer of heavier blankets for chilly nights.

At the door, I thank him. He looks at me again, squinting before he shakes his head. He pulls a piece of paper out of his back pocket, along with the stub of a pencil, and jots down his number, telling me to call him if I ever need anything.

"Thank you. If there's an issue with the house, I'll get in touch," I say, taking the paper and sliding it into my pocket.

"Anything," he repeats, holding my eyes.

"Anything," I say, rubbing my arms against a chill breeze.

He pauses before the gate at the bottom of the stairs, glancing first at me, then past me to the bedroom window. I can't be sure from here, but it sounds like he says, "See you soon, Emma," before disappearing onto the street.

5

I LOOK AROUND THE rest of the house to make sure nothing is amiss. Not that Claudio would have done something nefarious. If anything, he seemed determined to make sure I was comfortable and safe, even if my presence appeared to be a little disorienting for him.

The door to the teddy bear room is ajar, and I push it open wider with my toe, staying on the other side of the threshold. A small blue table lamp has been switched on, casting a circle of light against the shuttered window. I turn it off, hurrying down the stairs and closing the door firmly behind me when I walk out, exhaling only when I hear the solid click of the deadlatch.

Matteo pulls up in his car as I step onto the street, and I hop into the front seat. “Were you waiting for me?” I ask. “Or do we just have impeccable timing?”

“The latter,” he says, smiling. “How early did Edoardo have to leave this morning?”

“I’m not sure, but before the sun came up. He has that meeting with the Swiss investors and wanted time to prepare.”

A shadow crosses Matteo's face, but all he says is, "Hopefully it goes well."

"How was your morning?" I ask. "Did you win any more Hottest Wine Producer awards or find a new model to date? Tibi told me about Rachele. Regina? It's hard to keep track," I joke. But it's not *really* a joke. Matteo goes through relationships like I go through therapists.

"Renata." He smirks. "That ended a while ago."

"Tibi told me about her two weeks ago."

"And we broke up shortly after."

I flop back onto the seat. "Matteo, what has a woman got to do to get you to stick around?"

He shrugs, a curl falling across his brow. I'm sure there's not much his partners haven't tried. Or maybe...

"Oh my god, are you secretly the worst boyfriend ever, and they can't wait to get rid of you?" I ask, twisting in my seat to face Matteo so I can poke him on the shoulder.

Matteo laughs—the best laugh—and nods. "You figured me out. Worst boyfriend ever. Who would want to date *this?*" He gestures to his face, his body.

I roll my eyes. "Terrible, you're right. Those poor women." Glancing out my window, I see the Paglia River running slow and steady south toward the Tiber, passing along the edge of Graziano Vineyards.

"The rain will be here soon," Matteo says. "If you want a river day, we should probably make that happen in the next few weeks."

As kids, we spent countless hours sunning and splashing along the banks of the Paglia during the summer. "That would be fun," I say, my breath catching with the memories. It's been ten years since the last time we were all at the river together.

A loud bang pulls my eyes back to the windshield. The car grinds to a stop.

"*Che cazzo*, Tibi!" Matteo shouts, slamming his palm against the horn.

Tibi's hands are on the hood, and she's grinning like a maniac. Her honey-brown bangs fall into her lashes, her choppy waves a nimbus around her face. I throw open the car door and jump out, pulling her into a hug.

"Thanks for calling me back, *stronza,*" she says, squeezing me so tight my ribs hurt.

"I didn't want to interrupt the divorce proceedings. Matteo implied the custody battle over the poems was getting pretty ugly, and you know how well I do with confrontation."

"It would have been less ugly if Jasper hadn't cried all over our beautiful work."

"What spell do you and your brother weave in your relationships that leaves your exes so devastated?"

"It's called indifference. Guaranteed to break hearts every time."

Tibi makes for the front seat, but I beat her to it, and she slips into the back.

"No Edo?" she asks, resting her chin on my seat so her face is beside mine.

"He had to be back in Florence this morning for a meeting."

She hums. "Shame."

"Tibi," Matteo warns.

"You're no fun," she tells him, hooking her thumbs in the straps of her rust-colored velvet overalls and sprawling across the back seat. "It's not like I was going to invite myself into their bedroom again. I know how to take a hint."

Tibi and Edo, much to Matteo's chagrin, dated for a few months when she moved back to Orvieto after university. It didn't last long, but as she tells it, it was still the best sex of her life. Matteo and Edo's friendship never fully recovered.

"Maybe next time." I wink at her. She blows me a kiss. Matteo groans.

"So, what do you think of your new place?" she asks.

"It's cute," I say. "The owner was there when I got back from my walk today."

Tibi and Matteo exchange a look in the rearview mirror. "Inside?" Matteo asks.

"Yeah, he was checking the heaters. I figured he'd talked to you about it."

Tibi leans over the center console. "Don't worry about Claudio. He's entirely harmless. But he's been off his rocker ever since—"

Matteo stiffens, and Tibi cuts herself off, which isn't something she's usually capable of.

"Ever since what?" I press. "Tell me."

"Ever since he lost his daughter," Tibi says, defiantly holding Matteo's gaze in the mirror.

"Emma," I murmur.

Matteo swings his head to look at me. "How do you know—"

"Something Claudio said," I say quickly. "But back up, what do you mean *lost?*"

"It was a long time ago." Matteo's voice is edged with something I can't quite identify—irritation, defensiveness?

"What happened?" I ask.

"The Paglia. Accidental river drowning," Tibi answers matter-of-factly before adding, in a stage whisper, "That, or murder."

"It wasn't murder, Tibi," Matteo insists so suddenly and so loudly that I press myself against the door.

"Sheesh," she says. "He's weird about it because they were *friends."* The way she enunciates the word friends makes her implication obvious—they were more.

"How have I never heard about this?" I ask, catching Matteo's eye. I'm scandalized, on the verge of being offended, that such an enormous thing has evaded my awareness. That none of them told me.

Matteo looks away, his grip on the steering wheel so tight that his fingers are whitening.

Tibi reaches forward, tugging a piece of hair behind my ear. "It was the summer after Alex—"

"Got it," I snap. It wasn't just my parents who thought the best way to protect me from things was by not sharing them with me.

Matteo's jaw pulses. "I'll call Claudio and make sure he remembers to check in before going into the house again," he says, trying to steer the conversation back as we pull around a turn, and the Grazianos' house—really a Renaissance country palace that they've painstakingly restored, stone by stone—comes into view, sweeping rows of grapes radiating from the property on all sides like a sunburst.

"Home," Tibi says, and my heart pounds in agreement.

As soon as I swing my legs out of the car, Castor, their giant, goofy segugio, sticks his snout between them. I brace his face in my hands, giving his floppy, fawn-colored ears a solid shake, and kiss him on his head. In a desperate search for long-overdue cuddles and scratches, he presses the rest of his body into me hard enough that I have to plop back on the seat.

I laugh when he licks my cheek and then pout when Matteo whistles, and Castor remembers himself and his intensive training and turns back into the serious boar-hunting dog Matteo raised him to be.

"Come on," Tibi says, weaving her arm through mine and leading me through the open French doors at the front of the property. Inside, June Murphy-Graziano is sitting at the table peeling roasted peppers. When she sees us, she stands, immediately bursting into tears as she walks toward me with charred pepper skin and seeds stuck to her fingers. I cry, too, because, well, June—Matteo and Tibi's mom—is one of the only reasons I'm a semi-functional human being.

June and my mom grew up together outside of Los Angeles, and they have been best friends since before they could even form memories. Theirs was an inherited friendship, their mothers having also grown up together. And thus, similarly, I inherited Tibi. One of the few accidental kindnesses my mother ever bestowed upon me.

How June tolerates Mom is beyond me. Perhaps it is a case of opposites attract. June is warm and soft and so overflowing with pure, unconditional love that you're sometimes worried you'll drown in it, but she somehow manages to buoy instead of suffocate. Her children consider her a best friend, and not in the slightly questionable way my mother always tried to be mine. June Murphy is perfect, and Meg Lancaster is, at best, kind of fake.

It would be hard to be best friends with my mother, a woman whom I barely know, even if she is, for better or worse, the one who mostly raised me.

"Mom," Tibi calls from where she's perched on the tiled kitchen island, the heavy rubber heels of her boots knocking against a marble mosaic of black and white stars, "you're worse than Castor."

June pulls back, keeping one hand on my shoulder as she wipes her eyes with the back of her arm. "Don't be ridiculous, Tibi. I've never once stuck my nose up Tori's butt by way of greeting."

Tibi quirks an eyebrow. “I bet you would, though.”

June smiles at me and shakes her head. “Can you believe this daughter of mine?”

“I wish we could trade,” I say as she leads me to the chair beside hers. “I’d get you, and we could all sit back with a glass of wine and watch as Tibi and my mother try to survive each other.”

“Your mom *loves* me,” Tibi says, pulling a chair up so close to mine they touch.

“She does,” I agree. “Though I think that is primarily because you are a.) not her daughter, and b.) an exceedingly unique example of the human psyche’s scope.”

Tibi, flattered, presses her hands over her heart. “Meg said that about me?”

“Direct quote.”

June squeezes my knee. “Meg loves you the most, Tori.”

Tibi and I both burst into laughter, and June rolls her eyes. “How’s the apartment?” she asks me, peeling another pepper. “I haven’t been there in over a decade, but Matteo tells me it hasn’t changed much.”

I imagine a teenage Emma, her form and features unclear but vaguely familiar in my mind, painting her toenails on the twin bed in the tiny teddy bear room. A backpack on the floor, her notebooks spilling out, covered in doodles. Maybe she’s written Matteo’s name or MG & EM on the inside covers. Maybe she’s tried signing her name as Emma Graziano, the same way I used to write Victoria Graziano in mine.

I shake off a tingle of undefined dread.

"It's perfect," I respond, picking at the charred skin of the pepper I grab. "I told Matteo and Tibi already, but I met Claudio this morning. He seems—"

"Troubled," Tibi offers.

"Nice," I counter.

"He is nice," June says, shooting a look at Tibi. "And given what he's been through, first with Emma and then his wife, I think he deserves more grace than most give him."

Tibi scoffs. "These mortal souls of ours contain multitudes, Mother. Being nice and being a little out of your mind are in no way mutually exclusive."

I tilt my head toward Tibi. "She would know," I confirm.

"Thank you, Tor." Tibi flashes me a toothy smile. "And Claudio is lovely, but you have to admit that it is objectively a bit odd, even by my standards, for a man to wander around town talking about his dead daughter, like, well...like she isn't dead."

"He thinks she's alive?" I ask, goosebumps rising under my clothes, making my shirt itch against my back.

June shakes her head. "He misses her, girls. Any parent would. You might survive the tragedy, but you will always feel like part of you is missing." She squeezes my hand, and I feel it right in my own heart of missing pieces.

"He looked up at the house when he was leaving," I tell them, "and he told Emma he'd see her soon."

"I stand corrected." Tibi twists her hair into a bun, an elastic between her teeth. "He doesn't merely talk about his dead daughter; he talks *to* her as well."

I chew my lip. "I used to talk to Alex," I say quietly. "When it first happened. I used to talk to her out loud like she was still there." People thought I was crazy then. And maybe I was. Crazy with grief and anger, if nothing else.

I haven't spoken to Grandma Mir since I lost her, but she's had plenty to say to me.

If Claudio is out of his mind, I likely am, too.

"We know, *patatina*. But that's different," Tibi says.

"Is it?" I ask, arching an eyebrow.

"Probably not. But to be very clear, I have absolutely no issues with anyone speaking to dead people. In fact, maybe we should try. Get some answers. Then we can know for sure one way or another if you are sleeping in the home of a murdered girl."

"Jesus, Tibi," Matteo says, shutting the fridge door with enough force to make me jump. I wonder how long he's been in the kitchen. He sets a bottle on the counter, four wine glasses clenched between the fingers of his left hand. He lets out a long, tense sigh. "Can we not do this again?"

"Do what?" Tibi asks, raising her chin at him.

He drops his head, his shoulders rising on a deep inhale before he looks up at us. "Emma was *not* murdered," he says firmly, his voice a mix of sadness and anger.

"Fine," she responds before mumbling so only I can hear, "but if that's true, why is that apartment so damn haunted?"

6

LUNCH IS DELICIOUS. THE Umbrian sun slants onto the terracotta-tiled porch, the blue wood table highlighted against the stone walls, which are cast in shade by the trellises that span the open roof, heavy with gnarled, ancient vines.

Twisted olive trees are interspersed among the fields of grapes. The lush rows amble along the hillside, and beyond them, rising from a bed of green, is Orvieto. The entire town is a monolith of tufo and travertine looming over the surrounding Umbrian plains.

I slurp another umbrichelli noodle into my mouth, giggling and tipsy on carbs and a glass (or three) too many of Matteo's wine. The pasta is thick and chewy and covered in freshly shaved black truffle.

"I'd like this to be the last thing I taste before I die," I announce to the table.

"But not today," Matteo says, topping off my glass.

"Thanks," I tell him. "For the wine and for not wanting me to die today." My eyes are squinty as I smile and reach for my glass. I stick my nose in it before taking a sip. "Wait. Maybe *this* is the last thing I want to taste before I die."

"I'm happy to arrange for both the umbrichelli al tartufo and the wine," Tibi says, swallowing a gulp from her glass. "I'll just need some advanced notice."

"I'll do my best," I promise with a hiccup.

Across the table, Francesco Graziano reads the newspaper with one hand, the other resting on the back of June's chair. June's leaning forward with her chin in her hands, looking at us all like we are the apples of her eye.

"Tori, if you want to take a little nap here before Matteo drives you back into town, you can have his bedroom."

I snort at Matteo's feigned look of disbelief, tossing my head onto his shoulder. I've been getting him kicked out of his bedroom for naps for decades. I could never stay with Tibi. She always slept with the dog, and no one else was welcome in her bed. This seems to be a consistent issue in her relationships.

Of course, Matteo no longer sleeps in his childhood bedroom. He's renovated the old stable. What was only a rundown pile of stones when we were children is now a three-bedroom, two-bathroom dream cottage with a view of Orvieto from the kitchen window.

"As wonderful as that sounds, I should probably get back sooner rather than later. Edo—"

"Mmm, Edo," Tibi murmurs around a mouth full of pasta.

I giggle, and giggle harder when Matteo shudders beside me. "Edo," I go on, "is coming down as soon as he's done with his meeting, and I still have to unpack."

June's eyes flit between Matteo and me, and she looks like there's something more she wants to say. She taps a finger against the table once. Twice.

Matteo stretches his hand out, stilling her. He smiles softly. "I'm good to drive, Mom," he says. I glance sideways, and his glass is still half-full. It seems that Tibi and I took it upon ourselves to prove just how drinkable this vintage is.

I scoot my chair back and get a touch of the spins.

Way too fucking drinkable, it turns out.

"Are you sure you don't want to stay?" June asks, her voice a little beseeching.

I start collecting empty plates, and she stands to help me. "I'll stay long enough to get the kitchen cleaned up and then be back for lunch again as soon as you'll have me."

"We'll have you always," June says, snagging Tibi's fork out of her hand. "And not just because you are the only one I don't have to force to do the dishes."

"Hey," Matteo protests. "I do dishes when I can."

"Oh, Matteo. Is it super *duro* to find the time to do the dirty *piatti* with all the photoshoots?" I ask, reaching over his shoulder for his water glass.

Tibi grimaces. "Super *hard? Do* the *dirty piatti?* Your Italian continues to be quite bad and strangely sexual."

Matteo chuckles.

I lean to keep the silverware from falling off my stack of plates as I shoot him a dirty look. "Tibi, you could make anything sexual."

She grins. "That means a lot."

Inside, I stack the dishes near the sink and help June scrape the last bits of our meal off the plates and into the *umido* bin. Every time I look up, June is watching me.

"What?" I ask.

"How are you really doing, Tor?"

"Fine," I say, hoping my smile hides how tense her question makes me. I set the plate I'm holding down to take June's hand. "Better now that I'm here with you all."

She drops my fingers and pulls me into a hug, her arms so tight around my back that it's almost hard to breathe—a sensation I crave, having grown up with a mother who didn't have time on her calendar to pencil in physical affection. "Listen, your job is not to reassure me that you are doing all right. Do not do me that disservice."

"Never," I murmur into her shirt.

"Good." She releases me and dips her hand into the soapy sink water. "And *we* are all better now that you're here, too."

"Everyone seemed to be doing pretty great before I arrived." I grab a towel and start drying. "Other than Tibi's breakup, it sounds like school is going well. And Matteo is doing so much with the vineyard."

She sighs. "If only he were as successful in other areas of his life as he is in business."

"He'll figure it out. One day, someone's going to stick."

"Someone," June hums, a sound that both lacks conviction and is heavy with insinuation.

I wonder if things were more serious with Regina or Rachele than he let on.

Or maybe it's something else.

I think about how well he knew his way around my apartment, Emma's old home. Tibi's implication that they'd been together. I think about his outbursts earlier—or what count as outbursts for Matteo—when Tibi was talking about Emma. "Was Matteo close with Emma?"

June pauses, the sudsy sponge pressed over the rim of a wine glass. "They were good friends."

"Is it weird for him that I'm staying in her house? He seemed upset when Tibi—"

June shakes her head, and I stop talking. "It's not that. When everything first happened, there was an investigation." She clears her throat. "A murder investigation. There were two suspects, and Claudio was one of them. He was already destroyed after the loss of Emma, and in the middle of the investigation, Silvia, his wife, just checked out. She picked up and moved to Spain to live with her sister. She left everything behind. She didn't tell anyone she was going. Or why. It didn't look good for Claudio, but there was insufficient evidence to convict anyone, and everyone was cleared."

"A murder investigation?" I repeat. When Tibi had mentioned murder, it sounded like teasing, like her own Tibi riff on a tragedy that was probably pretty distressing for her as a kid. Distressing for all of them.

Maybe, especially, Matteo. On top of losing a friend, watching their grieving parent put through the wringer would be awful.

I think of finding Claudio in my apartment today, and my breath catches. Why would he have been questioned? There must have been something that made the police think he was involved—some shred of evidence that pointed to Emma's father as her potential killer.

But he was cleared, I remind myself, *and the Graziano family wouldn't have me living in the home of an accused murderer if they thought he was guilty.*

"Anyway," June says, looking away from me. Part of a story she hasn't fully told me is still stirring in her eyes—a sight I'm familiar with after being shielded by others' half-truths my whole life. "It was a difficult time. Matteo is protective and loyal and still holds on to a lot of that, I think. You two are, unfortunately, alike that way. Two peas in the grin-and-bear-it pod."

Matteo walks in with the rest of the glasses and sets them on the counter beside me. "Who's in Tori's pod?"

"You are," I tell him, stepping closer to June. "You're the other pea."

"And what is this in reference to?" he asks, following my lead and putting more space between us.

Before June can answer, before Emma's name comes up again, I blurt, "The summer after my first year of high school, in Newport Beach with Grandma Miriam. You slept on the fold-out for two weeks and never told anyone the cat was peeing on your sheets. You washed them every day. We all thought you were..."

I trail off, feeling a little warmer in the face than I did before starting my story. June's shoulders shake beside me as she dries her hands. "I'm going to see if anyone wants an espresso."

Matteo's voice drops as she walks away. "Thought I was what, Tori?"

"Thought you were experiencing abnormally excessive nocturnal emissions," I say in my best professional nurse voice.

"Huh," he says, leaning back against the counter. "Every night. Is that considered excessive?"

"Abnormally excessive," I say again.

"Compared to what?"

"Normal rates of nocturnal emissions."

"Did you study this in nursing school?"

I pop a hip against the sink. "It's common knowledge."

Matteo laughs and pours himself a glass of water. "Good thing it was just cat piss then."

As we pass the river on the way home, I no longer feel nostalgic for summers on the warm banks of the Paglia.

I feel unsettled. I imagine the top of a girl's head bobbing along with the current. I imagine her water-bloated limbs beneath the rapids. I wonder who found her. Where. I wonder if her body was as ruined as Grandma Miriam's, or worse, from the battering of the waves. The animals.

I jump when Matteo's hand squeezes my shoulder, letting out a cry that somehow sounds both agonized and excited.

"Sorry," he says, returning his hand to the gear shift. "Just wanted to make sure you were still with me."

I chew my lip, watching him push a sandy brown curl off his forehead. He is watching me back. I want to ask him about Emma, but I don't. I saw how upset he got earlier. He smiles, and I relax against the seat of the car. "I think I fell asleep with my eyes open," I tell him.

"Nightmare?" he asks.

"Aren't they always?"

"Tor," he says, the car slowing as he takes another switchback on the way up the hill, "when you say those things, it makes me worry. I don't want you to go through that again. I don't want—"

"It was a joke," I say with more bite than I mean. "I'm not sixteen anymore."

He glances at me, his eyes skittering too quickly in too many places. "I know you're not."

And despite what everyone thinks, I'm not that fragile girl anymore. I'm not broken like I was when I lost Alex. "I just need a nap," I say, rubbing my hands over my face. "And more self-control when it comes to your wine."

"I brought a case for you to have at the apartment. Be careful." He winks. "Especially since Edo won't drink it."

I jerk my head around to look at Matteo. "I totally forgot he doesn't drink white wine. Not even yours?"

"Not even mine."

"What's wrong with that guy?" I ask, crossing my arms.

Matteo shrugs, but his jaw tightens. "Just his taste in wine, it seems."

"Yeah." I think about Edo. His perfect dimple and his blue eyes. The way he whispers my name into my neck before kissing me. His sweet gifts and his patience. I catch myself smiling. "Just his taste in wine," I agree.

7

MATTEO PARKS ON THE one-way street in front of my gate and turns on his hazard lights so he can carry the wine up into the apartment. I open the front door, peeking up the stairs as I step into the house behind him. A damp chill has settled in the air, like the sun can't quite penetrate the thick stone walls. It feels like walking into a cave.

"Want me to check things out before I leave?" Matteo asks, studying me.

I lean against the railing. "What's there to check out? Do you think my sweet landlord is lying in wait upstairs?" My voice is light and teasing, not at all how I feel when I glance toward the landing.

I shiver but don't voice the actual question fueling my disquiet: *Do you think he had something to do with the death of his daughter?*

Matteo steps closer and cups my face with his hands, his palms warm and reassuring against my jaw. He leans down to meet my gaze. "Nothing. There's nothing."

I drop my eyes from his and nod. "I know." Outside, someone honks. It's a polite double tap that will probably turn into a real laying-on if Matteo doesn't hustle downstairs to move his car. "See you soon?"

"Anytime, *patatina*. You just let me know when you want me."

He chucks my shoulder as he passes me, closing the door behind him and leaving me alone in the apartment. I bite my lip, one foot frozen on the first step, before turning on every downstairs light I can find, even though it's barely three in the afternoon. I lock the exterior shutters in place, and rectangular bursts of daylight flood the space, highlighting the stylized portraits on the walls. The women in the frames look starker, their eyes more indignant.

I wonder what they've seen in this home, what they've heard.

What truths they know.

When I can no longer put it off, I take the steps upstairs two at a time, mostly to convince myself I'm not afraid of this house. My home, now. I reach with a trembling hand for the light switch in the bathroom, and the glow spills into the hallway. My breath steadies. Matteo was right, of course. There's nothing here.

I open the windows and the shutters in the larger bedroom and start putting away the rest of my stuff. Everything I packed takes up barely a fourth of an armoire, which is convenient because the other is locked. I shipped some books and heavier winter clothes before my flight. Nothing summery. That felt like looking too far ahead, and my position with the twins is only set to last through May when the family goes to Porto Ercole for the warmer months.

It's late afternoon when I finish organizing everything, and I still haven't heard from Edo. I run my hand along the end of the bed, knowing that if I give into the temptation of a nap, it will make sleeping tonight that much more improbable. Determined not to nod off before sunset, I wander downstairs to find something to keep me occupied.

I read the titles of the books that line the shelves beside the fireplace, the spines displaying a collection of Italian, Greek, and English—titles probably left by students after their semesters abroad, realizing too late that something would have to be sacrificed to make room in their suitcases for their newly purchased souvenirs and semi-illegal cheese hauls.

One of the books, a brown hardcover copy of Sophocles' *Antigone,* has a barely visible piece of paper protruding from between the pages. Reaching up, I wheedle the book out from where it sits on the shelf, firmly entrenched among other classics. At last, I release it with a corresponding burst of dust that makes me sneeze.

I finger the yellowing edges of what I can now tell are envelopes bursting from the pages—at least twenty. When I flip the book open, I see they are all the same: telegrams addressed to Claudio at this address.

They've all been opened, the glue now dried and useless. I take the book to the table and sit, negotiating with myself. If Claudio were worried about people seeing these, he wouldn't have left them in a house with rotating tenants. And surely I'm not the first of those tenants to be a little bit curious.

Who knows how many American students have already sat precisely where I am now, poking into the life of their landlord?

I grab the envelope tucked between pages sixty and sixty-one, push the flap open, and peer inside. A surprising wave of relief hits me when I see it is just a single piece of paper.

Not a lock of hair or an incriminating photograph. Just a telegram, as advertised. I reach in to pull it out, and as I unfold the paper, searching for a date, a clash of wood and glass peals through the house, reverberating through my bones.

The space goes dark.

The downstairs windows have slammed closed, and the shutters with them.

I set the letter back between the pages and shut the book. My legs shake as I rise to my toes and thrust it back into the vacant space on the shelf.

My fingers tug at the red string on my wrist, my heartbeat louder than my footfalls as I ascend the stairs. In my head, Grandma Miriam laughs at me. *The dead won't hurt you, Victoria, if you give them what they want.*

I know it was just a draft. I shouldn't have left all the windows and doors wide open. I understand that the movement of the air, the pressure, the flow, can be startlingly powerful.

But when I twist the knob on the bedroom, flipping on the lamp by the door and peeking inside, I still get chills.

The windows are locked, and the shutters outside them are also latched.

However, the armoires are wide open. The mirrored fronts catch the light from the hall, casting glimmers around the room.

I close the one holding my things. Then I close the other, which it turns out is empty. And, it is interesting to note, no longer locked. Or perhaps it was never locked, and I'm—as usual—more tired than I realized.

Regardless, I don't linger in the room.

I find Matteo's wine from last night in the fridge and whisper, "screw it," as I pour most of what's left into a cappuccino mug, carrying it out onto my patio with a blanket I yank off one of the couches.

I rarely drank at home, not even after Grandma Miriam passed. I was too busy with work, too focused on keeping going, and then on my move. And even though I know coming to Orvieto was the right decision, my nerves and heart could use some buoyancy. They crave that sweet breach, a moment of lightness in the space that the wine offers between all the things that have been and this perfect moment I'm determined to have on my sunny Italian veranda.

The house isn't unsettled, I reason as I pull my chair into the sun and settle into it with the blanket over my shoulders. *I am. I have been for months.*

I yawn and blink up at the sky, savoring the crispness of the wine on my tongue.

And then I hear the screaming. The same child-like wailing that filtered in through my open window with the sun this morning. The sound bounces off the far side of the patio, dulling when it strikes the tufo. I drag my rickety chair over to the other wall and climb on, pulling myself up and over the cascade of flowering jasmine that spills across the stone to see what is beyond.

On the other side is an orchard.

I feel a swoop of disorientation, a spatial dissonance like someone slipped a Wonderland 'Drink Me' potion into Matteo's wine. Because an orchard *can't* exist here. The medieval district of Orvieto has been built up and built into itself for hundreds of years, and yet, next to my tiny apartment is an impossibly large garden, hidden by high walls on all sides so it's invisible from everywhere except, I suspect, the small room upstairs—the teddy bear bedroom.

The screaming starts again.

My toes are balanced on the very back of the chair, and I try to push myself up further so I can see more of the orchard, my body sinking into the dense green leaves and starry clusters as my shoe slips on the edge of the seat and sends it skittering sideways, landing with a clattering thud.

"Hello!" someone calls in a heavy accent from inside the forest of yellowing trees below me. "Are you all right up there?"

I scan the dense nursery, but it is hard to distinguish anything beneath the canopy of reds and ambers.

"Over here, darling," the voice rings out again, the tightness of the *es* and heaviness of the *l* distinctly not Italian. "By the pergola."

I see her then, an older woman with a pale moon face, black hair bound up into a wild, unruly beehive of escaping waves, and Venetian red lips. "I'm so sorry," I say, grimacing as I cling to the jasmine. "I thought I heard screaming, and—"

She waves a cigarette in the air, the smoke zigzagging in front of her face. "Oh, yes. That was Paul."

"Paul?" I repeat, looking around the garden for another person who might be the source of the crying. Perhaps this woman's very loud grandchild. I see no one else, and when I glance back at her, she nods toward what looks like a tiny house in the corner of the yard. I squint and barely see the massive bird through the screened-in door. My mouth falls open.

She blows out a perfect ring of smoke. "He's very nice to look at, but he's terribly dramatic."

"Paul's a peacock," I confirm.

"Would you care to meet him?" she asks, pressing her cigarette into a blue and white ceramic ashtray brimming with butts. "I was just about to make a coffee. You can join me."

"Sure," I say. "I'm Victoria, by the way. Your new neighbor."

"Mirësi." She says it like Meer-see, extending her hand palm down into the air as she introduces herself like she expects me to blow it a kiss from where I dangle precariously on the wall between our properties. "Shall I meet you at the gate, or would you prefer to proceed from there?"

I glance back over my shoulder and decide the fall onto my patio is far shorter than the dive into her garden. "I'll be over soon."

8

As I step out onto the cobblestone, it occurs to me that I'm not sure how to find Mirësi's gate. Walking up the slope of my street, I tilt my head back, keeping my gaze on the tops of the walls, which rise at least thirty feet into the air where they intersect mine. Every step I take is dizzying, the wall above me contracting as the street rises up to meet it. I follow the spilling greenery up and around the corner, where the stones taper to almost nothing, and the jasmine takes over, forming a solid screen.

There's a fountain set into the basalt pavers where the street curves, a cast iron *nasone* that is old but relatively new compared to the medieval palazzi surrounding it. Perhaps it replaced something ancient—a hole that sunk deep into the tufo, where thousands of years ago, people could crawl into the earth to get water since there was none on the hill.

I wonder if the same water that feeds the Paglia, the water that carried Emma away from her family, runs below me now.

A few feet ahead, a dark wooden door is set into the vines, suspended in the cloud of green, framed by constellations of white blossoms. There is no buzzer or bell, so I reach for the brass knocker. Marks from fingers on the ring make the metal shine against the tarnished, grotesque face of a bloated gorgon. The thud against the door is hollow, the sound swallowed by the pores of the stone built up along the narrow streets. I wait, hoping I've found the right place.

I hear a car heading my way and squeeze closer to the door. I'm sure it can get past me, but the one-way streets were built for carriages, not full-size vehicles, and even at that, the walls bear the marks of too-wide wheels, concave reminders carved over hundreds of years. As the car comes into view, I raise my hand and grin, stepping into the middle of the street. Edo had me help him pick the black Audi last spring.

Well, not so much help as make sure I liked it—since he'd hoped I would be driving it too. He chose the special order Audi Black Edition finish, though. Because why not get the Bat Mobile version?

It seemed appropriate for Edo, the son of wealthy Italian royalty, who also happens to be out in the world fighting for justice by heading the green and sustainable lending program at one of the biggest banks in Italy.

The car doesn't slow, instead making a quick turn onto the street of my apartment before it reaches me. I drop my hand, staring after it. Is it possible he didn't see me?

It is far more likely that I am incapable of telling different Audis apart and am admittedly still not entirely sure what Black Edition means.

"Victoria?" a voice asks at my shoulder, and I startle, laughing as I turn to face Mirësi. She is even more spectacular up close. Pink puffs of blush on her cheeks, dark, thick lashes that match her brows and hair. Older but ageless.

"Thank you so much for the invitation," I say, clasping her hands in mine as I kiss her cheeks.

Her delicate fingers circle my wrists, and she studies the red string on my arm as I pull back, a slight smile pulling on the corner of her painted lips. "I've been in need of some fresh blood. The town is small. Sometimes, it feels especially so." She glances over my shoulder and hooks her arm around mine, leading me through the gate and under a canopy of paling leaves. "Paul," she says when a cry peals out around us, tipping her head toward a semi-enclosed pergola in the corner of the garden. The peacock has his tail feathers raised and spread, shaking them at us as we pass.

"Ah, yes, Paul." I stop to watch the bird for a moment, his colors as loud as his voice. The iridescent blue of his chest catches the soft afternoon sun, and he practically glows against the muted, buttery stone walls. "Is he...a pet?"

"A pet?" She shakes her head. "No. He is just visiting." I don't question her. But I am happy to hear that the screaming is only temporary.

Inside, the house is dark, with lights casting pools of illumination over busy bookshelves and heavy tables set under vaulted stone ceilings. The old electricity makes the lamps flicker, creating the illusion of candles dancing across the walls. Mirësi leads me down a few steps into a kitchen filled with the thick perfume of simmering coffee.

"Have a seat," she instructs as we pass a large dining table. I pull out a chair and settle onto the upholstered cushion. Mirësi continues to the stove, where a Turkish coffee maker is bubbling softly.

The table is covered in crystals and bundles of sage. I glance at Mirësi. She's holding the wooden handle of what looks like an ancient copper coffee pot. The metal is engraved and so dark that it's almost black.

It is all giving serious witch energy. I think of Grandma Miriam, who would either love Mirësi or find her performance completely intolerable, which makes me enjoy this surprise encounter even more.

"That's a beautiful coffee pot," I say, leaning forward on my elbows.

"Ah." She clucks, circling the pot over the flame. "This belonged to my great-great-grandmother, and since the war, it has traveled with me from Kosovo to nearly every continent." Mirësi places two gold-rimmed cups on white saucers on the table. "Watch out, it spits," she says, returning with the coffee maker and tilting it first into the cup closest to me and then into the other.

"Thank you," I say, lifting the cup for a tiny taste. The liquid is steamy and thick, bitter but creamy.

"Drink only from the one side," she directs with a raised eyebrow, and I do as she says.

Mirësi asks me questions while I sip, and I tell her why I'm here and how I've been visiting Orvieto since I was old enough to walk. The coffee is strong, and my heart beats harder the more I drink. When I ask her about herself, she only says, "Later."

"And the house?" she inquires after I finish my coffee. She takes the cup from me, turning it upside down on the saucer and setting it between us.

"My rental?"

"Yes, the Mancini home. Is it..." She trails off like she's searching for the right word. In lieu of finding it, she waves her fingers in the air.

"It's great," I say, smiling brightly, even if I'm starting to wonder why it feels like I'm constantly reassuring people that the house is just fine.

She sighs as she leans back in her chair, her eyes drifting to a window that looks out over the garden. "Good. That's good, darling."

"Did you know any of the previous tenants?" I ask; this time, she doesn't rebuke me or press on with her own questions.

"Yes, many. From what I've been told, Signor Mancini moved off the hill and began renting the space out when he lost his job teaching at the Liceo Classico. It's been filled with international students, almost all young women, since we moved here six years ago." Knowing Mirësi is part of a *we* makes me immediately curious. But instead of elaborating on how she ended up here and who she's here with, she adds, "I've been acquainted with a number of them, and they all agree."

A tickle of a chill traces my spine. "Agree on what?"

"That the home is haunted." Her eyes sparkle as she clutches the pendant-shaped amethyst dangling from her neck.

I laugh, and it sounds forced even to my ears. "My friend Tibi said the same thing."

"When many voices rise with the same story, it is perhaps worth listening to." She holds my gaze, not quite in challenge, but like she's waiting to see if I will step up and play along. Mirësi is sweet and has been very welcoming, but I'm uninterested in reinforcing the belief that my apartment is haunted by anything more than one man's sad memories.

Death is death.

We don't have the good fortune of keeping our loved ones around in any real way once they've left us. And I should know—because I tried.

I shrug. "Seems to me that strong drafts and moody artwork are enough to sway impressionable minds towards the supernatural."

"You don't believe in ghosts?" she asks, folding her hands on the table. When I shake my head, her eyes dart from mine to the space over my shoulder. I resist the urge to turn around. "That surprises me."

I'm not sure what to say to that, but we become aware at the same time that I'm fidgeting with the red string on my wrist. I laugh, and so does Mirësi, and I'm not sure if we are laughing for the same reason, but it helps to dissipate the uncanny chill that's settled on my shoulders.

Mirësi smiles at me in a way that makes it feel like she's just teasing, her eyes kind in a wondrous, Baltic mystic-on-the-side sort of way. A reminder that it's all in fun.

I grin back. "You almost had me going there for a—" My phone buzzes against my leg, interrupting me. I pull it out to see a text from Edo. He'll be in town in half an hour and wants to take me to dinner. He also has other ideas about how he'd like to spend the evening that make my cheeks heat.

"Sorry," I say to Mirësi, writing a quick text that I'll be ready and waiting. "I have plans and should probably be going soon." When I raise my head, Mirësi has my cup in her hands, her gaze focused on the grounds stuck to the porcelain.

"True love," she says, winking at me. "A few obstacles, perhaps, in the coming months, but by the time the stone fruit ripens, all will be settled."

My pulse skips, my phone vibrating again in my lap as she speaks. I ignore it and prop my elbow on the table, resting my chin on my hand. "You're a fortune teller then? Not a witch?"

Mirësi chuckles as my phone buzzes again. "Can a woman not be all things?"

"She certainly can."

She tilts the cup. "I prefer *messenger*, in any case."

"Any more messages before I have to head out?"

Mirësi bites her lip, raising the glass again and swallowing a deep breath. Her face crumples.

"What is it?" I whisper, leaning forward to see the grounds, dried and amorphous on the white porcelain.

Her gaze snaps to mine. "It's you, Victoria."

9

"ME?" I ASK, PRESSING a finger into my chest. "In the coffee?"

"No. Well, yes. But not just in the coffee." Mirësi sets a plate-sized quartz crystal between us, the pointy side facing me, and I can't help but feel a little offended that she seems to be warding herself against my presence. "It's *you* who has come to settle something."

I snort. "The coffee thinks I came to Orvieto for revenge?"

"Didn't you?"

"Um. No. I came for—"

She holds up a finger and squints into the porcelain. "Not revenge." Her lips purse, and then she nods. "It's justice. You came for justice."

"I did?"

Mirësi gives an elegant shrug and smiles. "The coffee thinks so. And according to this spot, here—" she shows me a round smudge near the handle "—you will have a lovely evening. Get going, child. I don't want to make you late for your date."

She walks me back out through the garden, lighting a cigarette after I hug her goodbye and thank her for the coffee. I turn back before the street curves to see her still watching me.

I can confirm that Grandma Miriam would *adore* Mirësi, more so for the dramatic divination. Laughing to myself, I check my phone to see if Edo has responded and find two unread texts from Matteo: the first asking if everything is okay and the second checking in about my plans for dinner.

June is undoubtedly at his side, unwilling to bother me herself, not wanting to seem overprotective or overly concerned. She probably asked Tibi to text me first, and Tibi refused.

Tell your mom I am FINE, and I love her, I respond.

Date night with Edo, but hopefully, I will see you all very soon.

He sends back a thumbs-up emoji—just one. I chew my lip, waiting for more. A smartass jab or even a *yeah, hopefully,* or a *have fun* would do. Something more *Matteo*.

"Tutto bene, principessa?" a familiar voice croons, deep and smooth as midnight. So hot. Just like the rest of Edo.

My face splits into a grin, and I turn, tossing my arms around his neck. "You're early," I gasp as Edo lifts me off the ground, his hands pressed into my back.

"I couldn't stand another minute away. Now that you're so close, it is especially hard not to be able to do this whenever I want to." He presses his lips to mine, firm and very intent. His mouth moves to my ear. "Are you starving, or should we go upstairs for a bit before heading to dinner?"

"Mmm," I hum. "You can help me get changed."

He puts me down, reaching for my hand and brushing his lips over my knuckles, eyes locked on mine. "I didn't think it was possible."

"What?" I ask, studying his soft smile.

"To miss you even more now that you're here."

I laugh. "That makes no sense."

"Doesn't it?" He leans against the wall as I fish the key out of my pocket. "It feels like I have so much more to lose now."

My hand pauses as I turn the key in the lock. "More to lose?"

"By spending so much time at work." He shrugs and smiles. "Away from you."

"Well, you are here now, and I propose we make the most of it," I say, pushing open the gate and pulling him inside.

The apartment is just how I left it, and I realize that the breath I let out is one of relief. The house is not haunted. Obviously. And for the next thirty minutes, the only spine-tingling noises to be heard are the ones Edo elicits from me with the astonishing things he does to my body.

After a quick shower, I emerge from the steamy bathroom and return to the bedroom, where I find Edo has laid out some clothing options for me on the bed. I never anticipated enjoying having a man pick out my outfits, but it turns out I very much do.

"How's your mother?" I ask, slipping into a strapless, black crepe jumpsuit. Edo steps up behind me, pushing my hair over my shoulder to zip up the back.

"The same." His voice is a little melancholy. Edo is almost endlessly optimistic, probably the most positive, confident person I've ever met. There has never been a challenge or a problem that I've seen get him down—except for his mother.

Caterina Mazza is what someone might informally refer to as a nervous wreck. My mom, Dr. Meg Lancaster, would probably say she has panic disorder, agoraphobia, and generalized anxiety. But since Caterina is scared of doctors, their opinions are irrelevant.

Edo and his mother moved to Orvieto because her husband, the elder Edoardo Mazza, traveled a lot for work, and in Orvieto, Caterina could be closer to her sister. For the first year, while Edo was finishing high school, Edoardo Sr. would come to stay with the family on the weekends. Once Edo went to university, his father's visits became less frequent. Then, Caterina's sister passed, and from what I've been told, she hasn't left her home since—in over half a decade.

That home, at least, is gorgeous. It is essentially a livable museum that occupies the entire second floor of one of Orvieto's most lavish Renaissance palaces.

I've only met Caterina once, very briefly. Something about the disquiet in her eyes broke my heart.

"You're such a good son," I say, turning in Edo's arms and kissing him. "I'm sorry she's not doing well."

He tugs the end of my hair and smiles softly, reassuringly. Maybe more so for himself than for me. "My father is coming to stay for a while next month, and we have several appointments lined up so we can have her condition professionally assessed and make sure we have her in the safest situation possible. Find her the best care."

Edo adores his father.

The elder Edoardo Mazza is just as dashing as his son, but where Edo's is a cooler self-assurance, his father is all swagger. He isn't a bad guy. Tons of people admire him, and he's never been anything but friendly to me, but I will say I am grateful that his son didn't inherit the same air of aristocratic entitlement. Of course, I'd never mention to Edo that something about his dad sets my teeth on edge.

He winks at me. "And he has mentioned more than once how delighted he will be to see you again." I shiver in Edo's arms. "Cold?" he asks, rubbing his hands down my bare arms before collecting a linen blazer off the bed and holding it out for me to put on.

I thank him as I slide my arms into the sleeves. "If I can help at all with your mother—if you think she'd like some company while everything is getting worked out—I'm happy to stay with her when I'm available. I'll only be nannying part-time and can assist with meals and housework."

"Amore mio," Edo says, cupping my face. The look he gives me says it all, so he doesn't even have to utter a word to make it clear in the gentlest way that that kind of work is for *the staff*. He wants me to do something I love. Or even to do nothing at all—if that's what I need.

"I'd like to get to know her," I insist against his silent argument.

Edo has heavily hinted at the seriousness of our relationship and our future as a couple, going so far as to imply that my mother, the over-the-top and in-your-face Meg Lancaster, would be his ideal mother-in-law—granted, they haven't spent much time together, and for the sake of maintaining this belief, I plan to keep it that way— and that was all before we were even living in the same country.

But I'd like to have some sort of rapport with my potential mother-in-law. I'd like for her to be able to trust me.

"Mamma is delicate." Edo sighs. "And complicated. You know her mind isn't quite right. I'd hate for her to say something that might hurt you."

I place a hand on his chest. "I've worked with people much meaner than your mother. I think I can handle it."

"We'll see," he says, circling his hand around my wrist and running his thumb over my pulse. "But for now, I want you all to myself, and if you want to eat this evening, we should get out of here immediately before I'm forced to take you back to bed."

"Yes, Count Mazza." I give my best curtsy. "Or is it Duke? Marquis? I can never remember."

He kisses my forehead. "It's Edo."

As we walk out the door, my phone rings, and I pull it out of my clutch. Matteo's name flashes across the screen before the call ends after only two rings.

Edo's watching me with a slight smirk, and I unfurrow my eyebrows. "Must have been a butt dial," I say, shoving it back in my bag. "Matteo never calls." As soon as I say the words, the phone pings, and I pull it out again.

"But he does text," Edo teases without even a hint of irritation, and I'm struck again by how wonderfully, how fully, he trusts me.

Because I feel surprisingly guilty.

Edo knows as well as I do that nothing has ever happened between Matteo and me. But he doesn't know how in love I was with him for most of my adolescence. If I am being perfectly honest, that little spark never really burned out, but it was redefined. Matteo will always have a special place in my heart. We grew up together. He's been through the worst with me. We'll always have that. And that is enough.

The phone pings and then pings again. Two more texts from Matteo. "I'm sorry," I mutter, chewing my lip and setting my ringer to silent.

"For what?" Edo asks, his voice so sincere, I question why I said the words in the first place. He brushes my hair back from my face and gazes into my eyes, his own a deep ocean blue, calm and beautiful, before taking the keys to lock the door and dropping them in his coat pocket. He reaches for my hand. "If Matteo is jealous, I can't blame him."

"Jealous!" I cackle.

Edo squeezes my hand, drawing me closer. "You have no idea how perfect you are, Victoria."

I open my mouth to argue, and he kisses me before I have a chance. I let myself melt into it, into all Edo offers. A guarantee of safety, security, and a sense of separateness from all the darkness of my past. The hope of a future far away from the things that still hurt. If I can just let myself learn to let things be easy.

Maybe being taken care of wouldn't be the worst thing.

"Besides, it wouldn't be the first time," Edo says as he pulls out of the kiss, his voice so quiet that I can hardly hear him over the heaviness of my breathing. He grins, dimples highlighting his gorgeous mouth, and I grin back.

10

When I wake up, my heart is pounding in my chest. Sweat coats my bare skin, the residue of an already-forgotten nightmare. I shiver. Freezing air filters into the room, along with moonlight through the window. The *gaping* window—creaking slightly as it rocks with the breeze. The same way I found it when I woke up yesterday morning.

I'm almost entirely sure it wasn't Edo's doing in either case. It seems the latches don't work to keep the windows in this house closed the same way they don't work to keep them open.

Edo is sprawled beside me, his dark hair falling into his lashes. I kiss his temple before extricating myself from the twisted sheet and locking the window, hoping it will hold until the house warms up so at least one of us can get another few hours of comfortable rest.

We came home late from dinner and talked for hours in bed, me snuggling into his side as his fingers traced my ribs. I get what he means about missing someone more when they are close.

About having more to lose.

I shudder against the cold, against the thing that is so much more than fear, as I quietly get dressed, grabbing a down jacket from the closet and then tiptoeing downstairs to the kitchen to boil water for tea. The sun won't rise for nearly an hour, but I love the stillness of the stone town in the pre-dawn morning. The muffled, muted way the world feels almost pretend, like walking through a fairy tale where the words haven't been written yet.

However, when I head down the stairs and find the dense morning fog still clinging so tightly to the cobblestones that I have to use my free hand to find my way down the street, it feels like one of those fairy tales they don't tell children anymore.

The kind with the not-at-all-happy endings.

I return to Porta Maggiore again but turn left instead of right, heading east for a good view of the forthcoming morning along the ring path. The street I follow into the trees is called *Salto di Livio,* Livio's Jump. Or Leap. I roll the name over in my mind.

There were always stories, growing up, of people who had plummeted to their deaths from the edge of the hill—accidentally and otherwise. I wonder now if Livio was one of them, if the road commemorates a man who lost his life here. If the unmarked turn-off is a memorial to someone who the cliff claimed centuries ago. I glance up at the towering stone, the light of the streetlamps only reaching a quarter of the way up the rock face. At the top, I know there is little protection, nothing to minimize the risk of the drop.

It would be so easy to fall.

Accidentally or otherwise.

I considered it once. The year we visited after losing Alex. But I knew she'd have been furious, and that was enough. Enough for me to step back from the edge, figuratively and literally. That was when I knew I chose life, even if I went on to fill that life, through my work, with death.

That's also how, years later, I knew I had fallen in love with Edo: when I told him about that summer, about that moment. His eyes welled as he held me closer, whispering about how grateful he was that he hadn't lost me before he'd had a chance to love me.

The trees keep the fog at bay, and as I emerge into a clearing, I see it has lifted. I can make out the pink-tinted hills of the Umbrian countryside, ripe with olives and grapes.

When I arrive at the crossroads for the Cannicella Necropolis, I drift closer to the base of the hill, the awareness of not being alone, of being watched, pricking at my skin. I see them, then.

An entire sounder of wild boars, ambling down a path of their own making, barely twenty feet in front of me, towards the nesting area I had stumbled upon yesterday.

A pair of piglets pass by, and I hold very still, barely breathing, as a large female follows behind them. She surveys me, her beady, black eye catching the first rays of the rising sun as she turns her head back. The boar grunts and continues, and the rest of the group follows her, paying me little attention, apparently appeased by her estimation of my lack of threat.

I smile. I could never fight a wild boar. I'm not physically strong or powerful or fast. I am harmless, and even the wild pigs know it.

And anyway, if I were forced to scream for help, there would be no one around to hear me.

I stay where I am, sitting on a tree stump as the boars disappear into the brush, settling into the grass and their dens as night draws to a close. Their smell trails them, a delicate musk that sticks in the dense air. The perfume of sweet, damp earth. Nothing like the smell on the train.

Once the sun has fully risen, I make my way back onto the hill, following an enclosed spiral staircase. The walls are adorned with colorful street art, and couples' names are scrawled in Sharpie on the concrete. I emerge at the communal gardens, where I'm surprised to find Claudio sitting on a bench and staring into the distance. I follow his gaze to the Paglia River, which glints like liquid gold on the horizon.

"Buongiorno," I say as I sit down beside him.

He smiles and pats my arm. "Buongiorno, Em—" He shakes his head, and his eyes cloud. My heart clenches. "Good morning, Victoria."

"Did you wake up too early, too?" I ask, admiring how the sun casts the landscape in the warmest shade of blush.

"Always," he responds, turning to face me. "You?"

"Always." I smile, trying to read his expression, wondering if the haunted look in his gaze is one of loss or something more. The urge to ask him about his daughter is almost overwhelming.

We both turn back to the view, sighing in unison as the sun sweeps higher. The shadows of dawn melt away as the light overtakes the valley. The smell of pastries, pizza bianca, and espresso comes alive with the day, reaching us even at this far corner of town.

"Can I buy you a coffee?" I ask. I should just go back to the apartment and leave the poor man alone. But I can't.

He rises and offers a hand to help me stand. "It would be a pleasure. But I insist on offering."

We walk side by side in silence, my mind spinning with where to begin and what I could say that wouldn't be horribly intrusive. But everything feels delicate: the teddy bear room, the painting, even acknowledging that I know about Emma somehow feels like overstepping.

As we turn into the piazza, someone raises a hand and shouts, *"Buongiorno, professore."*

Claudio's face lights up, and he dips his head in a slight bow. It's the first time I've ever seen him look happy.

"Professor?" I ask, even though I already know, thanks to Mirësi.

"Yes, I taught at the Classics high school for almost twenty years." He chuckles softly. "My old students like to remind me."

"What did you teach?"

"Ancient Greek studies," he says, and the words are sharp, almost derisive. He clears his throat. "Mostly literature," he adds more softly, holding the door to the bar open for me.

"I've never been very good at languages," I confess after Claudio orders our coffees.

His eyes brighten with the challenge of an educator facing an unpromising student. "Perhaps you just haven't found the right language."

I shrug. "Ancient Greek, though?"

"Here," he says, grabbing a napkin and reaching over the bar for a pen. Suddenly, the man who seemed so old when I first met him in my apartment is spry and capable. His shoulders, no longer stooped, look strong under his coat.

It is so strange how grief transforms us, how heartache can diminish us in so many ways.

Guilt can do the same.

I lean closer to see what he's writing. It is a list of books and plays, I think. All in English. He has filled almost the entire napkin when he hesitates, taking a deep breath as he studies me. I see him start to wilt again, to turn inward, before he rights himself and adds one more title: *The Orphic Hymns.*

He slides the napkin to me along the bar.

"How will reading the stories in English help me learn Ancient Greek?"

"You will fall in love with them, and then you will need to know them more deeply. And that need will be enough." I raise my eyebrows doubtfully, and he grabs the napkin, setting money down for the coffee on the counter. "You'll see."

He walks me back to the apartment, and we talk about nothing in particular. But for today, I got enough. I saw a version of Claudio as he existed before, and that already colors his story in a bit more. He was a passionate teacher whose students still call out to him on the street—not exactly 'kill-your-daughter' material.

"May I have the napkin? I'll begin my studies immediately, Professor Mancini, so I'll be ready to report back by our next meeting."

He laughs, and the sound is so honest and unexpected that I feel my eyes water. As he pulls the list of books from his pocket, a shadow falls across us on the street, and I look up just as Claudio does to see Edo leaning over the wall and grinning down at us.

Claudio's face registers momentary surprise and a hint of wariness before he beams back at Edo. "Signor Mazza," Claudio says, stepping back to see him better. His posture shifts, his shoulders dropping. "I didn't know you were in Orvieto these days."

Edo gestures to me. "As often as possible, now that Victoria is here."

"Ah." Claudio winks, and it seems at odds with the sudden fragility he displays. Like he can't let others see the hardiness he still possesses, the competence of his mind and body. "Of course. I will let you two get on with your morning, then. Have a beautiful day, and give my regards to your mother, Signor Mazza."

"I will," Edo says, unconsciously rubbing a hand over his heart.

Claudio collects the mail from the box on the gate and shifts his gaze to me, holding the letters under his arm. "I appreciated the company this morning, Victoria."

"Thank you for the coffee."

He inclines his head and turns to walk away. My brows furrow as I try to interpret this strange performance. "I forgot the nap—" I start to call after him, and he stops suddenly and gives a tight smile, an almost imperceptible shake of his head.

"Call me if you need anything at the apartment," he says, dipping his head. Old and delicate. Transformed back into the broken man I first met.

"I will," I tell him, even though I now feel like I'm promising a stranger.

At the top of the stairs, Edo wraps me in his arms, kissing the top of my head. "Didn't sleep well?" he asks.

"As well as usual." I warm my hands against his chest. "How do you know Claudio?"

Edo rests his chin on my head, pulling me in closer. "He was my teacher."

"*You* studied Ancient Greek?" I pull back to see him better.

He chuckles. "I tried."

"Did you..." I hesitate, playing with the hem of his sweater. "Did you know his daughter? Emma?"

Edo's features turn thoughtful, a little sad. "Yes, I knew her. Claudio was accused of her murder when she went missing. It was terrible."

"How could people possibly think he'd do something like that?" Even as I say it, I think of Claudio's unsettling transformation—the disguise of meekness he dons in front of others.

Edo pushes his dark hair back from his face, his blue eyes impossibly vivid in the morning light. "It was a weird time. There was a lot of talk of devil worship and Satanic cults and blood rites."

"What?" I scoff. "They thought Claudio was part of a cult?"

"Well." Edo chews his lip, looking almost guilty. "He kind of was."

11

"EXCUSE ME?" I PRACTICALLY shout. "Are you telling me that people thought my landlord sacrificed his daughter?"

Edo rests his hands on my shoulders. "It was never as explicit as that. There were rumors."

"You," I say, poking Edo in the chest, "just made it sound like he was definitely in on the Satan worship."

"What I meant was that Claudio was part of a group or a club of some sort. Mostly men. A little secretive. And at the time, in the area, there were a number of documented cases of cult activity."

I cross my arms. "Like teenagers wearing Leviathan crosses on their hoodies? Listening to offensive music?"

"No, like brainwashing and mental manipulation, especially of women and children."

A tremor of cold rolls through me. "That's sick and terrifying, but it's not murder!" I insist.

"No." He looks away. "It's not murder. Not that was ever proven, at least."

"That isn't reassuring at all."

"The police had nothing on Claudio other than a few stories from students about a coin he carried around with a pentagram on it and an alleged affair."

"An affair?" I whisper. "With who?"

"Alleged," he repeats. "And no one knows. They found a bunch of letters during the investigation, but there was never a return address, and whoever had written them used an alias."

My mind wanders back to the telegrams stuffed in the copy of *Antigone* on the bookshelf, and my breath quickens. Could those also be from his mistress? Blood rites are one thing, but what if it were simpler than that? What if Emma discovered something Claudio didn't want her, or others, to know? I look over Edo's shoulder to the upstairs window and shiver. Didn't June say that Silvia, Claudio's wife, left him during the investigation?

"That is incredibly sketchy."

"Victoria," he says, his broad hands circling my hips and drawing my attention back. "Do you think I'd let you stay in this apartment if I thought he was dangerous?"

I wrap my arms around his neck. "You have been quite persistent about trying to convince me to stay somewhere else since before I arrived."

"That's for purely selfish reasons, *amore mio."* He runs his thumb along my bottom lip.

And right now, with everything I've just learned, I'm tempted to take him up on the offer.

We spend the rest of the morning lounging in bed and watching the news, which I hardly pay attention to, on Edo's laptop.

I left my laptop in storage in San Diego. I had used it for work, and it was full of records, basically a digital grimoire of death and ways to die. Mr. Jain, 1:13 am, liver failure. Mrs. Abara, 3:02 pm, heart disease. Mr. Copeland, 5:11 am, morphine overdose. I didn't write that, though. His death certificate cited stroke as the cause of death.

When Edo runs out to grab a couple of pizzas for lunch, I'm drawn downstairs to the bookshelf. The temptation of the telegrams needles my thoughts. Knowing they are right there is like an impossible itch, and I've hardly thought about anything else since Edo mentioned Claudio's affair.

I want to read them all and snoop through every drawer I can find in this house.

But Edo has to leave tomorrow afternoon to return to Florence for work on Monday, and I will have the apartment to myself then.

An awful part of me wishes he'd leave sooner.

I open a bottle of Matteo's wine and sit on the patio while waiting for Edo to return, saying a silent hello to Paul when I hear him scream over the wall. Mirësi and her coffee were right about one thing: my evening with Edo was terrific. All our time together is. I should try to appreciate it more.

Edo lets himself in with my keys and grins at me over armfuls of pizza boxes. His smile falters when he sees the wine glass.

"I know," I say, raising a hand before he can comment. "You think that the drinking isn't helping with my sleep, and you may be right. And I know you don't drink white wine, so I can't convince you to join me. But, Edo. Matteo's phenomenal."

He raises a dark eyebrow. "Is he?"

"Yes." I stumble a little over the word. "At wine."

My phone pings face up on the table—a text message. I wince.

Edo laughs as his eyes drift to my screen. "And his timing isn't bad either."

I couldn't agree less.

"He only texts me because of his mother," I explain, ignoring the message and passing Edo a plate. "You know June is right there beside Matteo, threatening him with withheld lunches...or worse."

"You actually believe that, don't you?" he asks, cocking his head.

I put a slice of zucchini pizza on my plate and one on Edo's, not meeting his eyes. "It's true."

He sighs as he sits down, and I freeze. It is the first time he's ever expressed sincere hesitation about my relationship with Matteo. He's teased and smirked and playfully shaken his head, but he has never sighed.

"Edo?" I say quietly.

"Victoria?"

I pull my chair closer to his. "If it bothers you, I'll ask him to stop."

"I only want to make sure that..." He trails off and takes my hand, twisting his fingers through mine. I press my leg into his under the table. "I just want to make sure you're okay. I know that this is a big change and that you're still grieving Miriam's loss. And I want you to know you can talk to me. I want to be the one you turn to."

I'm trying, I think. But since Alex, I've never turned to anyone. Not my family. Not Tibi. And not Matteo.

"I am so lucky." I kiss his jaw. "And I know it."

"Me too. And if Matteo tries anything, friend or not, I'll have to have his production license revoked," Edo jokes.

I flick him. "I thought you swore to use your nobility only for good."

"Does *my* good not count?" he asks with fake hurt in his voice, and I laugh before biting into a delicious slice of warm pizza.

He winks and takes a bite of his, too. We sample a slice of each pizza he bought, which is about four too many, before I go in to make espresso.

When I return with our coffee, he's standing in the corner of the patio, looking over the road. He has his phone to his ear and swings his face to me when he hears me set the cups on the table, closing the call as he smiles. "The office," he explains without prompting. "Something came up, and they want me to come in tomorrow."

"On a Sunday?"

He chews his lip guiltily. "On a Sunday."

"Does that mean you'll have to leave in the morning?" I pray my voice doesn't sound as hopeful as I feel. Good lord, I do not deserve this man. I'm practically giddy at the possibility of trading him out for the chance to rummage through a near-stranger's hidden telegrams.

Edo shakes his head, dropping his eyes. "I need to go now. I have to get all the documents together this evening. I'm sorry, *principessa.*"

"No worries," I say, too quickly, too brightly. His brow furrows slightly. "I mean," I go on, aiming to make my voice more thoughtful, "you'll be back soon, right? And then next month, we'll get a good stretch of time together when you come to handle the stuff with your mom."

My stomach twists a little when I remember his dad will be here, too.

"I will be," he says, stepping closer and tugging a strand of my hair between his fingers. "I have to make sure Matteo doesn't have a chance to steal you from me."

I smack a hand against his chest. "Don't be ridiculous."

"Am I?" he asks, running the back of his hands along the line of my waist. "Being ridiculous?"

"Very," I murmur.

Edo leans in and kisses my neck. I press myself into him, my fingers clinging to his sweater. "I hope so," he whispers into my hair.

He leaves me on the porch to get his things together, and I keep my phone tucked in my pocket, imagining, in a way that feels a little crazy, Edo watching me from the bedroom window, waiting to see if I'll text Matteo back. I make sure he can see my hands when I sit down. So, if he does look down, he can be reassured that I am here for him—no one else.

Paul screams, and I wonder for a moment what it means that I feel like I'm acting for Edo. Trying to play the part of a perfect girlfriend.

It's easier this way, I tell myself.

Yes, Matteo will always make my heart flutter with teenage infatuation, but nothing ever has, or ever will, happen between us. I love Edo. And he loves me. If my little performance makes him feel better, then no harm, no foul. Because the truth is, I have no idea how to play this part.

I startle—real, not pretend—when Edo lays a hand on my shoulder. "I'll walk you to your car," I say, standing. "Where'd you park?"

He studies me, reaching for my wrist. "Victoria."

I raise a hand to shield my eyes against the sunlight that frames him. I remember hearing somewhere that in Ancient Greece, it was believed that looking directly upon the full splendor of a god would destroy you. That a human was so incapable of comprehending the magnificence of the Olympians that they'd just, *poof,* be dead if they witnessed their undiminished glory. Seeing the way the sun shimmers gold at the edges of Edo's skin, his eyes scorching, fiery blue, it's hard to imagine anything more striking.

I chuckle, grateful I'm still standing.

He smiles, and I'm half-inclined to turn away in case his perfect teeth are what do me in. "Something funny?"

"Not funny at all." I gesture to him. "This is very, deathly serious. You are leaving me, and I don't know when I will see you again. After what happened in our bed last night, it is going to be especially hard to simply fall asleep." I hope he forgets that it is, unfortunately, always hard for me to fall asleep.

"*Our* bed," he repeats, his hands tightening around my upper arms, thumbs rubbing back and forth.

I grin up at him. "Our bed. Our Batmobile. Our..." I trail off, not sure what else to add to the list.

"I have some ideas," he says before kissing me. "But they will be more easily realized if I still have a job."

"Go," I say, pushing him toward the stairs. "When you get into Florence, let me know so I won't worry."

"And you, stay in touch."

"Of course."

"Please," he adds, his voice low.

I nod, a funny feeling in my chest at recognizing how much he cares. I hope I'm ready. For Edo, I hope I can do this.

12

I REST MY ELBOWS on the low patio wall, chin in my hands, watching Edo walk up the street. His navy sweater is snug against his back, the strap of his leather overnighter cutting across his shoulder blades. My boyfriend is very attractive.

"I love you," I shout before he turns the corner. Even from here, I can see his chest rise with a soft laugh. His smile is devastatingly tender when he faces me, and a touch of disappointment that he's leaving snakes its way into my belly, though it's not enough to temper the excitement bubbling there. It is the same feeling I used to get when my parents would leave Alex and me at home alone when we were young, an exhilaration that borders on panic.

He waves, and I blow him a kiss. Then, he takes a right at the crossroads and disappears behind three stories of medieval palace. I count to three, slowly, with a double Mississippi. I'm not sure what I am trying to prove or to whom, but knowing I have some agency over my burgeoning obsession with Emma *is* reassuring.

About six months after I lost Alex, when things got really bad, I started to develop compulsions. Well, I started developing fixations, and those fixations led to compulsions. It seemed silly at first, trivial—a misplaced need to know everything about something, to fully understand. But then I'd forget to eat. I'd stop sleeping. I'd bury myself in it.

And I'd feel an impossible yearning to talk about it—to Alex.

So I did.

My mother said the fixations were a way to control input and focus on something external. With the internet at my fingertips, it provided a constant flow of dopamine, a hit of feel-good that I was desperate for. I was a sixteen-year-old addict who spent hours speaking out loud to her dead sister.

My mom explained that away, too—Complicated Grief Disorder.

Difficulty accepting the loss. Mourning. Heartache.

She wasn't entirely wrong. But what she didn't account for was the anger. The hate. She could tell me whatever she wanted to, but I knew, and I think she did too, that I would never trust her again.

I top off my wineglass and carry it into the house, making my way straight to the copy of *Antigone* on the bookshelf. Now that nothing is standing between me and the telegrams, I am a little skittish. Claudio was so kind this morning. So warm. And it feels like a betrayal to sit here and dig into his world without his permission.

But then again, he encouraged me to read several translated Greek works, *Antigone* among them. He knew they were here, and he knew I would see them.

Could he want me to find the telegrams? Is it some sort of test? A game?

A chill settles on my neck.

Claudio called me Emma the first time we met. If these telegrams have something to do with her disappearance, am I digging my own grave by exhuming the past?

If I am, do I care enough to stop?

I reach for the book and flip it open to page sixty again, not hesitating to pull the telegram from the envelope. According to the date in the corner, it was sent almost exactly six years ago. The message is written in Italian, which I should have anticipated. I skip the body and go straight to the bottom.

Saluti,

Diche ed Orfeo

Diche and Orfeo? Diche and Orpheus?

I stuff the telegram back into the envelope and between the pages, then flip further back into the book and take out the next. It is signed the same way. I keep going through the book, opening each envelope. The bottom of every telegram has the same salutation.

Edo said they could never confirm Claudio's affair, that the letters they found had been signed with an alias, and that the writer was never identified.

But there is seemingly more than one writer who sent these telegrams—Diche *and* Orfeo—and with names like these, it is probable that they are also using pseudonyms, which, based on the documentaries I've seen, strikes me as a pretty cultish thing to do.

And if these were sent years after the investigation, the police never would have seen them. These could be the key to discovering who was responsible for Emma's disappearance.

Because maybe it wasn't an accident after all.

I chew my lip, wondering if I should call Edo and have him translate for me. "No, he's too busy," I say out loud. "Matteo or Tibi?" I question the silence of the house, half expecting it to creak or slam or for a light to flicker in response. When nothing happens, I decide I shouldn't involve them, either. For multiple reasons. Best case, they will worry about me. Worst, someone might mention it to June, who would tell my mother.

I'll just have to figure it out on my own. Maybe I can ask Mirësi.

I shut the book, and when I pick up my wine glass, I discover it's empty. After I refill it in the kitchen, the bottle is also empty. Leaning against the counter, I open my unread messages. Speaking of making people worry, I'm surprised June hasn't shown up at my gate yet when I see the number of unread texts from Matteo.

I take a sip off the top so the wine won't spill and call Matteo as I walk up the stairs, telling myself the timing is coincidental and that I don't need the company to make me feel safe on the second story of this house.

"Patatina?" he answers after a single ring.

I tuck the phone against my shoulder and shut the door of the teddy bear room, which refuses to stay closed. "In the flesh."

"Are you..." His voice drops. "Is Edo with you?"

"He had to leave," I say, dropping onto the wide windowsill in the big bedroom. "Some work thing came up, and he had to go back to Florence."

Matteo is silent for a full five seconds.

"What's up with you two recently?" I demand, drawing my legs up. The breeze is soft and scented with jasmine. I lean my head back. "I know things never quite recovered after the Tibi situation, but that was years ago. Did something happen between you guys that I don't know about?" *Has everyone decided to keep something else from me?*

"No." Matteo clears his throat. "Nothing happened. I'm just..." He trails off, and for a split second, I let myself consider Edo's words. His hilarious and misguided belief that Matteo is envious of our relationship.

"Just jealous?" I ask in a voice that's more rhetorical than teasing, a voice that screams *I am joking, and we both know it.*

Matteo doesn't laugh.

Or he does, but it sounds more like a grunt. An angry, annoyed grunt. What the hell? I decide I probably shouldn't mention that he texted me over ten times in the past twenty-four hours. Or maybe I should; maybe since he clearly isn't interested, now is a good time to set some boundaries. For Edo's sake.

"Matty—"

"Are you still up for meeting the twins tomorrow?" he asks, interrupting me.

My heart catches, and my eyes drop to the red string on my wrist. "Of course. I can't wait." I raise the glass and swallow a gulp of wine.

"You know, Tori, it's okay if you want to take some more time to settle in. They'll understand."

"I'm fine." I yawn, the sun warm against my skin. "Really."

"I'll come by at nine to walk you over."

"If you want to give me an address, I'm sure I can manage on my own."

"I also have a ton of food to drop off for you. Mom is worried you don't have enough to eat at the house."

I groan. "I told Edo that's why you were texting. He was being so weird."

"Weird?"

"Don't worry. You can let June know she can just call. I won't get mad if she checks in on me. I'm not Tibi. See? Problem solved."

"Yeah. Right."

I hiccup.

"Tor?"

"Yes?"

"Do you want to come to the house for dinner?"

I gaze out the window, the light casting long shadows on the wall of tufo across the narrow street. There's an open window, the room dark through the frame, and I imagine someone looking back at me. "I should stay here and get some stuff taken care of."

I smile, thinking of Edo's concern. Knowing I'm doing the right thing. And this time, it doesn't even feel like pretending. I take another sip of wine.

And then, I'm fighting to breathe, a leaden weight saddling my chest, compressing as I sink underneath the burden. I open my eyes, and everything is dark. My arms and legs are frozen. All I can do is blink into the gloom, desperately sucking air into my throat as I rack my memory for the prayer Grandma Miriam taught me when I told her ten years ago about the nightmares.

I shout the words in my head, a version of the prayer that isn't quite right but close enough to offer comfort. In the chanting, I hear Grandma Miriam reciting the lines beside me. *You have returned my soul within me,* she sings, and I feel her holding my hand, stroking my fingers as my body returns to me.

I take a deep breath, the amber gilt of the streetlamp outside slowly bringing the world to life around me. The beating of my heart is so ferocious that the room seems to echo with it. I'm in bed, in the teddy bear room.

When I can finally sit up, I scramble for the lamp on the bedside table and then rush out the door. In the big room, I find an empty wineglass and my cell phone on the windowsill. I pull the blanket off the bed and wrap it around my shoulders to ward off the chill of the night air. I feel dizzy when I reach for my phone, realizing how dangerously low the window is and how far the drop is to the patio outside.

How stupid it was of me to be drinking there.

I don't remember saying goodbye to Matteo. I don't remember finishing my glass or getting into bed.

It's not even eight p.m.

Edo called about three hours ago. Twice. Probably to let me know he'd made it safely. He also texted me: *Did I lose you already?*

I type as fast as I can, my fingers still shaking from the nightmare, the surprise of waking up and finding myself in the dark. *I fell asleep as soon as you left,* I lie. *I'm sorry I missed your call.*

Bouncing dots appear almost at once, and I hold my breath. But just as quickly, they vanish.

Miss you already, I write.

Nothing.

I consider calling, but he's probably deep into his work, ensuring everything is perfect. He's so careful. I don't want to distract him.

Matteo texted, too, but I leave his message unread.

I close the window, latching the shutters even though I know they won't hold, and head downstairs, flipping on the lights as I go. *Antigone* is still sitting on the table. I know I won't get back to sleep tonight, not with the pressure of the nightmare still heavy in my lungs, so I might as well start reading.

I flip to the first page and shudder. Already, death and loss pervade the story. Already, I know I will have the perfect excuse to see Claudio again.

13

THROUGH THE NIGHT, I doze on the couch, constantly waking with a gasp, a jolt, as my conscious mind draws me violently and wholly out of the tumult of the unconscious. By sunrise, I've read *Antigone* twice, and now I'm even more curious about what the telegrams say.

And why Claudio chose to store them there, in a story about a woman trying to properly lay a loved one to rest. Even without knowing more about what happened to Emma, it is hard not to draw parallels between Antigone's story and Emma's, which is incentive enough for me to tiptoe upstairs, get dressed, throw on Edo's heavy jacket, and march out into the lightening morning.

I march through town, hoping to catch Claudio in the gardens again. I wait half an hour before giving up and getting breakfast at a nearby cafe. Instead of cutting back through the piazza to get home, I return to the gardens, descending the spiral stairs and wandering toward where the wild boars should now be settling in for the day.

The brush is dense, and the shadows are still heavy in the early morning light. Sticks crack under my feet, and I swear when a branch snaps back and scratches my cheek. My approach is anything but delicate, which is good. I'd rather they know I'm coming.

Their rustling reaches my ears before I see them, the soft grunts breaking through the greenery. I know I am closer than I should be, and slow as I near them. These aren't massive males like the boar that got stuck in the train's undercarriage. Their tusks aren't as conspicuous, not protruding and vicious—the threat of their mouths not on display. They are females, sisters and mothers and aunts, with their piglets.

And they are, in many ways, much more dangerous.

We watch each other, and when I make no move to get closer, they tumble onto their sides, sprawled and vulnerable in the grass and first fall of leaves, their young piled against their bellies. As their breathing steadies, one raises her head and eyes me, her pupil deep black, her gaze almost pensive. I wonder if it's the same sow who studied me yesterday. I wonder if she remembers me.

If she doesn't, she seems to reach the same conclusion.

I pose no risk.

Soon, she too seems to be asleep, and I wander back through the woods and onto the hill, with plenty of time to shower and caffeinate before Matteo is at the house.

When I get back, the teddy bear room door is open, and the doors to the armoires are open in the big bedroom. The house is showing off again now that Edo isn't here to see it. I grab a towel and step out of the bedroom, pausing as cold creeps into my bones when I see something else is open now, too—a crawl space above the stairs, the door just barely ajar.

I rise onto my toes, teetering at the edge of the top stair, and push it closed before ducking into the bathroom and locking the door.

The steam from the box shower once again consumes the bathroom. Despite the chill in the air, I crack the window mid-shower to combat the sense that something is concealed in the haze. That something is in there waiting for me.

When I get out, the mirror is almost entirely fog-free, except for the top right corner, where a cloud of moisture lingers. It almost looks like someone has swiped a finger through the condensation, the inkling of a capital T barely visible as the steam dissipates. I watch my weary reflection drag the edge of my towel over the spot before I brush my hair.

I do my best to cover the dark circles under my eyes with makeup, then put on a bright, striped sweater I brought to Italy specifically for this moment. It screams, *I love kids. I am fun.* This seemed like the kind of messaging I should be leaning into as someone who has worked in death for half a decade and is suddenly looking to nanny.

Downstairs, I prepare one last coffee and finally take the time to acknowledge what's happening.

Twins. Two little girls.

It feels poetic, me finding myself again in this facsimile of my origin story. Me, building a new life, alone. Letting things go. Finally letting Alex go.

The dead never leave us, Grandma Miriam argues. I half-heartedly consider a glass of Matteo's wine to help quiet her. I don't want to show up to my new job with ghosts in my heart and on my shoulders.

I don't drink, of course, because I haven't completely lost it.

I hurry to the street when I see the time. I still can't get over Edo's sigh and the palpable distress he felt around my relationship with Matteo. He let the facade crack, and I appreciate the honesty. I know it isn't easy for him to show that side of himself, to be anything other than positive and supportive. The least I can do is make sure I'm not giving him anything to worry about. Having Matteo in the house, being alone with him somewhere private, feels like a betrayal of Edo.

Matteo pulls up, grinning at me as he leans across the center console to open the door.

"Thanks," I say, my voice strained by my guilt. And I know sitting in a car doesn't make me guilty, but the quickening of my pulse when Matteo's fingers graze my sweater does. The tightening of my chest as he studies me, his hazel eyes tending toward amber today in his gold-rimmed glasses, might, too.

His hand moves from the console to the gearstick, but he doesn't drive. "Hey," he says softly. "You all right?"

"Didn't sleep great, but I'm fine." I clasp my hands between my knees and look out the window, the wall not much more than a foot from the glass.

"If the house—"

"No," I blurt, turning to him. "The house is great. It's...perfect." I chew my lip, suddenly feeling protective of the house. Protective of the things I want from it. The crawl space door, the writing on the mirror, all of that aside, I feel like the house and I are similar, somehow. It's the one thing I'm sure of right now. I need to be there.

He runs a thumb under my right eye, and my breath stutters on an inhale. I know what he sees there: the darkness. A confession of exhaustion, a lack of peace. "I just want to make sure you're okay."

I duck my face, his hand falling away. "It's just jet lag, Matty."

He nods, not in agreement or acceptance. It's a nod of seeing something more, of seeing through me, but telling me that he will pretend for now if that's what I want. He puts the car in drive.

"Wait," I say, "why are we driving?"

Matteo shrugs. "Couldn't find parking."

"Edo didn't seem to have a problem when he was here."

"It seems Edo is just a luckier guy than I am." I feel his gaze on my face, but his eyes are on the road when I turn.

"Tell me about the family again. The dad is your friend, right? Have I met him?"

"Maybe, once. You'll like his wife. Lucia is a writer. She's a blast. Even Tibi agrees."

"I'm excited to get to know her," I say, and I mean it.

"And the girls." He reaches over to squeeze my knee, but pulls his hand away quickly. "The girls are adorable. You're going to love them, Tori. They are going to love you."

I don't respond.

Matteo eventually finds a parking spot near the elementary school, and we walk, mostly in silence, up to the cathedral and then down Via del Duomo to the center of town. He turns right down a small side street and then walks us into the courtyard of a familiar building. "This is..." I whisper, trailing off.

"Where Edo used to live. Yeah. You've been here before. Caterina Mazza is still here."

"I know," I say, looking over my shoulder.

His eyebrows furrow.

I tilt my head toward the vines growing up the walls and the tables set in the sunlit courtyard, trying to appear more curious than paranoid. "It looks different than the last time I was here."

"Sure. I bet." He chews his cheek, his eyes darkening, and then presses the buzzer for the Riccis'.

Lucia buzzes us up, and we walk up the stone steps together to the third floor, passing the ancient, dark wood door to Caterina's apartment on the way. The top floor of the palace is split into four separate apartments, all surrounding a massive central courtyard.

Lucia opens the door for us, shaking my hand and placing kisses on Matteo's cheek. Her husband, Carlo, is changing the twins' diapers in their nursery. She offers us a coffee while we wait.

I glance out the window and, based on the view, determine that the Riccis' apartment is above Caterina's dining room and kitchen.

"You have a beautiful home," I say when she hands me an espresso. At this point, after just three hours of sleep yesterday afternoon and approximately none last night, caffeine might be the only thing keeping me alive. "How long have you been here?"

"Carlo and I moved in after we got married. But he grew up here. You didn't tell her, Matteo? About how poor Carlo chased you and Edo around in high school?" She looks at me and playfully shakes her head. "Lucky for me, he couldn't keep up."

"You all went to school together?" I ask, leaning against the wall.

Matteo pulls out a chair for me, and when I don't sit, he stands beside me. "We did. But Lucia was always in Porto Ecole during the summer, so she was never fortunate enough to meet you."

"I heard plenty, though," Lucia says wryly, raising her eyebrows. Matteo grins down at his feet. A curl falls over the rim of his glasses.

Great. I'm not sure what there would have been to hear. I'm guessing Matteo didn't share the part about me going crazy. I'm guessing he didn't tell them much about my dead twin, either. Neither seems like the kind of thing that would recommend me for the position.

I laugh, albeit nervously, and finish my espresso, my fingers shaking, the porcelain clinking against the small white plate when Carlo walks into the kitchen with a small girl on either hip: Ada and Ileana.

They look almost identical. At this age, so did Alex and I. Matteo takes my cup, and Carlo sets the girls down. I move closer, squatting before them. "Ciao," I say. "I'm Tori." They look at me, confused and a little startled. I try to scootch back and fall on my ass.

Their eyes widen in unison. I pretend to fall again. They burst into giggles, reaching for each other's hands.

And I don't feel any of the things I expected to feel. There is no torment in their joy. No pain in witnessing their togetherness—no regret or guilt or emptiness.

I feel something so new and surprising that I almost fall again. I feel an ache I never thought I would—for *this*.

Smiling, I glance over my shoulder. Matteo smiles back.

14

"DID YOU SEE THAT?" I ask Matteo, slightly out of breath from a heated game of toddler tag, as we walk back to the car. "I am a kid person! Mutual fun was had. No one cried."

"You're an everyone person, Tor." He pulls his keys out and unlocks the doors. "I told you they'd love you."

"But I didn't think you meant it." Matteo starts to open the passenger door, and I reach out to stop him, unintentionally peering up at the row of windows that line Caterina's apartment. "I'll walk."

"I still have all the food Mom sent with me. I have to come by anyway." He reaches past me, pulls the handle, and gestures to the seat. *"Patatina."*

"Thanks," I say, sliding past him and grimacing as our arms brush.

Matteo shuts my door and walks around to the other side of the car, the sun catching the strands of light in his sandy brown waves.

"Do you have dinner plans?" he asks as he starts the car.

"Nope." I lean back and close my eyes. My only plans for the rest of the day include a long nap, and if that succeeds, an attempt at translating a telegram or two.

"There's this new place down in Ciconia I want to try."

"Will they have anything Tibi can eat? At lunch the other day, she told me she was sticking to strictly locally grown wheat for the rest of the week. Only carbs from within a kilometer of the hill."

"Then she's going to be very hungry for the next few days because she took the train back to Rome this morning."

I sit up. "Everything okay with her and the Irish poet?" I have about thirty texts sitting in my messages from Tibi. I should probably check them. Since she can be a bit of a spammer, I generally assume she'll call if it's important.

"Everything's fine. Maybe very fine? Very Tib, in any case. She seemed excited to see Jasper. I'm not sure if it's because she's aching for a fight or something else."

I chuckle. "Very Tib," I confirm.

"What time is good for you this evening? I could come by early and take you to the house first. Mom would be thrilled to see you."

"Won't I see June at dinner?"

"My parents can't make it. They have their weekly date night, and I thought—" he stops talking, chewing his lip as he meets my eye.

"Shoot," I say. "I completely forgot I'm supposed to meet a neighbor at seven."

His shoulders drop slightly. "A neighbor?"

"Yes," I lie. "She lives in the house at the corner. I met her the other day. She has a peacock. Well, it's not her peacock, but he lives there. Paul. She's a witch. Probably."

"Sounds interesting." He grins. "I'm glad you're making friends

"She tells fortunes from coffee grounds."

He smirks. "How does tomorrow look?"

"You'd have to ask Mirësi."

"I mean for dinner." He nudges me with his elbow, and I drop my gaze to my hands.

"Edo might be back by then."

Matteo's hand seems to tighten on the gear shift. He clears his throat. "Of course. If he isn't, though, and you want to get out..." He trails off, then adds, "My parents will be available."

"Yeah, maybe," I offer.

I would love to see the Grazianos. I would love a night out with Matteo, something the two of us have never done before. Not alone.

Wherein lies the problem.

I am not savvy enough at relationships to honor Edo's concerns, which I am very willing to admit are not entirely unwarranted, and navigate a new, more intimate friendship with Matteo. Maybe if I weren't clinically sleep-deprived, I could reason my way through it, but from where I'm sitting in Matteo's sun-warmed leather seat, there's no way to reconcile the two. A one-on-one dinner is definitely out of the picture for now. Perhaps even a family night out.

Matteo pulls up to my gate, and we unload everything onto the exterior stairs—huge packs of carbonated water, twenty types of Umbrian cookies, anything June could find that was relatively fresh but with a long shelf life and zero prep time. Matteo invents a very illegal parking space and leaves the car so he can help me carry it all up into the house.

"Paul?" he asks after a loud scream as I unlock the front door.

I gape at him. "How did you know?" *Is it common knowledge that peacocks wail like possessed infants?*

"I guess I was hoping it was Paul. I mean, the alternative is—"

"A screaming child." I nod. "That's what I thought the first time I heard him."

"Exactly. Much less romantic." He winks as he steps into the house with the packages of water.

"I don't know," I say, peeking into a bag of biscotti as I follow. "Nothing like a touch of horror to set the mood."

He opens the cabinet under the sink. "You always were a strange one, Tori Jacobs."

After putting everything away, Matteo asks if he can use the bathroom before heading out. He jogs up the stairs, and I clean up the dishes on the counter before heading upstairs to grab a phone charger.

When I arrive at the landing, the doors to the bathroom and the teddy bear room are open.

"Matteo?" I whisper, pushing the teddy bear door wider—like maybe a monster ate him and is now waiting to pounce on me.

Matteo straightens, his eyes swinging to mine.

"What are you doing?" I ask.

"The door was ajar, and—"

I glance over his shoulder. The front of the child-size armoire in the corner is flung wide, and the three drawers at the bottom are pulled out haphazardly. I cross my arms. "And you decided you'd come into Emma's room and go through her stuff?"

"What?" His mouth quirks at the corner.

I gesture at the armoire, and he shrugs. "That wasn't me. I just wanted to make sure the window was shut. They tend to unlock."

"I've noticed," I mumble, my eyes still on the open drawers in the corner. I hug myself a little tighter. Could I have done that? Did I come up here last night and start going through things? It's more than possible.

It is also possible that someone else has been here. Or that Matteo is lying.

I squeeze my eyes shut, trying to remember, and practically jump out of my skin when I feel Matteo's warm hand on my cheek.

"Tor," he says softly, his face just inches from mine.

He drags his fingers down my jaw before pushing my hair from my temple, his eyes never leaving mine.

I shudder. "What are you doing here?" I ask.

"Making sure you're okay."

"Stop," I say, shaking my head. "Whatever this is..."

"What do you mean?"

"Matty, we've been friends forever. You've never asked me out to dinner before or done—" I mirror his actions, running my fingers along his jaw, pushing a curl off his forehead. His chest rises, his eyes darkening, and I draw my hand back. "You've never done *this.* And I don't want to be a pawn in your bullshit with Edo. That's not fair to me."

He reaches for my wrist, and I tug my arm away. He looks hurt, as he should be. And then he looks angry, but he rolls his neck and plasters on an apologetic smile. "You're right. I'm being a dick."

"But why?"

He bites his lip. "Forgive me?"

"If you do it again," I say, narrowing my eyes, "I'm telling Tibi."

"Anything but that." Matteo throws his arms up in surrender.

I cock my head. He has a pill bottle in his left hand. "What's that?"

"This?" he says, looking guiltily at the orange container. "This is from your mom. I was going to put it in the bathroom. Just in case."

He passes it to me when I put my hand out. I read the label.

Sleeping pills.

My heart sinks. "You've been talking to my mom?"

"Not really," he says, shifting his feet. "But my mom has."

"She only saw me one time, Matteo. I was fine. I am fine!" Tears prick my eyes, an ugly feeling of betrayal landing in my gut.

"You know she likes to worry about you." His eyes are pleading, and he slips his hands in his pockets like he's worried he'll reach for me otherwise. "About all of us. And Meg, your mom, she loves you so much and she is really—"

I glare at him.

"But, Tor, she said you've—"

"Please, just stop." I sink onto the bed, holding the bottle of pills. What Matteo doesn't know is that they aren't just sleeping pills. They are the same antipsychotics my mother put me on after Alex died. My mother has prescribed me antipsychotics again without so much as speaking with me, assuming, I presume, that I am the same broken mess I was ten years ago.

My cheeks warm in embarrassment. It is not my mom's lack of faith in my mental fitness that is so disappointing; it's the Graziano's and the fact that Matteo and June hatched a whole plan with her to deliver the drugs. That no one believes me when I say I'm all right.

Actually, that's not true.

Edo believes me.

"I think you should go," I say, standing.

"Tori, look—"

I put my hands out, the pills rattling in their cage. "I don't want to hear it."

Matteo bows his head and sighs, walking out of the room and down to the front door. I watch from the landing as he pauses with his fingers on the handle. "I'll call you tomorrow about dinner?" It's a question, gentle and a little bit beseeching.

I shake my head. "Thanks for helping me get set up with the apartment and introducing me to the Riccis'. But I've got it from here."

He studies me and then looks around the room, delaying. Or, more than that, it's almost like he's looking for something. Like he doesn't want to leave the apartment as much as he doesn't want to leave me. His eyes land on the table.

"Go then if you must, but remember, no matter how foolish your deeds, those who love you will love you still," he says softly.

I follow his gaze to where the book is lying. "Excuse me?"

"Antigone."

I don't respond, mainly because the way he says it makes it feel like he knows something. Not just about the story, but also about what else it might mean. Maybe even something about the secrets stuffed in the copy not ten feet from us.

Matteo exhales, slow and heavy, and leaves without another word. I lock the door behind him and flip through the book, counting all twenty telegrams to ensure they are still there, and then hide the book behind the cushions on the couch.

It's not quite noon, but I make a plate of cookies and pour myself a glass of wine, hoping it will help me relax enough for a few hours of good sleep. I glance at the bottle of pills beside the sink on the kitchen counter and consider flushing them down the drain, but I think better of it.

They may be handy to have around.

As I sip the wine, I scan the books on the shelves, looking for evidence of more telegrams but finding none. I silence a call from Tibi. And then a second call.

When the glass is empty, I'm still not tired. I go back upstairs to put Emma's room back together. The crawl space door above the landing is open again.

This time, I smile.

It's time to give Claudio a call.

15

CLAUDIO SAYS HE'LL BE over soon to check the latches and the crawl space door. It takes about twenty minutes for him to arrive, a tool bag in hand. His arms seem to strain under the weight of the leather tote.

"Need help with that?" I ask, opening the gate for him. I know he has his own set of keys, but I don't plan to force him into showing his entire hand at once. He's smart enough not to let himself in while I'm here.

When he squares his shoulders, he consumes almost the entire width of the steps. His face opens, brightens. He reshapes himself in a moment, and I stumble on the step above me.

"Careful," he says, looking amused as he waits for me to right myself.

I laugh, and it sounds nervous. "I hope I'm not bothering you."

"Not at all, Victoria." He nods toward the upstairs as we step onto the patio and raises his voice like he doesn't intend the next part for my ears alone. "I'm sorry the house has been giving you problems."

"The house has been great," I argue. "I just want to make sure that nothing shatters or falls apart on my watch."

Claudio hums. "Ah, well, sometimes nothing can be done. Sometimes, it is just time for things to fall to pieces."

"Not the windows, though, I hope," I tease, ignoring the way his words settle like cobwebs on my skin.

He sets his tool bag on the table, and I'm glad I moved the copy of *Antigone*. "Preferably not the windows."

"Can I get you a coffee, water...wine?" I walk into the kitchen, watching him from the corner of my eye. "Have you tried Matteo's award-winning Orvieto Classico? Can I pour you a glass?"

"I'm not much of one for drinking alone." He pulls a hammer from his bag and studies the weight of it in his hand. "Would you be willing to join me for a toast?"

I consider for a moment the wisdom of being two glasses of wine deep, after not sleeping for nearly twenty hours, alone in a home with my landlord, who I suspect may be involved in the murder of his daughter and who, at the very least, appears to suffer from some sort of borderline personality disorder.

If my mother and the Grazianos already think I've lost it, what pretense is there to maintain that I haven't? Besides, if Claudio is like most people, he will be more open after a drink.

And I have questions.

"That sounds lovely," I say, swooping two stemmed wine glasses out of the cabinet and filling them nearly to the rim.

I carry them back out, handing the fuller glass to Claudio. *"Salute."*

Claudio clinks his glass against mine. "To life," he says, taking a deep drink.

I sit at the table, sipping my wine and observing him while he tinkers with the downstairs shutters. He is capable and, it occurs to me, relatively young. I'd go so far as to say that this version of Claudio is kind of handsome, the reminders of an attractive youth still visible in his strong jaw and cheekbones.

He rubs his forehead before reaching for his glass and finishing it. He smiles at me, a literal, albeit disarming, sparkle in his eye. I realize I'm staring.

"Refill?" I ask, feeling a little dizzy when I stand up.

"Why not? I don't think I could be any more useless than I already am with a hammer." He brings me his glass, and I feel his eyes on my back as I walk into the kitchen. I top off his glass, open another bottle, and top off mine.

"No luck with the shutters?" I ask, passing him his wine. We clink our glasses together again, no toasting this time.

"Seems I'm better with languages than with tools." As he says it, he looks over his shoulder at the bookcase. His head tilts, and I can almost swear he sees it, that he's noticed the empty spot on the shelf where *Antigone* should be. "But let me take a look at the crawl space door before I finish this glass and see if I can get at least one thing taken care of today."

I trail him up the stairs, our glasses in my hands, and lean on the wall beside the bedroom door. "How is your English so good?"

"I studied it in school." He tests the door, swinging it open and then closing it again. "And taught it later."

"At the high school?"

"No," he says, pulling a nail from his pocket. "Mostly private lessons. Kids of wealthy parents. Businessmen hoping a handle on English would equal more money. Bored housewives."

"That's not a very generous description."

"I know." He shrugs guiltily. "But in some cases, it was true. That doesn't mean they weren't some of my best students, though."

I snort at the implication in his voice, at the thought of a hunky language professor going into these women's homes, thrilling them with his attention. "Is that so?"

Claudio smirks, and I tense as he turns back to the crawl space, the glasses wobbling in my fingers. An affair doesn't seem so unlikely, so *alleged* after what he's shared. But what does that mean for Emma? How does it relate to what happened to her?

"I think I found the problem," he mutters, reaching his hand high above him and into the crawl space. He strains for a moment and then pulls something out. I set the wine glasses on the floor and take it from him.

A knit plushie, a pink little piglet with a blue felt scarf.

"Claudio—" I start to say, desperate to ask a question I shouldn't, but he's already got a nail between his teeth and another between his fingers, banging it into the wood beside the crawl space door, ensuring it stays closed.

I pass him the glass when he's done, along with the piglet, and on the way down the stairs, he stops on the landing, taking in the small portrait of Padre Pio, the single earring, the collection of things that seem random to me but might tell entire stories for him. He sets the plushie in an empty spot and exhales.

"I miss her," he says, sipping his wine. "I miss them."

That's right. Claudio lost Emma and his wife. Possibly because he was cheating on the latter, but just because you're responsible for something terrible doesn't mean it won't break you. In my experience, it means the cracks run even deeper.

"Did you paint that?" I ask, and he knows I mean the nightmarish figure in the woods, the painting that's haunted me every time I've come up and down these stairs.

"No, a friend gave it to me." He chuffs. "A *student*."

I drain the rest of my wine, and Claudio does the same.

"It's...dark."

Claudio nods and straightens the painting. "So was she."

"Where is she buried?" I whisper.

"Who?" he asks, turning to face me.

I swallow, caught off guard by his question as much as he was likely caught off guard by mine. "Emma," I answer softly.

Claudio shifts his feet. "She has a headstone in the cemetery, but..."

"But what?" I push when he doesn't go on.

"She's not buried there."

I blink at him, not understanding. "Why not?"

He looks away, and for the span of a second, a smile tugs at his lips. "They never found her."

Ice cascades down my limbs, down my spine, and I take an unsteady step away from Claudio, the wine and the lack of sleep catching up to me all at once. I start to sway on the step, and he catches me, my entire body going rigid at his touch.

"Let's sit you down," he says, lifting me bodily into his arms. "We don't need any more accidents."

I don't resist. I can't. I suddenly feel like I took the pills Matteo brought. My body is useless, and my mind is nearly as ineffective. He carries me to the couch and lays me down, grabbing a throw blanket and placing it over me while I watch him wide-eyed. He adjusts the pillows, his hand disappearing behind cushions and reappearing with the copy of *Antigone* clutched between his fingers.

"You've been reading?" he asks, flipping through the book just like I did after Matteo left, surveying the telegrams, all in their places.

"Yes," I answer, my voice barely audible. My vision goes hazy at the edges. I'm so tired. The human body has mechanisms in place. It can't run forever on alcohol and zero sleep. It can't run on grief.

"Good," he says. "Very good. I suspect you are quite an excellent student. Now get some rest so you can start on something new tomorrow."

"Okay," I mumble, letting my eyes drift closed.

"And Victoria…." I feel his breath on my ear. I sense his body close to mine as he leans over me. "I didn't hurt my daughter."

I cling to the last shreds of my consciousness, squinting at Claudio and meeting his eyes where he crouches beside me. "I know," I say before letting the exhaustion have its way with me.

Everything is quiet when I wake up, but the light is on in the kitchen. I come out of sleep slowly, calmly, like I just closed my eyes and opened them again. There's no bad dream for me to fight my way out of, no suffocating fear weighing down on my chest, no clamminess causing the throw blanket or my clothes to stick to my skin.

The sensation is so strange and unfamiliar that I almost feel like *this* is a dream. The easiness of it is nearly as disorienting as finding myself laid out on the couch downstairs. I try to piece things together: the visit with Claudio, the wine. I raise my head off the pillow to listen for footsteps or creaking or anything that might indicate I am not alone.

There's nothing—just the sound of my breath, the occasional distant noise of a car.

Stretching, I extract myself from the couch and get a glass of water in the kitchen, noting the copy of *Antigone* in the center of the table as I pass. Beside the sink, the medicine bottle Matteo brought is lying on its side, open, little pink pills sprawled across the counter in a constellation of narcotics.

I remember considering dumping them down the drain at some point, but I don't think I was in here between the time Claudio left and when I woke up on the couch. I don't think I've moved at all since I lay down, if the soreness in my muscles is any indication.

Maybe I knocked them over when I was refilling our wine. Three glasses and no real food wasn't a great idea.

I leave the pills where they are, still not sure if I should sweep them directly into the trash or back into the bottle, and after finding no sign of my phone, I head up the stairs, freezing on the landing.

My fingers graze the thick acrylic, the form of the screaming woman in the painting. I hold my breath as I lift it off its wooden stand, turning it over slowly and tilting it to catch the light from upstairs. I can just make it out, the name sketched in faint pencil in the corner.

My mouth falls open.

Caterina?

16

THE CHANCES THAT CATERINA Mazza, Edo's *mother*, painted this and gifted it to Claudio are slim. There must be several Caterinas in Orvieto. But it's not impossible. I want to call Edo and ask. He'd know if his mom ever took English lessons, wouldn't he? Especially if she'd taken them with Claudio. But it quickly dawns on me that that would be a bad idea. Because maybe Caterina was more than just Claudio's student. Some things in the past are best left buried.

I shiver, replacing the painting as I remember Claudio's comment about Emma never being found—his strange, incongruous smile. But something else he said has nestled deep into my gut with absolute conviction.

He didn't hurt his daughter.

At least not directly. Or intentionally. There are a lot of ways to hurt people. But I know he didn't kill her.

I know it with the same certainty that I knew I shouldn't go to spring break camp the year I was sixteen. The way I knew that the kiss I gave Alex before I left would be the last, despite my mom's insistence that it was fine, that Alex was fine, that it was good for me to be with friends for a while.

I came home to find Alex's hospital bed already moved out of our shared bedroom and Alex's body in a cold room at the crematory, my mom having taken her off life support while I was away.

The same certainty that told me what I'd find before I opened the door to Grandma Miriam's house three months ago.

My phone is on the floor of the small hallway, almost dead, and I am astonished to discover it's just past midnight. I slept for nearly ten hours, which almost has me convinced that I drugged myself with the sleeping pills between glasses of wine. If I did, and that's why I finally slept so well, I have no intention of telling my mother and the Grazianos they were right. At least not right away.

I'm tempted to take one more and see if I can squeeze in another ten hours to offset the steep sleep deficit I've been racking up, but I have to be at the Riccis' at nine, and I can't risk it. So I grab the phone charger, wash my face, and go downstairs to find a new book.

The next time I see Claudio, which will hopefully be soon, I will ask him to write the books down for me again that he'd scribbled on the coffee shop napkin. There's only one other title besides *Antigone* that I remember him noting, and I drag a dining room chair over to the bookshelf to see if I can find it.

The black and orange spine is set back on the top shelf, dulled by dust that I wipe away with my fingers. I read the title aloud: *The Orphic Hymns.* The back cover tells me that the book is a collection of eighty-seven poems addressed to various gods and attributed to the mythical poet Orpheus, or Orfeo in Italian—the same name from the telegrams.

I smile. I no longer feel the need to scavenge the house for evidence of Claudio's wrongdoing, but what if...

I know it sounds crazy before I fully formulate the thought.

What if the house is trying to tell me something? What if Emma is trying to tell me something?

Antigone is the story of a woman fighting to lay her loved one to rest. Something that hasn't happened for Emma, either. It is also the story of a woman silenced by a man for standing against him. I tug at the red string on my wrist. I never have believed in ghosts, but Grandma Miriam did. And I've been wrong about other things.

What if Mirësi and her coffee reading were right, and I am here for justice? I laugh because it's ridiculous. But also, kind of not ridiculous? What if I'm here for Emma, for the justice she deserves? Just because her disappearance was a terrible accident doesn't mean she isn't also looking for peace.

I carry the book to the table and set it down next to *Antigone.* There are no envelopes breaching the pages, no telegrams. There is a photo, though—black and white and blurry, printed on computer paper that's been folded into fourths, the seams thin and delicate. A copy of a sonogram. I slide it back in and close the book.

After a coffee and a plate of cookies, I curl back up on the couch and start reading. The hymns are numbered, the titles simple: To Protogonos, To Ether, To the Stars, to Kronos. Below that, before the poem begins, it lists the type of incense to burn while reciting the words. Things I've never heard of, like storax and manna, and others more familiar, such as frankincense and saffron and myrrh.

The words flow easily, prayers pouring out of my lips as I recite them one by one out loud. It reminds me of a Greek Mythology for Kids book Alex and I had when we were little, each page introducing a new god with unthinkable beauty, strength, or smarts for us to be enchanted by.

Halfway through, I flip back to the beginning to start again, reading until the faintest hint of dawn creeps across the windowsill. I clean up the pills, counting only twenty-seven of the thirty that should be there, then change into a new pair of jeans and leave the apartment to watch the wild boars come home. It is, I realize as I walk down the hill, the only thing I have in Orvieto that is just for me—my mornings in the forest, alone with the sunrise and the pigs. The only thing I don't have to share or that someone else hasn't procured for me.

I like that no one knows I come here. That no one in the whole world knows where I am right now. That whatever happens here is only mine, belongs only to me.

And something about being near the powerful animals, acknowledging each time they pass close, each time I sneak closer, how delicate the line between life and death is, facing the fragility of my existence, makes me feel more solid, more real.

It also makes me feel nearer to Alex and Grandma Miriam, in a physical sense, like the space that separates us could be as nominal as the width of a boar's tusk. The ragged slice it makes through an artery. They are just a misstep away.

The animals ignore me as they settle, my scent familiar and my meekness ceaselessly inoffensive. When the rustling and the grunting give way to quiet, I pick my way back out of the brush and go home to prepare for my first day of work as a nanny.

The bathroom fills with steam as I shower, but after my conversation with Claudio, I no longer feel worried that something's lurking there. I don't reach for the window with a racing heart to clear the haze. When I get out, the cloud slowly dissipates, but I see it again, more clearly this time: the T near the corner of the mirror, the beginning of an H beside it. It is as clear as if someone dragged their finger through the moisture and wrote it there.

"I'm listening," I say out loud, my blurred face reflected in the mirror. "I'm here." I used to tell Alex the same thing when she'd cry out in pain and panic in the night as her body stopped obeying her.

As I walk to the Riccis', I call Edo, my phone disconnecting twice before we finally manage to talk. He remembers Carlo.

He knows they live above his mother. He doesn't throw out a "you should pop in and say hi" or a "she'd love it if you stopped in for a quick visit," and I am neither disappointed nor surprised. When we last spoke about her, he made it clear that he doesn't think she's doing well.

If she painted the piece on the landing in Claudio's home, I'm not sure she's been well for a long time.

Edo asks about what I did yesterday. I tell him that after meeting the twins, I slept and read. "That's it?" he asks as I press the buzzer for the Riccis' apartment.

I grimace. But it's easier this way. What am I supposed to tell him? That I shared what could almost be construed as an intimate moment with Matteo after he asked me out to dinner and after I accused him of going through Emma's things? That I invited Claudio into the house and got drunk enough to ask him where he buried his daughter? That he convinced drunk me he didn't do it? That I possibly swallowed an abundance of sleeping pills and spent ten hours nearly unconscious? "That's it," I say brightly as the door opens. "Will you be back this evening?"

"No, maybe tomorrow. I'm sorry."

"Miss you."

"Miss you too, *amore.*" His voice drops deeper. "And the thought of you playing with kids all day, the thought of you with babies at all, it makes me want to—"

I interrupt him with a hushed laugh as I pass Caterina's door. "Save it for the bedroom."

"I'll try. I love you, Victoria."

"Love you too," I say quickly before closing the call. Lucia is already waiting for me with the door open. The girls run out to greet me, each with a toy to share, each reaching for a hand to pull, and my heart wants to combust at the sound of their synchronous giggles.

Edo wants kids. I've always known that, and as I load up the girls to get to the park, zipping their tiny jackets and slipping miniature gloves over their chubby fingers, the thought of having a family one day fills me with something other than dread for the first time since I was a teenager.

By noon, the twins are exhausted and hungry and very close to ready for a nap. I feed and change them, and Lucia takes them into her arms, kissing the tops of their heads and thanking me for providing her with the most productive morning she's had in two years.

"Again tomorrow?" I ask, folding a pink blanket and laying it on the end of Ada's bed.

"Please, yes. I'm already worried about what we'll do without you over the summer."

I smile at her and whisper goodbye to both girls before slipping out and shutting the door as gently as possible behind me. My footsteps are nearly silent on the stone steps. The only betrayal of my presence is the swish of my jacket and the whisper of my pants. I pause beside Caterina's door, far from where she could see me from the peephole, and listen.

There is the drag of feet, the clank of something, perhaps a key in a dish, and then stillness. Like Caterina is frozen on the other side of the door, listening too. Waiting for someone—me? —to walk by as she lingers with her eye pressed to the tiny window, scanning the hall with depthless brown eyes that are so unlike Edo's.

The thought makes me feel trapped, and my heart beats as I press myself against the wall, thinking of those same eyes following the lines of the figure in the painting. Eyes that brightened as she filled it in with horror.

Delusions, I think, the word arriving in my mind with the force of everything Meg Lancaster decides is true. But this time, I appreciate it.

Caterina is not hiding behind the door.

I take a deep breath and step in front of the door, not looking back when I hear the marked sound of a lock clicking open just as I pass, and refusing to turn when I hear the distinct shuffle of slippered feet behind me as I hurry for the last flight of stairs. I don't study the windows when I'm out of the building.

Because as far as I can tell, Caterina *was* hiding behind the door. And I'm not sure I'm ready for us to be alone together.

17

On the way home, I stop at the bookstore, housed on the bottom floor of a 14th-century palace beside the ancient Torre del Moro, the clock tower that sits at the town's major crossroads, dividing the hill into four quarters. Matteo dragged me to the top once, Tibi making it only halfway before she decided the view from the slant window was just as poetic as what she'd see from above.

She was wrong. From the top of the tower, you could see all of Orvieto unobstructed. I surveyed the tiny alleys, the rooftop patios, the secret gardens—like Mirësi's—concealed behind walls and unknowable from the street. The perspective felt almost lurid. Invasive. Godlike. I could see every car entering Orvieto and every car leaving. I could trace their exit for miles, deep into the green horizon. The same way I could follow a single person through the streets.

The woman shelving books speaks English. I ask her if she has a Greek Mythology primer available in English, an Encyclopedia, or even something like the book Alex and I had as kids. *The Orphic Hymns* are easy to read and beautifully translated, but that's not enough. I need to understand them, and I can't do that if I don't know who the Curates, Nereus, or the Oneiri are.

The bookshop doesn't have anything in stock at the store that fits the bill, not in English, anyway, so she helps me place a special order for a textbook-looking, three-hundred-page hardback. If I end up leaving Orvieto someday, it will fit in nicely with the rest of Claudio's collection, which is good because it definitely wouldn't fit in my suitcase.

Three days, she tells me, and it should be here. Maybe even sooner. She'll text when it arrives.

I walk home slowly, enjoying the way the sun-heated cobblestones contend with the cool breeze. As I let myself into my apartment, Paul screams. His wailing feels familiar now, something I've grown accustomed to, like my own unique welcome home. I don't rush to turn on all the lights or open the windows when I step inside. I'm no longer scared of the space; we've reached an understanding. As I hang up my coat, I wonder how Paul would feel if I screamed back one day. I wonder if people would realize it was me, and not the bird, crying out.

The Orphic Hymns and *Antigone* are both on the table, and out of habit, I count the telegrams in the copy of *Antigone*. My phone rings when I reach eighteen, and I pull my cell out of my pocket, answering as I peek into an envelope.

There's no hello. Just an exasperated, breathless Tibi, berating me before I have a chance to utter a single word. "I can't believe you moved across the world to Orvieto just to be an asshole, Asshole."

"I thought you were busy with Jasper," I offer in my defense, even though it doesn't justify the multiple missed calls and unanswered texts—and those are just the ones I'm receiving. My phone is still playing hide-and-seek with my notifications.

"Please." She sighs. "Do not say that name."

I close the book and sit down. "Matteo made it sound like—"

Tibi groans. "Oh, god, or that name."

"Who am I allowed to talk about?" I ask, smiling. I've always been enchanted by how acutely Tibi lets herself live things and how fully she gives herself to her whims. I don't think I've ever permitted myself to experience a feeling as deeply as Tibi does—not since Alex was diagnosed twenty years ago.

Except maybe grief, but that wasn't a choice.

"Actually," she says, her voice perking up, "yes, let's talk about Matteo."

Now, it is my turn to groan. "Do we have to?"

"You started it. And since we are now officially on the topic: what the hell, Tor?"

I wince. "What do you mean?" *What did he tell her?*

"Matteo is, like, refusing to text you, and my mom is trying to make me do it."

"That is what this is all about? Can someone please tell June that I'd prefer at this point if she were the only Graziano to contact me."

Tibi gasps. "You do not mean that, Victoria Jacobs."

"I do a little bit." I pick up *The Orphic Hymns* and flip to a random page. "But only right now because you are being mean to me."

"You deserve it," she insists.

My finger runs over the dedication of poem number seventy, *To Melinoe*, and then the note below it about burning aromatics. "I might," I agree, only half paying attention.

Tibi starts talking again, but I'm stuck on the words of the hymn: *Terrestrial queen expel wherever found the soul's mad fears to earth's remotest bound...*

"Uh-huh," I mutter when she ends a sentence with what sounds like a question.

"I knew it," she exclaims. "I told them you'd be pissed."

"Wait." I push myself away from the table and the distraction of the poems. "Pissed about what?"

"The meds, Tori. Mom and Matteo talking to Meg. The whole situation."

"You were in on it, too?" I wander into the kitchen, the pill bottle still beside the sink.

"No. Of course not." She hesitates. "I mean, I knew what was happening—"

"Aren't you the one who told me that inaction is equal to immorality?"

"That was different. That was you standing by while Matteo stole the first joint I ever rolled and very nearly smoked and not doing anything about it."

"You were thirteen, Tib. The court of public opinion might argue that Matteo's inaction would have been more problematic."

"You two are so obnoxiously responsible. But, speaking of drugs—" her voice softens "—did you take the ones your mom prescribed? Did they help you sleep?"

I give the bottle a slight turn like it's an hourglass, watching the round, rose-colored medication spill down as I think about the three missing pills. Maybe they dissolved in the sink drain. Maybe they fell under the fridge when the bottle toppled over.

Or, maybe, I swallowed them. I did sleep very well. It's the answer everyone is looking for and the best way to ensure Meg Lancaster doesn't show up here to doctor me. "Don't tell Matteo and June, and definitely do not tell my mother, but yeah. I did. And they helped a lot."

She will undoubtedly tell June immediately, who will then tell Matteo and my mom. Then, everyone can move on.

I ask Tibi about Jasper again as I head upstairs to change into sweatpants—I have no intention of leaving the house again for the rest of the day—and she's more forthcoming than she was at the beginning of the phone call: They are still in love. He is still gorgeous and Irish. And they are still broken up because there is no way it will ever work between them for reasons that lean more towards vibes than logic.

"When will you be back in Orvieto?" I ask, relatching the window in the big bedroom.

"Tomorrow? I'm staying in a hostel tonight to feel young again, single, a little bit foreign."

"Right, since you are not any of those things in real life. Are hostels even—" I freeze when I leave the room. The crawl space door is ajar. Open only an inch, but an inch more than makes sense with the nails Claudio drove into the wood.

"Tor?"

I reach up on my tiptoes to tilt the crawl space door wider, trying to see how it's come undone. "Do you still have that Ouija board we brought you from the States the year you decided you were psychic?"

"Of course." She takes a bite of something and keeps talking. "I have the tarot deck, too. Plus a few others I've acquired since."

"Do you know how to read the cards?"

"Not at all, but..." she makes a sad sound reminiscent of a sniffle. It's hard to tell if it's real or just for show, but because it is Tibi, I assume the latter.

"But what?"

She takes a deep breath. "Jasper does. Or, he did."

"He isn't dead, Tibi," I say, staring at the solid blackness beyond the door. "When you get back to Orvieto, I have a neighbor I want you to meet."

She snorts. "The one you ditched Matteo for to have dinner with last night? He might have mentioned something about that."

It takes me a second to understand what she's saying and connect it with the lie I told Matteo to avoid a night out alone with him. "Did he also mention that he was acting incredibly weird and..."

"Jealous," she offers, and when I don't respond, she continues, "If you'll allow me to play devil's advocate for just a mom—"

"Nope. I don't want to have this conversation." I lean against the wall. "Text me when you're back in town."

"You don't answer my texts."

"Call me, then."

"I've called like one hundred times—"

"I'll be better," I promise. "If my phone behaves. It's been doing weird shit."

"Don't make excuses."

I shake my head. "Be safe at the hostel."

"Oh," she shouts before I can hang up. "You have to forgive Matteo. Don't forget."

I laugh. "I'll put it on my to-do list."

"Good, because the *vendemmia tardiva is* coming up, and it's super fun. You two aren't allowed to ruin it."

"And what exactly is the *vendemmia tardiva*?" I flip on the hall light and step back into the bedroom, trying to peek inside the crawl space. I can't.

"That's right," she says. "I forgot you've never been here in the fall. *La vendemmia tardiva* is the late harvest—when we collect the last of the grapes while sampling the first bottles of vino novello from the initial harvest. It is an immersive wine experience, a fifteen-acre, interactive exploration of the Graziano terroir. Plus, we all get drunk and eat a lot."

"Can I invite Edo?" I ask, looking around for something to stand on and finding nothing.

Tibi scoffs. "Like I'd say no to a chance to watch that man perform manual labor."

"I'll be there," I tell her. Edo can't feel weird about me spending time with the entire Graziano family, especially if he's there, too.

When we finally hang up, I open the door to the teddy bear room, running my hand along the unmade bed before walking to the window. The shutters are open, and I can see Paul lounging near the pergola in the corner of the garden. I can see Mirësi's door.

I turn to look at the armoire, the bottom drawers still open. I crouch and pull at a piece of blue and white striped fabric, my pulse quickening when I free it from the drawer and discover it's a set of baby pajamas.

The teddy bears. The baby clothes. The knitted piglet.

This can't be how Emma left her room. It's as if, after her disappearance, everything reverted. Like Claudio was trying to hold onto his little girl, and maybe now, she's trapped here in some sense. Unable to move on.

Maybe people do stick around sometimes.

Maybe all those moments when I felt Alex beside me, I wasn't crazy.

I return to the window, scanning the garden for Mirësi or signs of someone home inside the house. I think it's time to talk to her again. I think it's time to ask her what she knows about ghosts.

18

I GRAB MY KEYS and a bottle of Matteo's wine, hoping that Mirësi will excuse my questionable ensemble: a slouchy lavender sweater that I paid too much for and sweatpants that are nearly worn through in the butt and knees, and not appropriate for either athletics or leisure at this point. At least not if either requires being seen by another human being.

When I reach the garden gate, I knock the gorgon's head against the brass plate and hope that Mirësi has excellent hearing or that Paul alerts her to the sound. Unfortunately, peacocks don't function quite the same way as dogs, and despite multiple solid blows to the knocker, there's no response.

I continue further down the street to the first door I find and scan the buzzer. Only four names are listed, and since none of them are Mirësi, and I don't know her last name, I can either leave or play a round or two of doorbell roulette and see what happens.

Mirësi mentioned my house being haunted when I met her.

She knows things I don't. She's heard stories from people who lived there before me. And she might have some insight into whatever is happening in the house. Maybe a way to bring to light the truth of what happened to Emma.

We can find out how much a person can see in a cup of coffee.

I press the top button and get no answer, but I can hear the bell ring somewhere above me. I press the bottom button, and the sound is much closer this time.

Static breaks through the speaker, followed by a deep voice with a wholly American accent: "*Scusi.* Or, rather..." There's a pause and the sound of rustling paper. "*Come...posso... aiutarla?*"

"Oh, I'm sorry," I say, wondering if either of the remaining buttons will land me in the right place or if my new fortune-telling friend is unreachable on terms that aren't hers. Or worse, I dreamt the entire thing, and there is no Mirësi. But Paul is real, at least, because he's wailing on the other side of the wall. "I was looking for Mirësi. I must have pressed the wrong button."

"Not at all." The stranger speaks much more confidently in English. "You pressed the perfect button. Let me find her for you."

"If she's busy, I can come back another time."

"Dear, Mirësi is always busy with something. Now is as good a time as any. Here—" the lock clicks open "—Why don't you come on inside the building, and she can meet you at our door."

I can hear him walking away, the receiver, I imagine, suspended on its spiral cord from the intercom unit, spinning in a slow circle. It's probably too late for me to shout that I don't know where their door is, but I'm sure I won't be left alone to wander the hallway forever.

There's no need to worry, it turns out. As soon as I'm three steps inside the entrance, she throws her door wide, a glazed chocolate cake in her hands, a sprig of flowering white freesia on top.

"What fortuitous timing," she says, smiling curiously at me before calling over her shoulder to the man who answered the intercom, I assume, "Victoria has brought the wine, Tony."

I raise the bottle. "Cheers?"

"Cheers indeed. Come in. I've been hoping you'd be by again." Mirësi looks much the same as the last time I saw her, her hair pinned in a chaotic but somehow contained nest of curls, round smudges of bright pink on her cheeks, and crimson lips. Her dress is such a dark shade of red that it's nearly black, and the fabric is stiff and unforgiving. But today, instead of coffee, she's bearing cake.

"Special occasion?" I ask, nodding to the cake.

She winks. "Isn't it always?"

"I don't want to interrupt. I just have a few questions about what you mentioned last time...about the house."

Her red lips turn up in a knowing smile, her dark eyes twinkling. "I thought you might." She sets the cake on the table and gestures for me to have a seat. A man, his white hair and beard stark against his dark skin, walks into the kitchen whistling, two wine glasses in one hand and a bottle opener in the other. He's wearing a blue oxford and khaki pants. His eyeglasses hang from a cord around his neck. He is all practical to Mirësi's magic.

"Victoria!" he says, setting an empty glass down to shake my hand. "Tony Walker. It's a pleasure to meet you."

"Nice to meet you, too, Tony." I pass him the bottle to open.

Tony's eyes widen when he sees the label. "Graziano's award-winning vintage."

"It's good, right?"

He studies me. "How'd you get your lucky hands on this stuff? I haven't been able to find any in town for months. Someone on eBay was selling bottles for upwards of 500 dollars American."

Great, and I've been going through bottles like I'm drinking water—so far, over half of the twelve Matteo brought, or what could potentially be three thousand dollars ' worth of wine in the U.S. market. "The Grazianos are old family friends."

"Good friends to have," Tony says, raising his eyebrows in a way that makes me feel like he somehow knows I haven't been entirely generous with Matteo. "Thank you for sharing."

"Thank you for letting me be part of the celebrations."

His gaze turns to Mirësi and softens, the small knife of the corkscrew frozen on the neck of the bottle. "Every day is a celebration with that one," he says, echoing Mirësi's words from minutes ago as I followed her into the house. She blows him a kiss.

I can't help but grin at their obvious, easy affection. Their mutual *joie de vivre.* "I need to try more of whatever you two are doing because it's obviously serving you well."

Tony smiles at me. "A good night's rest and meaningful work."

Mirësi wrinkles her nose as she slices into the cake. "New adventures and boundless curiosity."

"Chocolate?" I offer.

"And chocolate," they both agree.

Tony pulls out the chair beside him for Mirësi. They face me across the table, a silver tray covered in purple crystals between us. "To chocolate," he says, clinking his glass against mine. Mirësi, who isn't drinking, raises the bite of cake on her fork to our glasses. There is a general hum of delight as the cake is sampled and wine is sipped.

Mirësi waves her fork in the air the way she'd waved her cigarette when I met her in the garden. Like a wand. "Has the house woken up a bit since we last spoke?"

"I think—" I hesitate, glancing at Tony. He is a very friendly person, but everything about him shouts *sensible*. Confessing out loud, in front of Tony, that I think there might be supernatural powers at play in my apartment is a little mortifying.

Mirësi rests a hand on his arm. "Do not worry about Tony, darling. He is a lawyer—"

"Retired," Tony interjects.

"He is a lawyer in his heart," Mirësi amends, "and doesn't believe in anything. But he is smart enough not to judge the beliefs of others."

"I believe in personal truths," Tony contends with the authority of a veteran attorney. "Because the world is subjective. I am not a non-believer; I am an agnostic. In the wise words of T.H. Huxley, one can never truly know any ultimate truth because it is beyond human comprehension. Thus, all things are possible and impossible at once."

I chew my lip, smiling. "Does that include ghosts?"

Tony folds his hands on the table and leans forward. "Let's hear the evidence."

I tell them what's been happening at the house: the windows, the crawl space door, my phone acting weird since I arrived. When I lay it out, it doesn't seem like much—a few small recurrences that can all be mostly explained away. I don't mention the writing on the mirror; it seems too far-fetched. "It's probably nothing," I finish.

"Something is never nothing," Tony says. "That is one thing I am almost certain of."

"It's probably not a ghost," I correct, meeting Mirësi's eyes, a desperate, surprising hope lodged in my chest that she will tell me I'm wrong. That it definitely is a ghost. That the dead don't leave us, we just fail to hear and see and feel them most of the time.

She's been quietly watching me since I started speaking, running the obsidian pendulum charm on her necklace along the gold chain. "I've seen a lot of tragedy, and sometimes, we are the ones who are haunted, and what we are witnessing is the repression of our shadows."

"Like, we attract unsettled energy?" I ask.

She shrugs, the fabric of her dress rustling. "Or we create it."

"So, *I* am haunting my apartment." I nod, laughing a little. Honestly, it seems like the most reasonable explanation, and Mirësi doesn't even know how messed up I am. If she did, there'd be no question.

"Ah," she leans back in her chair, setting her palms on the table. "I didn't say that. Remember, Victoria, you are not the first person to find the apartment disquieting. Energy is a lasting, physical thing; unresolved energy is the most forceful. It searches for a conduit, a means of putting things to rights."

Tony chuckles, tilting his head in my direction. "Look at her, honey. Now she's worried the house is going to possess her."

"Not the house per se," Mirësi says. "Whatever is stuck inside it."

I groan. "And what, or who, do we think that is, exactly?"

"We'll have to find out. In the meantime, maybe you should explore what—or who—you brought with you." She raises an eyebrow and a single finger at me, not permitting me to argue. "Because it seems the house is very interested."

Tony takes another sip of wine. "This is arguably the best wine I've ever had," he says, unintentionally diffusing the dread pooling in my stomach that somehow, I've entangled my dead sister and my dead grandmother in the tragedy of

Emma. "Do you think you could get me in touch with Matteo Graziano about acquiring a few bottles?"

"Want to meet him?" I say, grateful for the distraction, even if talking about Matteo elicits a mixed bag of feelings at the moment, guilt rising to the top, especially as I extend an invitation I have no right to give. "They are having the late harvest soon. You can come pick grapes and drink wine with the producer himself."

Mirësi's eyes narrow. "The coffee..." she mumbles before looking at me sharply. "Matteo is your lover?"

I almost spit my wine out. "Matteo? No, he's not my *boyfriend.*" I emphasize the last word because I refuse to refer to 'Matteo' and 'my lover' in the same sentence.

"Matteo is not your *boyfriend,*" she repeats. "Good."

My neck heats.

Good? *Good?* Did she see something about Matteo and me in the coffee? Why is it good Matteo isn't my boyfriend?

And oh my god, why do I care? I should be happy. I am happy. My boyfriend is not Matteo; it is Edo—as it should be. The coffee apparently agrees.

Tony passes me a personal business card. "Send us the details, and we will be at the harvest. Or I will, I shouldn't speak for Mirësi."

She spins the stem of the freesia, smudged with chocolate glaze, between her fingers. "I think I would like to be there, too." She smirks at me, her face teasing. Mirësi isn't solely reliant on coffee grounds to see to the heart of things. "As long as you are sure it's all right we come."

I'm not sure it's all right at all. But I know the Grazianos will tell me it is. "The more, the better, right?" I say, slipping the card into my pocket.

Mirësi shakes her head, dark curls spiraling through the air. "That depends entirely on the company, Victoria."

19

I LEAVE THE REST of the bottle for Tony when I head home, silently congratulating myself for consuming only a single glass of wine with my cake. This is the most sober I've been any afternoon since I arrived, which is good because I have to call Matteo and apologize. First, for how I reacted when he brought me the medication, and second, for having now invited three people, one of whom he may not like and two of whom he doesn't even know, to his house to harvest grapes and drink his wine.

Mirësi sends me off with a slice of cake for the road and a promise that we will meet again soon. Outside, beneath the jasmine, I prod the screen of my phone to try to get it to come alive, finally managing to get into my call log. I think I see a missed call from my mom, but by the time I move my thumb to hit Matteo's name, it's disappeared. Meg Lancaster, a missing mother, even in my imagination.

"Hello?" he answers, his voice unsure.

I wince. "Hey, Matty. Please don't hate me."

"What's wrong?" It sounds like he shifts the phone or maybe stands.

"I invited some people to the harvest. A lot of people." I clear my throat. "Well, so far, just three whole people. But I can't seem to stop."

He chuckles. "You're coming?"

I close my eyes, inhaling the scent of warm jasmine. "Is that okay?"

"Of course, Tori."

"Then yes, I am coming. And so are my neighbors, Tony Walker and Mirësi...something."

"And...?"

I let out a breath. "And Edo."

"Right." He pauses. "Sure."

"Sure?" I stroll to the corner.

"Whoever you want there is welcome."

"Thanks." I feel my shoulders relax. Matteo and Edo are fine. Matteo and I are fine. "I'm pretty excited to see what all the fuss is about."

"I hope it doesn't disappoint. And Tori, about yesterday—"

I drop my head. "Matty, I'm sorry. I shouldn't have been so mean."

"No," he argues. "I was way out of bounds. I had no right to...to touch you."

We aren't talking about my reaction to finding him with the medication, I guess. "It was barely a graze," I lie, shivering at the memory of his fingers on my face. "Just the barest hint of a touch."

"It won't happen again," he says, and my chest tightens.

I bite my lip, leaning against my gate. "It wasn't like you tried to kiss me," I say, and I have no idea why—because it seemed like he had been seriously considering the option.

I think part of me wants to hear him admit it.

"Who didn't try to kiss you?" My head snaps up. Edo is turning up the other end of my street with his hands in his pockets and a smile that doesn't reach his eyes.

"Holy shit," I say, dropping the plastic Tupperware holding the cake onto the cobblestone. I contemplate dropping my phone beside it but make a different, horrible decision instead, lifting it back to my ear. "Edo just got here. Call you later, Tibs?"

Matteo doesn't respond, but he also doesn't hang up immediately.

"Love you, too," I say, hanging up and shoving the phone into my waistband before wrapping my arms around Edo's neck. My heart is beating so hard in my chest that I feel faint. His hands circling my waist are the only thing keeping me from pitching sideways.

"Ciao, principessa," he whispers against my ear. "Bad timing?"

"Not at all." I pull back to look into his sharp blue eyes, pressing the rest of my body closer, hoping to drive out the lingering uncertainty there. "This is my favorite kind of surprise."

He kisses me, slow and hungry. "I had a chance to get away from the office and just jumped in the car and got straight on the A1...I'm sorry. I should have told you I was coming."

"Edo," I say, pushing a hand into his hair. Thank god Matteo didn't call me back. "I'm happy you're here."

Edo grins, his hands drifting to my hips. "Does that mean I can take my girlfriend out to dinner before I have to go back?"

"You can't even stay the night?" I ask, pouting.

His face falls. "Trust me, there's nothing I want more. Well, that," His eyes darken, his lips turning up as his fingers slide into my waistband, "and to get you out of these truly alarming sweatpants."

I laugh, stepping back to pick up the fallen cake. "I'm happy to make that happen. Just maybe not in the street."

He takes the Tupperware out of my hand so I can unlock the gate. We only make it to the couch before I lose my sweatpants. And everything else I'm wearing. I know I should feel guilty as he trails kisses along my ribs. When he pushes into me and says he's missed me.

And I do feel something, but it is something adjacent to guilt. More abstract. I feel worried that he'll find out how bad I am at relationships. How little I deserve to be in one with him. How unequipped I am to share myself with another person.

I love Edo, and I am not sure I am capable of not hurting him. Because deep down, I'm scared to be with anybody. I'm afraid of what it might do to me if I lose them. Not in a figurative way, the way Edo talked about with our newfound proximity.

I'm scared of what will happen to me if they die.

If he dies.

Could I survive losing Edo? Or would it be the thing that finally, fully broke my mind and sent me teetering into full-blown crazy? I was close after Alex died. I don't think I've taken enough steps away from that edge since then to risk it. Not after seeing how far back Grandma Miriam's loss pushed me.

Maybe that's what's holding me back. Why I am struggling to set that firm line with Matteo. Because, for Edo's sake and mine, I know, in some ways, it would be easier for this to fail.

Edo kisses me as he comes, wraps me in his arms, and says he loves me. I say it back, snuggling into him, trying to prove that I can sustain something precious, even if it is just for a moment.

I catch my breath as he presses his forehead to mine. "I don't want to leave this couch, but I have to feed you before I go back to Florence."

"I can feed myself," I say, biting his jaw. "Thank you very much."

He laughs and pulls me closer. "If this were all the sustenance you needed, trust me, I'd be thrilled. But unfortunately for me, I think an occasional meal might be necessary."

"Can't we just stay here until you have to go?" I protest. "I had a slice of cake earlier. I'm golden."

"You're not doing a great job of making me feel better about your eating habits." He grabs his briefs, slipping them on before heading for the kitchen. "And how are we doing on the hydration front?"

I wonder if coffee and wine count. I hear the water running, then the tap goes silent—a pregnant pause that precedes the faint rattle of pills against plastic.

He walks out holding the orange bottle, his brows furrowed. "What are these?"

I wrap a blanket around myself and stand, taking the medication from him and setting it on top of the copy of *The Orphic Hymns* on the table beside my cell phone. "My mom prescribed them. They're for sleep." I don't add: *And clinically insane people.*

Edo's eyes brighten, and he takes my hand, bringing it to his lips to kiss my knuckles. "I'm glad you are letting her help. She only wants the best for you. Just like the rest of us."

"Yeah," I murmur.

He nudges my chin up with his finger, so I'm forced to meet his gaze. "This also means I am not letting you get out of dinner."

"Since we are on the topic of mothers and all," I hedge, tracing a finger down his chest, "what if we invite Caterina to join us?"

He drops my hand. "I told you, she's not doing well. She rarely leaves the house—"

"Then we can take dinner to her," I insist. "Pick up her favorite meal. Give the staff a night off."

Edo's jaw tightens, and he presses his eyes closed, opening them again after a deep breath. "I know your heart is in the right place, Victoria, but she doesn't want to see y—" It sounds like he's about to say *you*. Edo's mother doesn't want to see me. "Anyone," he corrects quickly.

"Oh," I whisper.

"It's not personal, *amore*. She feels embarrassed, I think. She's so feeble, physically and mentally, she can't even take care of herself anymore. She can hardly get out of bed."

"I understand," I concede, pulling him into a hug and pressing my ear against his heart, the unruffled beating of it so unlike my own. "I'm sorry for pushing."

He holds me even tighter. "I love how much you care. Now go get dressed so I can feed you."

I flash him a smile over my shoulder as I walk up the stairs, my eyes snagging on the creepy painting when I turn back toward the landing, feeling all at once very convinced that Caterina Mazza is the one who painted it.

Something twisted in her matches something twisted in me. And I think Edo is wrong. I think his mom is perfectly capable of getting out of bed. I think she's even capable of hiding behind doors and spying on her son's girlfriend.

But that leaves me to wonder why he believes otherwise. There's no reason for him to lie about his mother's condition, so why is she trying to convince him and his father that she's so helpless?

I grab a button-front midi dress I know Edo loves from the closet and slip on a pair of suede Mary Jane flats, my fingers stilling on the buckle of the shoe as I peer up at the swinging shutters.

Caterina isn't the only one pretending.

Claudio has also been playing a part. I don't know why, but I do know that he lets the mask fall a little when it is just the two of us together.

I just need to find a way to get Caterina Mazza alone.

"Ready?" Edo calls from downstairs as I twist my ponytail into a low bun.

"Coming," I call back, shoving a single pin into my hair, everything held precariously in place.

Edo meets me at the bottom of the stairs, offering me his arm. He sighs. "You're so beautiful, *tesoro.* Sometimes I worry it will overwhelm me—that you, Victoria, will be the death of me."

I laugh, putting the house keys in my purse. "I don't think that's quite how that expression works."

"I don't know," he says, handing me my cell phone. "I think it may be exactly how it works."

20

I WAKE UP IN the teddy bear room, my mind blurry and heavy, like my consciousness is surfacing from the bottom of a lake.

Or a river.

Staring at the wall, I try to put together what happened last night.

I know that Edo walked me home after dinner, and when he left, instead of reaching for the wine like I wanted to, I did the responsible thing and took a sleeping pill. I remember trying to read for a while after, calling someone. They seemed upset.

I roll over in the twin bed, pulling the baby blue and white checked sheets up to my neck, my face pressing into something soft. I reach one hand out of the covers and lift the pink knit piglet off the pillow. My stomach tightens.

Shit. Was it Matteo? Did we fight about something? I have a vague memory of holding something. The stuffie, I think. I have a memory of crying.

It is light outside the window—the shutters are open, but thankfully not the glass. I'm in my bra and my undies, my dress in a puddle beside the bed, my shoes nowhere to be seen. Yawning, I force myself upright and my feet onto the ground, then wander into the bedroom, where I discover I had the wherewithal to plug in my cell phone, though it's still at thirty percent.

I rub my eyes, squinting at the screen, at the missed calls from Tibi, Edo, and most recently, Lucia. I squint, focusing on the time, and realize I was supposed to be at the Riccis' house thirty minutes ago.

I call her back, throwing on the same lavender sweater I wore the day before and a pair of leggings. "I'm on my way," I tell her as soon as she answers. "I'm so sorry, Lucia." My voice trembles. I sound like I'm about to cry again. I've never been late for work. Not once.

Letting myself down in life is one thing. Letting down Matteo's friends, who are also my employers, is entirely another.

I should be used to the feeling, the sliver of icy shame that threatens to incise my self-worth, cut it clean from the rest of me. Between everything that has happened with my mother and sister and grandma, it's incredible that this part of me has survived at all.

Lucia shushes me like I'm one of the twins. "I just wanted to make sure you were okay," she says. "I brought the girls to the park. Why don't you meet us here?"

"Be there soon," I promise, slipping on my sneakers and closing the call, disappointed that because of my lateness, I'll miss two opportunities to walk past Caterina's door.

And do what? Fake an emergency and hope she opens up? Press my ear against the wood and see if I can magically hear her being a functional human, proving she's lying to Edo? I need to come up with a plan—something not entirely ludicrous.

Trying to hang out with your boyfriend's mother shouldn't be this difficult.

I pop into the bathroom before leaving and glance at myself in the mirror. Last night's makeup doesn't look too awful, and I can hide the worst of it with sunglasses.

On the way to the park, I check my outgoing call log. It's empty, or it's not loading, but either way, there's no evidence of any phone call last night. No insight into what happened. I can only pray that it was Tibi, and they were tears of mirth, and I have nothing to feel bad about this morning other than standing up the kids I'm supposed to be babysitting.

I could call her back now to confirm, but I know deep down that her missed calls this morning have nothing to do with whatever happened last night, and I'd like to maintain the fantasy a little longer.

Lucia spots me and waves as I walk up to the park. I jog the last few paces to her, apologizing and reaching for the diaper bag. Ada and Ileana sit in a small structure that looks like a house, feeding bits of grass to a doll laid out on a blanket. I wave at them when they look up, and they smile. "They are precious," I say.

"I know," Lucia agrees. She inspects me, then reaches out and pulls something from my hair—my pin from last night, tangled in the length of my ponytail. I'm sure I look exhausted and messy. Maybe even hungover, which, ironically, I'm not for the first time in days. But she seems pretty damn tired too. Tired enough to decide that leaving the twins with me for a few hours is worth the sleep she needs. The quiet time. The uninterrupted shower.

When she goes, I crawl into the little house with the girls. I feed the doll and put her to bed. We all pretend to read her a book. Ada crawls into my lap to flip the invisible pages, and Ileana rests her head against my arm. The weight of their bodies, the tickle of their hair, their voices like birdsong—all together, it is life concentrated, so vital and delicate that for this moment, nothing else exists.

It makes my heart break for Claudio. It makes me wish my parents could have acknowledged what we lost when Alex left us, what my mother took from me.

When the girls get fussy, I pack them up in the stroller. I get them some pizza bianca up the street and order myself a much-needed espresso and a chocolate croissant to go. On the way up the stairs of the Riccis' apartment, I leave the pastry at Caterina's door, knocking three times but moving on before I expect her to be able to answer.

Lucia looks refreshed when she greets us at the door. The twins are happy but tired. Just the way she wants them. "Again tomorrow?" she asks as I help her prepare them for their nap.

"I'll be here. On time. I'm going to buy an alarm clock as soon as I leave this building." And I mean it, because my phone is as unreliable as I am after a glass of wine.

I take the stairs slowly, quietly, chills dappling my skin as I approach Caterina's door.

The bag is gone, and in its place is a small, black star painted on a scrap of paper.

And just like that, we've made contact. As I bend down to look closer, my phone rings at full volume. I panic, rushing down the rest of the stairs as I try to extract it from my bag. "Hello?" I pant into the receiver, leaning against the wall beside the door outside the building.

"I'm back!" Tibi says.

I glance up, wondering if I'm visible from any of Caterina's windows. "One night in the hostel was enough?"

"For the rest of my life, I suspect." She hums, considering. "Or until my next bad breakup."

"Only time will tell," I say, slipping onto Via del Duomo as a group of students passes. "What are you up to the next few days?"

"Preparing for the seance, of course."

"The seance?" I ask.

"I have my cards, my board. You have a witch and a haunted house. It's a seance. And Sunday is a full moon."

"Sunday is the harvest."

"And what better time to perform a seance than when wine drunk and very full?"

"I don't know; it's my first seance."

"What are you doing right now?" Tibi asks in a way that makes me think she could be somewhere on the hill, stalking me.

"Trying to figure out where to buy an alarm clock." I step around a pair of older women standing in the street.

"Why can't you use your phone like a normal person?"

"Because when I said my phone has been doing weird shit, it wasn't just an excuse for being an asshole."

"Wild," she murmurs.

"My ability to recognize my failings as a friend?"

"Hardly. What would be wild is if you did something about them. But no, I meant your phone malfunctioning. That's a ghost thing, for sure. I read it somewhere. They interfere with electricity and manipulate technology to send messages or signs. Or, you know, *do weird shit*. It's science."

I pause, trying to remember how far down Corso Cavour the electronics store is. "Oh, yes, I think I saw that article in the *Smithsonian.*"

"Yeah, probably. They ran it right before your mom's paper about her smart-ass daughter."

"She called me smart?" I scoff. "You must be confused. Couldn't have been my mom."

"You're hilarious." I hear the sound of a page turning, followed by the sound of a pen on paper. "Do you have liquor in the apartment?"

"Does Matteo's wine count?"

"No."

"I have the entire contents of Claudio's liquor cabinet, then."

"Perfect. What about candles?"

"I don't think so." I scan the shop window for an alarm clock. Do people still make alarm clocks?

"Incense?" she quizzes.

"Not that either." I push the door to the shop open, a bell tinkling above my head.

"Photo of the deceased?" she asks, dismayed.

It surprises me to realize I've never seen a photo of Emma, but yet I have such a clear picture of her and who she was in my mind. I am curious if the two images will align. "I'll check the house."

"Please do. There is no point in me bringing my Ouija board if you don't create a welcoming atmosphere for the dead. We have to make her want to be there."

"With liquor? She was seventeen. Should we maybe consider something more age-appropriate? Fanta? Coke?"

Tibi sighs. "She's dead, Tor. She's ageless. And dead people like hard liquor. I don't make the rules."

"It's science." I press the buttons on an unplugged clock radio. Bingo.

"Finally, you're catching on."

"But the whole point is that she already *is* there," I say, gesturing to the clock when the shop owner comes over. He nods and walks to the back of the store, where he keeps the rest of his stock. "And I want to know why. I want to help her."

"Cazzate," she swears so loudly I startle. *Bullshit*. My Italian might not be great, but I know the essentials. "You want to find out what happened to her, just like everyone else."

"Did you know they never found the body?" I whisper, following the owner to the register to pay.

Tibi gasps. "Maybe it's in the house!"

"Shut up," I hiss. "I have to sleep in there."

"You're already sharing the space with her ghost. What's the big deal? I don't think you need to worry, though. The place is pretty small. Not many places for stashing corpses."

My pulse quickens.

Not *many* places. But there is the crawl space.

21

WHEN I RETURN TO the apartment, I set my new alarm clock on the table beside the books and, after taking a deep breath, haul a dining room chair up the stairs.

I know, of course, that there isn't the body of a teenage girl in the crawl space. But now that Tibi's put the thought there, I have no choice but to double-check.

The chair wobbles against the stone floor as I climb up, the back legs skimming the edge of the top step. The door is open, but just slightly, a few inches at most. Still enough to hide whatever is behind, enough to make me hesitate to slide my fingers over the side to open it further. I count to three, duck to avoid slamming the door into my head, and reach up to swing it open.

The light from the fixture in the hall falls flat against something lumpy and dark, and I reach for my phone. The flashlight won't turn on, but the screen cooperates, and I stretch my arm out to illuminate the space.

The crawlspace, which *is* decidedly big enough to fit a body, is filled with medium-sized black plastic trash bags stuffed to varying degrees of fullness. There's no body—not unless someone cut it into smaller pieces and packed them in separate bags. Unfortunately, there's only one way to know for sure.

I pull out the closest bag, and when I drop it to the ground, it makes a soft thud that could simply be the sound of bedding—or bones wrapped in bedding. The chair teeters as I step off, and for a split second, I have a vision of my own body, sprawled out and contorted at the bottom of the stairs.

How embarrassing would it be if I killed myself snooping through my landlord's crawl space storage? My hands shake as I unknot the bag, turning it upside down and dumping the contents on the marble.

It is neither bedding nor body parts. It is an entire bag of baby clothes, primarily shades of blue, green, and yellow. I scramble back up and grab another bag, dumping it beside the onesies and jumpers in the hallway once I open it.

Toys. Unused. Still packaged.

This stuff couldn't have been Emma's.

I can't safely reach the bags further back without risking my life, but I'm tempted to try. Why would Claudio have an entire crawl space full of baby stuff? Could his wife have been pregnant when they lost Emma? Could his lover have been?

And if so, where is that child now?

I pack everything back up and replace it as it was, more or less, when I found it. I jump off the chair and let it bump against the marble steps as I drag it back to the table, not bothering to push it in before I walk to the cabinet beside the fireplace.

Between the telegrams and the crawlspace, I forgot about the drawer I accidentally sent crashing to the floor on my first full day here. It seems as good a place as any to start looking for a photo of Emma—and maybe for some answers.

I pour a glass of wine and walk to the back of the room. The drawer resists as I tug the handle, just as it did last time, finally sliding free when I give it a good jerk. The contents are a mess, which makes sense since I shoved them all back in there in a panic.

I sit cross-legged on the floor and begin sorting. I pull out a pile of bills, all dated from at least five years ago; a postcard from Venice addressed to Claudio and Silvia Mancini and signed Mina with a heart over the *i*; copies of a newspaper I've never heard of called *Il Secolo XIX*, all over a decade old, the most recent among them printed almost a full year before Emma disappeared.

I also find pictures.

Obviously, I can't be sure that it is Emma's face I'm holding in my hand when I find the miniature square portrait, the kind of photo you'd use for a passport or school ID. But it is the same face on the slightly younger girl in a snapshot of Claudio and another woman, probably Silvia—his wife, Emma's mother. The threesome standing in front of a flowering tree, apricot, maybe, with bright blush blossoms, their smiles wide.

The girl's hair is a soft golden brown, and her eyes are dark, rich chocolate. She's pink-lipped, rosy-cheeked. She's pretty.

There's one more photo, but I don't spot her right away. The shot is of a group of teenagers, eleven of them. They are standing in front of the small lake by the train station, Orvieto looming behind them in the distance. I'm distracted at first by the boy at the center: a nineteen-year-old Matteo. God, he was cute, his waves a little lighter, his cheeks a little softer—his grin a little more innocent.

Then I see her gazing at him. Matteo's arm is slung over Emma's shoulders, and she's tucked in beside him, her mouth open on a laugh. It looks like late spring, sweaters tied around waists, probably a couple of months at most before Emma was lost.

I scan the rest of the group, recognizing Carlo and Lucia. My finger stops on another familiar face at the edge of the photo. Edo's blue eyes glitter, his dimples deepened by his broad smile. He stands slightly apart, still the outsider, the new kid in the group. It must have been hard for him to move to a new town and finish his last year at a new high school.

It makes me feel protective, angry almost. I wish Matteo would be kinder to him. Edo doesn't have anyone else here besides his mother. And now me. The Grazianos are the closest thing I have to family in Italy and, for all intents and purposes, pretty much everywhere else, too. Would it be so hard for Matteo to put on his big boy pants and relent a little? The whole protective big brother thing made sense with Tibi, but whatever his hesitation is now feels more like male posturing, an almost chauvinistic level of laying claim.

I feel the echo of Matteo's fingers on my face, the brush of his breath against my lips, and shiver, swallowing the rest of my drink. It was a laying claim that I didn't hate as much as I should have. But I did an okay job reasserting that boundary when we talked on the phone.

Or did I? Was I hoping he'd argue when I told him it wasn't like he tried to kiss me? What did I want him to tell me?

Why was I disappointed when he promised it would never happen again?

I shake my head and stand, setting the square portrait of Emma on the mantle before digging around in the glass liquor cabinet in the corner for an appropriate spirit, settling on a bottle of Disaronno. I find two rocks glasses and pour the copper-colored alcohol up to the rim of each, setting one beside the photo on the mantle and clinking the one I'm still holding against it.

"Cheers, Emma," I say, sipping the almondy, slightly sweet liqueur. Tibi said we needed the liquor for the seance, but if it's a question of making Emma comfortable, I might as well start now. I talk to her as I put everything back in the drawer. I compliment her sky-blue crocheted tank top. I tell her I wish my family ever looked as happy as hers does in the photo with the blossoming fruit tree. Sometimes, I pause so she can answer, going still as I listen for the definitive creak of a door or a window, the whisper of something being moved, but I hear nothing. I close my eyes to see if I can feel her, but the house and the air remain still.

You can't force her, Grandma Miriam scolds. *Give the girl some space.*

I chuckle, raising my hands in resignation. Outside the window, long shadows stretch across the tufo as the sun sets on the other side of the hill. The sky is already a bruised purple. I grab my coat and keys, leaving my phone and charger upstairs.

The small street down to Porta Maggiore is quiet, and the ring path even quieter. Most of the way is unlit, but I'm now familiar enough with the route to find my way. Between the glass of Disaronno and the inborn agitation of walking through a forest alone at twilight, I feel incredibly alive, the way you only can when you allow yourself to abide by a persistent awareness of death.

Most people shy away from their mortality. Those people are decidedly less fucked up than I am. Those people probably also wouldn't attempt to hunt down a sounder of wild boars in the near dark.

Those people would probably be smart enough to run when they found them, or at least to freeze. I do neither. We approach each other at a distance on the path, the boars at least a hundred feet from their nesting area. I can make out fifteen, but I am sure there are more in the brush and young ones hidden among the sows.

A growl rumbles through the group, cutting off the rustling and the soft grunts. The sound is deep, primal, so fully animal, so fully wild that it makes the hair lift up my arms and on the back of my neck. I see her then, the matriarch, the one who has been indulgent in the past, magnanimous in her acceptance of my presence when the boars were returning to bed but who looks stronger and less acquiescing after a full day's rest. Her ears are up, her tail twitching in the fading light.

She growls again, and I shudder as she approaches, her pace quickening to a trot as she ducks her head.

I throw myself at the ground, prostrating before the beast.

I am nothing. I am no threat. I am weak and vulnerable and not worth it.

I am already half-dead. I have been since I lost Alex.

The boar knows all these things are true. She can smell it on me, sense it in my blood and on my body. I have nothing to give and nothing to lose.

She walks past me, the others falling in line, dividing around my body like a parting sea. My forehead is pressed into the dirt. I wait until the sound of their hooves has disappeared, and then I face the rising moon, grinning.

I'm closer to Emma than she realizes.

"You can't hide from me," I call to her when I walk back into the apartment.

22

I HANG MY JACKET on the coat rack by the door and collect my dirty glass from the floor by the fireplace. In the kitchen, I fill it halfway with Disaronno and drink it in two gulps while I eye the open bottle of sleeping pills.

Did I take one before going out? I dump the pills out on the countertop—a yellowish plastic made to look like stone that's probably called something like lemonade nebula or sunshine mist in the U.S.—but don't bother counting. One pill has been split in two; only half is accounted for on the counter. I scoop the rosy tabs up and dump them back in the bottle, satisfied that if I did take the meds, I didn't take much.

Walking up the stairs, I pull my shirt over my head and drop it in the hall. In the bathroom, I wiggle out of my jeans, slide my panties off, and toss my bra over the back of the toilet before turning the shower water on as hot as possible.

As the steam starts to rise, I step in, letting the water scald my scalp, letting it burn away the chill of the fall night—the deeper chill of acknowledging for the first time that I've already met one death, my heart as good as ruined, but was granted the clemency of life.

The chill of seeing it all flash in the midnight dark of a boar's eye and being forced to wonder how clemency can feel so much like torment.

I let the water fall until it cools, opening the shower door to release a tempest of steam into the small room. Dripping, I walk to the mirror, wrapping my arms around myself against the cold. I hold my breath.

The letters emerge just as I knew they would, forming slowly as the moisture settles on the glass.

A *T*, an *H*, an *E*. And then what I was hoping for, the word blossoming to life, fading in instead of out beside the blur of my reflection, an invisible finger slicing through the haze.

DEAD.

The words are written on the mirror as clear as day.

THE DEAD.

I wait for more, but she's done, not ready to trust me entirely, to tell me all her secrets.

"It's a good start," I say, pressing my palm to the mirror, the glass like ice beneath my fingers. "Thank you, Emma."

I tug my unbrushed hair into a braid and walk naked into the large bedroom, keeping the lights off because the shutters are, unsurprisingly, wide open. My hands grapple with the handle on the armoire, and once it's open, I dig around inside, unseeing, for a pair of pajamas that I pull over my skin, still sticky and damp.

The alarm clock glows red beside the bed. I check that it's set before grabbing a blanket off the mattress and trailing it behind me into the teddy bear room, where I curl up in the bed, cuddling the pink knit pig to my chest and drift off to sleep while wondering who the child is who was meant to be sleeping here.

When I blink awake, my heart catches in my chest. He's there, in front of me, the early morning sunlight behind him. His smile is lovely, and small depressions shadow his cheeks. I notice the ball in his hands and sit up. He backs toward the window, pulling his arm up to pass the ball to me. I want to stop him, worried that he's too close to the open window, feeling a tug in my chest that almost hurts.

He releases the ball, and I rear back, squeezing my eyes closed. My arms frozen at my sides.

I blink again, and it is dark. The shutters are closed, and through the slits, I can make out the pale whisper of morning. My arms are still restrained beside me, the rest of my body just as immobilized, pinioned to the mattress by the weight of the invisible thing pressing down on me, holding me hostage in my own body.

Sleep paralysis, my mother would say, using big words to explain it away before telling me I need to get more rest. *No, it's not unresolved trauma; it's just stress*. I need to manage things better. She'd reassure me that the medication is not making it worse, even though I went online and saw on Reddit that it can be a common side effect.

Grandma Miriam thought it was my soul entering exile, stuck in some in-between, leaving my body deprived of its life force. She taught me the prayer to call it back.

I googled the phenomenon years ago and read stories of night*mares* and jinn, hags and demons. Maybe I'll ask Mirësi. Perhaps she has a crystal for that.

The alarm goes off in the big room. Paul screams. The feeling seeps back into my body, not slowly, but all at once in a rush that feels electric and itchy.

I wrap the blanket around my shoulders as I get up and wander into the big room to grab my phone and turn off the alarm. The house is freezing, and the metal is ice cold when I lay my fingers on the radiator. I turn on the sink in the bathroom, and there is no hot water. The burner must have gone out, but I have no idea where it is. Even if I did, I'm not sure I could do anything about it.

After almost thirty seconds of my phone not responding to my touch and opening random apps at will, I get into my contacts, only to discover I never saved Claudio's number. I manage to shoot a text to Matteo, including Tibi in the message, for no other reason than it guarantees I'll keep this text thread above board in all the ways that matter.

I'll get in touch with Claudio and let him know, Matteo texts back seconds later, followed by Tibi's, *Fuck you both. I'm sleeping.*

Downstairs, I make myself coffee, holding it between my legs as I blow dry my still-wet hair on the couch. My hands shake from the cold as I get dressed, but I take the time to swipe on some makeup and make myself look reasonably presentable before leaving the apartment early.

I'm at the pastry shop before the doors are even unlocked, shifting my weight back and forth and rubbing my hands together to keep from freezing to death on the cobblestones. The owner sees me and, taking pity, lets me in. I wait at the counter as she extracts cake rounds from the oven, the air filling with a sweet, warm heaviness.

I order two dozen bigné—bite-sized profiteroles dipped in chocolate. She separates them into two bags at my request. By the time I leave, the florist is set up in a portico that runs along the side of a Romanesque-Gothic church. Orvieto is so effortlessly picturesque that it sometimes doesn't feel real.

The florist makes me a small bouquet of coral Dahlias, and when I press my finger to the Riccis' brass bell, I'm a full three minutes early. Lucia buzzes me up, and on the way, I set one of the bags of bigné outside Caterina's door, knocking again three times like I did when I left the chocolate croissant.

Lucia is waiting at the Riccis' door with the girls, and she seems confused when I hand her the flowers and the bag of pastries. "For yesterday," I explain. "I am so sorry I was late."

"You're still adjusting," she says, and I think she means to the time zone, but I also don't know what Matteo's told her. "The only thing you need to be sorry for now is bringing these into the house." She peeks in the bag. "I'm going to make us some coffee, and you are going to help me eat them, so I don't finish them all on my own while you are out with the girls."

I put on the twins' socks and shoes as Lucia prepares the coffee. I brush their hair into matching pigtails and slip sweaters over their heads. Lucia sets the table: four plates—two blue and white china, two plastic—each with a pair of profiteroles placed in the center.

She winks. "I'm saving the other four for Carlo. Or at least, that is what I'm telling myself."

I strap Ileana into her booster and laugh. "He works a lot?"

"He does. His family moved off the hill after he graduated, and they have a business nearby that he helps run. I grew up outside Orvieto, so we don't have anyone in town. Granted, they are all within a five-minute drive. Sometimes, that little bit of distance is a blessing, but—" she smiles at me "—we needed some extra support."

I smile back and help Ada break one of the bigné in half, licking the smudge of chocolate off my thumb. "Are you close with any of the neighbors?"

"Not really," she says in between bites.

"What about Caterina Mazza?" I ask, wiping a spot of cream off Ileana's face in a gesture of forced indifference. "Do you know her at all?"

Lucia gives a teasing smirk, and I feel my neck heat. "It's perfectly normal to be curious about our potential mothers-in-law," she says. "Especially if she happens to be Caterina Mazza."

I'm not entirely sure what that's supposed to mean, but I take a bite of bigné to keep from asking.

"Carlo and I married relatively young, and we've been living here for just over six years. We saw much more of Caterina when we first moved in."

"What was she like then?" The only Caterina I've ever known has been fragile and skittish.

"A little quiet but friendly." Lucia shrugs. "She'd say hello in passing, ask after Carlo's family. Then, after her sister passed five years ago, we didn't see her for months, and when we did, she'd transformed. We've hardly seen her since."

"She's never out?"

"Rarely. When the twins were born, she knew somehow," she says, shaking her head. "When we got back from the hospital, Carlo checked the mailbox, and she'd sent us something, which I thought was funny because she lives one flight of stairs away."

"What was it?"

She laughs. "A telegram!"

Chills sweep across my skin, so violent it makes my skin hurt. "Is that a common thing to do?" I ask, trying to keep my voice from trembling.

"These days? No." She walks over to the sink, grabs two wet cloths, and passes me one. We rub the chocolate off the girls' hands and unbuckle them. "Oh, and there was one other thing," she says, lifting Ada out of her seat.

I turn to face her with Ileana in my arms.

"On the twins' first birthday, we found two gifts outside the door when we went out. I can't be sure they were from her, but we knew she'd been sort of a hobbyist at one point—painting, pottery, embroidery—so we assumed. And no one else in the building would leave something like that without a note."

Ileana squirms in my arms, and I set her down. "What were the gifts?"

"I'll show you," she says, and I follow her down the hall. "And don't you dare judge us. The girls nap well in their cribs, but we haven't figured out how to kick them out of our bed at night."

I chuckle. "I would never." Maybe I'd be better adjusted now if my mother had ever loved me enough to make sure I felt that kind of safety and security.

Lucia pushes the door of her bedroom open, and I see them immediately, lying lifelessly on the pillows.

Two pink, knit piglets, identical to the one I slept with last night in the teddy bear room.

23

WHAT THE ACTUAL HELL?

My chest constricts so violently I have to cough to breathe again, my mind going in a thousand directions at once.

Lucia looks at me, her brow furrowing, and I force my lips to turn up. "How cute."

"The twins love them," she says, closing the door. "I'm almost tempted to ask Signora Mazza to make another set in case they wear these out."

"Well, if I ever have the opportunity, I'll be sure to bring it up." Edo is determined to keep me safe from his mother, but I can't be this close to her every day and not try.

I pack up the girls and some snacks, my head still spinning, and we head downstairs. My heart sinks a little when I see the bag of bigné, untouched, outside Caterina's door. The girls and I visit the small playground near the barracks, where they take turns on the old, wooden horse spring rider before we cut across town to snack on the steps of the Duomo. The stone, warmed from a morning of sunbathing, chases the last of the morning chill from my bones, and I watch as the girls trace the lines of the red, white, and black mosaics—mostly stars—that skirt the church in their shiny saddle shoes.

After a morning of running through everything I've learned about Caterina again and again—between the piglets, the painting, the telegrams, and all of the other evidence accumulated in Claudio's home—it seems possible, especially after Edo's mention of Claudio's alleged affair, that Caterina and Claudio were somehow involved.

He did say she was his student. He also made other implications about how much the bored housewives loved their language lessons.

But a secret child?

Or maybe the child wasn't meant to be a secret. Maybe Caterina intended to leave her husband. Maybe Claudio's wife found out, and that's why she fled to Spain in the middle of Emma's investigation.

Why would he decorate an entire room for a child he didn't expect to have around? Why would he have bags of toys and baby clothes?

I know I'm missing something, but a part of me isn't sure I want to push. Edo would be devastated if he discovered his mother had been unfaithful. His heart would break for his father.

I squeeze my eyes shut. What Edo doesn't know won't hurt him.

When I open my eyes, I check the time. We need to head back to the Riccis', so the girls aren't late for their nap, but I don't see the twins. I stand, dropping a mostly empty cracker package onto the travertine, golden crumbs pooling at my feet as I scan the piazza. I jog to one side of the building, pushing through a crowd of tourists as my pulse threatens to beat out of my throat, and then to the other.

The girls are sprawled on their bellies in the grass beside the cathedral, and when I call out their names, my voice cracks. I sink to my knees as they run toward me, their tiny legs and arms pumping as they giggle. Ileana reaches me first, throwing herself against my chest. I pull her in, reaching my other arm past her for Ada.

Her body lurches, the rubber sole of her shoe sticking on the step. She drops, inches from my fingertips, and slams her face into the unforgiving stone.

My scream ricochets through the piazza, shrill and full of horror. All I see is red as I scoop her up, the memory of Alex tumbling down the stairs seizing my senses—the blood that spewed from her nose, smearing her face, dripping into her eyes. That's when Alex's body started showing signs. That's when I first started dying beside her. My ruin was not as conspicuous because it transpired deep inside me. Because I didn't want to, *couldn't,* consume the space and help and love that Alex needed. So I was okay.

And when she died, I tried to bury the part of me that wasn't okay along with her, but it refused to remain inhumed.

I'm clinging to the girls, Ada's face pressed to my chest as I cry into her hair. People surround us, a traffic cop pushing his way to the front of the crowd. He tries to get a look at the girls to see what's going on, but I won't let go.

"Le bimbe stanno bene, signora." The girls are OK, he says, before stating louder, *"Mi senta, signora? Stanno bene." Do you hear me, ma'am? They are fine.*

I shudder as I inhale, finally brave enough to pull back and examine Ada's face. He's right. There is no bruise, no blood, just a shocked look of terror as our eyes meet. "Sorry," I whisper to her, kissing her head and freeing her and Ileana from my grasp.

The people around us disperse, the cop staying behind to ask if I need anything. I pull myself together enough to offer a thank you in Italian and an apology for panicking in English, which he appears to comprehend absolutely no part of.

I hold the girls' hands extra tight as I lead them back to the stroller, smiling at them as I buckle them in, singing songs on the walk home, trying to dissipate their nervousness as much as my own.

"Ada took a tumble on the steps of the Duomo," I say to Lucia, who meets us at the bottom of the stairs to check the mail.

Lucia rubs Ada's head. "She's always been a little accident-prone. She's not like Ileana and me, always worried about what might happen," she says, adding with a touch of envy that I sympathize with, "Ada takes after Carlo; she exists in the moment, unaware of all the possible consequences."

I hope she's right and that it's nothing more—that her accidents are not the result of her body choking out precious nerve cells, that there's no mutation in her genes, a small, near-invisible marker on a single chromosome that is slowly causing her brain to drown in its own waste.

She's not Alex, I tell myself.

We part ways downstairs, Lucia telling me Carlo came home for lunch and would help get the girls down for their nap. It's not until I'm standing outside the building that I think again of Caterina and the fate of the bag of bignés. Is there another small painting in the hall for me? Something else?

I cross the street and glance up at her windows, my fingers going to my lips when I see her, standing in the glass, staring straight back at me. She tips her head in acknowledgment, a clear *I see you*. I drop my hand, inclining my head as she did. When I raise my face to her, Caterina releases the brocaded curtain and disappears behind it.

Well, one thing is certain. Caterina isn't as bedridden as Edo believes. What other secrets is she keeping from her family?

I'm still gaping at the window when my phone rings, and I wince when I see it's Edo calling, struck by a sliver of guilt and a greater fear: that he is in the apartment watching me gawk at his mother. That she's told him I've been leaving treats outside the door, that I've been harassing her. I worry he's calling to tell me to stop.

"Hello?" I answer, hurrying away from the building, like somehow running away now makes me more innocent.

"Amore." His voice is so deep and warm that I want to curl up in it. *"Quanto mi manchi."*

I look back once over my shoulder, and there is no evidence of Caterina in the windows. "I miss you, too," I say. "How's work?"

Edo sighs. "That's why I'm calling. I think I will be stuck at the office all weekend again."

"Seriously?" I ask, and the hint of dismay in my voice is—if I'm being honest—disguising a rush of relief. He's going to miss the harvest. Not to mention the potential seance.

"Once this deal is closed, things will change."

"Things are fine as they are," I reassure him, turning left at the clock tower.

He hesitates. "Are they? I've barely seen you since you arrived in Orvieto."

"I just mean," I scramble, my hand pressed against the door to the bookstore, "that I know you love what you do, and I'm not going anywhere. There's no rush."

"How are you so perfect?" he asks, thankfully not giving me time to attempt a response. "I have a meeting, but I'll be in touch soon."

The call cuts out as I'm saying goodbye.

When I walk into the bookstore, the woman who works there recognizes me immediately and meets me at the counter. She says she texted this morning. I never received it, but it doesn't matter. She ducks and reappears with a package wrapped in craft paper.

My book arrived.

On the way home, I stop at Mirësi's, feeling lighter, excited almost. Things are going well. The book came in early, *and* Edo won't be at the harvest. It's easier this way for everyone. He probably wouldn't enjoy himself anyway, not with work looming over his head. There will be no tension, no awkwardness. Edo will have the time he needs to work on his important Swiss deal, no distractions. It's the responsible choice with everything he has hanging on the line.

I swallow away the inkling of tightness in my throat. It's almost concerning how easily I convince myself that Edo's absence is the best thing for *him,* as if my problematic feelings are irrelevant.

Mirësi invites me in, but I tell her I can't stay. I relay the details of the harvest that Tibi first relayed to me—where to meet, what time, what to bring. "And me, if possible," I add. "I could use a ride."

"Happily. And for the seance?" she asks.

I laugh. "To be determined."

"All is well in the house, then?" she asks, raising a black eyebrow.

"All is…" I trail off, chewing my lip as I think about the message in the mirror, the dreams, everything I've learned, and what I still don't know about Caterina. "Actually, I have a question. What do you know about night paralysis?"

She pulls a thin cigarette out of a package hidden in the folds of her thick skirt and lights it with an engraved brass, flip-top lighter. "You mean Mokthi." She inhales, then tilts back her head and releases a cloud of smoke into the sky. "He comes for women, the tired and suffering, and stops you from moving."

"Is there anything a person can do to keep him away?" I ask, feeling a little called out at the way she eyes me during the tired and suffering comment.

She flicks her ashes onto the cobblestone. "Keep your husband's hat by your bed while you sleep."

"I don't have one of those." I cross my arms. "Any other options?"

"You'll figure something out, darling." Her eyes are full of mirth. "And if you are comfortable with half-lies, I'd appreciate it if you don't mention the smoking to Tony. We are pretending I quit."

I chuckle. "What smoking?" Mirësi might not know it, but her comment is just the reassurance I need. Relationships are nuanced, and sometimes the truth isn't what's best for anyone.

I'm sad you won't make it this weekend. I love you, I text to Edo when I get to my gate.

Followed immediately by a text to Matteo. *Really looking forward to the harvest, Matty G.* I don't mention that Edo won't be there.

24

I PRESS SEND AS I walk up the exterior stairs to my apartment, the book lodged under my arm. As soon as the text is delivered, my phone starts pinging. My hand freezes with the key in the lock as I see the messages come through, one after another.

Shit, shit, shit.

The messages appear out of order, and I read them just as arbitrarily as they arrive, but it isn't hard to realize I've made a colossal mistake.

Claudio is available at ten, Matteo writes. *Your phone keeps going to voicemail. It's full, by the way.*

We want to make sure you will have heat tonight.

He's going to head over now. I'm meeting him there.

Call me when you can.

And the most recent, sent less than an hour ago: *Heat is working.* That's it. Nothing else. Which makes me feel even more nervous.

Because I know what they found inside the house, and I know how bad it looks.

Maybe even crazy.

I open the door slowly, squeezing my book to my chest like armor, not wanting to witness the evidence of my folly. I imagine the scene through Matteo's eyes, god, through Claudio's, and my stomach knots so tight it makes my eyes prickle.

The photo of Emma is propped beside the glass of Disaronno on the mantle, the drawer I found it in partially open nearby. On the table, I have *The Orphic Hymns* splayed open to the poem about Melinoe, the copy of *Antigone* on top of the pages, holding them down. Worst of all, it's clear I've been messing with the telegrams, my sticky fingers all over whatever secrets they are hiding.

Secrets that probably belong in part to Caterina Mazza.

I set the book I'm holding down and pull out a chair, leafing through the pages of *Antigone,* freeing an envelope from between the pages. I carefully extricate the telegram inside, unfolding the delicate paper.

I already know what Matteo and Claudio found upstairs: the bed in the teddy bear room unmade and slept in, the pink knit piglet lolling on the pillow, just like Ada and Ileana's were in Lucia's room. In the kitchen, zero evidence of any food being consumed, and a half-empty bottle of Claudio's liquor next to my dirty glass, the meds beside it with the red warning label: a short sentence in Italian that cautions against the consumption of alcohol.

It doesn't paint a pretty picture—definitely not a picture of a healthy and stable and thriving woman. I'll have to call Matteo and explain it away somehow before he calls my mother. I'll think of something, maybe find a way to blame Tibi.

But right now, my eyes keep snagging on the names Diche and Orfeo at the bottom of the telegram I'm holding.

I tear through the brown wrapping on my new book and flip to the index, running my finger down the rows of names and places as I search for the page I need.

Orpheus, 211.

There is a photograph of an ancient mosaic, a man holding a lyre, surrounded by wild animals. A lot of the information was also in the forward to *The Orphic Hymns,* which I've skimmed. Orpheus was a legendary bard from Thrace, a prophet, a musician, and a poet who traveled with Jason and the Argonauts. He was the mythological founder of the Orphic mysteries and the author of *The Orphic Hymns.*

Nowadays, he is perhaps most famously known for the legend of Orpheus and Eurydice, in which he descends to the underworld to retrieve his deceased wife—one of only a few mortals ever to undertake a catabasis. He pacified Cerberus with his lyre and played a song so moving for Hades and Persephone that even the god of the Underworld himself was swayed to Orpheus's cause.

With one condition.

Eurydice had to follow behind Orpheus while they departed the caves of the underworld, and he was not to turn and look at her.

But he did, having lost faith at the faintness of her footsteps, and Eurydice was compelled to remain among the shades with the other dead.

I chew my lip, hooking a finger around the page and returning to the index until I find Eurydice. Below her name at the top of the page is the Greek spelling, Εὐρυδίκη, followed by the classical pronunciation. Focusing on the last four letters, I repeat the sounds out loud. Dee-kay. It's the same way you'd pronounce Diche in Italian.

Tearing a piece of the craft paper the book came in to use as a bookmark, I return to the page about Orpheus, reading the rest of the entry and then returning to his name, Ὀρφεύς, and its possible origin: the Greek word orphanós, meaning orphan. Or fatherless.

A fatherless boy who returned from the dead.

My head sags, and I press my fingers to my temples, trying to put it all together and make sense of what it might mean and how it might connect to Caterina. Could she and Claudio have sent their child away? But then, who would the Eurydice be, and why that name? The name of a dead woman?

When the doorbell blasts through the house, I lift my head so quickly that the room spins, and I have to press a hand against the table to steady myself as I stand. Before I can even reach the intercom, Tibi's voice trumpets up from the street.

"Litte pig, little pig, let me in!"

"Coming," I call back, rushing to replace the telegram and the envelope and shove the books onto a shelf with other books, perfectly innocuous. I'm out of breath when I ring Tibi up, standing in the doorway as I wait for her to come up the stairs. "What are you doing here?"

Tibi scoffs, looking offended. She has a large duffel slung over her shoulder, and if I had to guess, whatever is inside would be the young Italian non-conformist's equivalent to Mary Poppins's stash. "Having a sleepover with my best friend, who wishes she spent more time with me, but never invites me over."

"Has the grace period officially lapsed where I am no longer allowed to blame my social shortcomings on jetlag?" I ask, opening the door wider so she can pass.

She sets her bag in the middle of the now-empty table. "You thought you could explain away *your* social shortcomings with *jetlag?* That's funny. Here," she says, handing me a box she pulls out of the bag. "From Matteo."

"Is it a phone?" I ask.

She pauses, scrutinizing me. "No, Tori. It's the moon. He wanted you to have it."

"Generous." I stick my tongue out at her as she unpacks two bottles of prosecco. "Why did your brother get me a phone?"

"Because," she says, taking a deep, exasperated breath, "yours sucks. Matteo's already programmed in some numbers. Mine, of course, and Mom's, Claudio's, Lucia's, and Carlo's. Your mom and dad's. His."

I pull it out of the box and turn it on. There's a message waiting from Matteo as soon as it boots up—four words: *If you need me.*

"This makes me feel like a criminal," I tell Tibi, turning off the screen, "having a second phone."

She pops open a bottle of prosecco. "Or a spy," she says, wandering into the kitchen for glasses, I presume. I follow her in to help.

"Is it weird, though?"

Tibi laughs. "Why would it be weird? What are you going to do with it? It's a phone, Tori. It's only as weird as you make it."

"I mean..." I hesitate, watching the bubbles pop in the glass she pours. "Do you think Edo..."

Her brow furrows, and she lifts a glass, nodding for me to take the other one. "You know you can use it to call him, too, right? It's not like it has to be a secret. It's not a burner phone. It's just one that can actually send and receive text messages. I hear it makes calls and even rings when you get one. Top-notch stuff."

She nudges me, and I nudge her back. "Okay, okay. Point taken."

"Cheers," she says, and when she grins at me, I grin back. Whatever Matteo saw in this apartment today, whatever he thought, he didn't feel upset enough about it to tell Tibi. Maybe it wasn't all such a big deal? I glance at the mantle, and Tibi's eyes follow mine. "Holy shit," she murmurs.

I trail behind her as she hurries to the mantle, lifting the photo of Emma and studying it. "I haven't seen a photo of Emma in years," she says, her eyes turning thoughtful. "I remember her voice. I remember she had this Caparezza crop top with all the original concert dates listed on the back that I was so jealous of. It's still hard to believe she's just...gone."

I know by the look she gives me that she's not just talking about Emma, but I don't want to be sad tonight. "I mean," I shrug, looking over my shoulder at the staircase. "I'm not sure she is. Not entirely."

Tibi grabs the bottle, and we sit down on the couch. She insists I tell her everything, our legs curled up, knees touching while we finish the prosecco. I am vague at first, very aware of how absurd what I am telling her sounds, but Tibi buys in entirely from the beginning. Everything I say evokes a gasp. She nods, her expression grave, when I mention Caterina, the painting, and the possibility of some connection there.

The new phone pings, and Tibi helps me dig it out from between the cushions. It's a text from Lucia. The girls aren't feeling great, and she will hang out with them tomorrow. I don't need to watch them.

My mouth goes dry. What if this has to do with Ada's fall? What if Lucia no longer trusts me with her girls? I text her back, saying that I hope they feel better soon.

"No work tomorrow?" Tibi says, peeking over my shoulder. She walks to the kitchen and grabs the second bottle.

We keep talking about the house. I mention the mirror in the bathroom, the words appearing in the steam, and her face is the most excited I've ever seen it. She threatens to strip off her clothes. She asks me if we can go shower *right now*. Somehow, we've almost finished both bottles of prosecco. I convince her that she'll faint from the heat and break her skull. We laugh when she teases about becoming the house's second ghost—a tipsy Tibi terrorizing future study-abroad students.

"We need food, I think," I say, breathless from giggling.

Tibi rests her head on my shoulder. "And more wine."

"I have some of Matteo's left."

She pretends to gag. "You know that expression, don't crap where you eat...or drink, in this case...well, let me tell you—"

"Whatever you are about to say," I interrupt her, "I don't want to hear it. You will not ruin that wine for me."

She stands, wobbling a little as she reaches for my hand. "Suit yourself."

We get our shoes on and walk up the lamp-lit street arm-in-arm, the sun having set sometime between bottles. The wine bar glows gold, the light and the music spilling onto the black basalt street. Tibi orders three bottles of wine and convinces the bartender to give her a bag full of the lumachelle they are serving for aperitivo—snail-shaped bread with pecorino cheese and pancetta baked into the dough.

Tibi holds up a bottle of red and the bag of lumachelle. "All four food groups."

"I think there are five," I say, grabbing the other two bottles.

She pushes the door open with her butt. "Five? You're so American. In Italy, there are seven."

"But never four," I quip.

She sighs dramatically. "It was a joke, Tori."

And it wasn't particularly clever or funny, but I'm laughing all the same.

There's one more thing I want to share with Tibi. I want to show her the boars and sit with her as we watch them wake up for the night. But I don't, because ghosts are far less likely to kill you than an angry wild sow. And they don't know Tibi like they know me. Tibi wouldn't be safe.

25

Tibi and I share the bed in the big room. Neither of us says it, but we haven't shared a bed since Alex died. The last time was in Newport Beach when the cat kept peeing on Matteo's sheets. Alex was already in a hospital bed by then.

I dream of that summer, of all of us together. It isn't bad or scary. I wake briefly to relatch the shutters, and when I fall asleep again, I'm at the Paglia River, spraying tanning oil on my stomach as Tibi and I lay out on the hot rocks, bright pink towels beneath us.

In the dream, I'm the same age I am now, but somehow also sixteen. Matteo is nearby, talking to a friend, and I peek at him from underneath my sunglasses. Wanting him to notice me, wanting him to see me.

The friend shifts his face and smiles at me. It's Edo.

He's the one who sees me.

I feel bad and decide to jump into the water. I drop to the bottom of the river like a stone. Fish swim past, then an entire whale. I'm in awe at the depth of the Paglia. I'm in awe at my ability to breathe here. I walk along the sandy bottom to a small house that looks a lot like my apartment. I knock on the door, and Emma answers it.

"Shhhh," she says. "They can't know I'm here. They can't know." She starts to shake me. "Do you hear me, Tori?"

I open my eyes, my head pounding with the reminder of too much prosecco and red wine—and not nearly enough bread. Tibi squirms beneath my leg, one hand braced around my shoulder in an attempt to push me away. "Damn it, Tor, come on. You're squishing my bladder." She wiggles out from under me and runs to the bathroom, groaning the whole way, probably because she also feels like crap.

Every sip was worth it. Last night was the most relaxed I've felt in months.

"Do we hydrate first or go straight for the hair of the dog?" I call to her.

"Stop yelling at me," she whines through the open bathroom door.

She shuffles back to the room, eyes barely open, and curls up beside me in bed without another word. A few minutes later, her soft snores are the only sound in the house, punctuated occasionally by one of Paul's screams. I turn to face her, thinking about Emma in the dream. I shiver, imagining her body still trapped at the bottom of the river, nothing but a cage of bones now.

The Paglia, in reality, isn't deep enough to hide her this long. Bodies don't just disappear, though, so where *is* Emma's?

Thankfully, not in the crawlspace.

I doze until the nagging of Tibi's belly wakes us both up a couple of hours later. She raises her hands over her head, stretching. "Coffee," she declares.

We take our mugs and two big water bottles out onto the patio. We don't talk about Emma or Alex or ghosts at all. We catch up on the present, scrolling through Jasper's Instagram. He's cute and incredibly, stereotypically Irish, with red curls and freckles and eyes that shift between blue and green. We read his old Substack posts.

"He's the worst," she whispers, tilting her head after reading a stunning line that is, I can only assume, about her. She blinks, neither of us acknowledging the moisture in her eyes. Tibi is so strong and self-possessed, so sure of who she is, that sometimes I forget she is also sensitive. Part of the Tibi show is her costuming of her vulnerability in confidence.

I wrap an arm around her shoulders. "He's in love."

"You think so?" She looks at me, her features unguarded—cautious hope written all over her face.

I smile. "I sure do."

It feels good to be the friend on the other side, the one providing comfort. This is why I loved being a hospice nurse. I offered care. I offered what peace I could. I provided companionship. My patients, for the most part, offered only themselves, their last days, and sometimes their final minutes. Their families were too lost in their grief to ever even consider mine. I preferred it that way.

Tibi sighs, wipes away a tear like it's a bug on her face, and opens up the photo album on her phone. She shows me shots of her newest project: lino print portraits of street performers in Rome with famous monuments stamped in stark ink behind the detailed faces.

"What the hell, Tibi. Aren't you supposed to be a poet? One person shouldn't be allowed to be this talented. It's unfair."

Her cheeks flush a little, an unfamiliar look on Tibi. "I'm still learning," she says. "But it's fun."

"You're an amazing artist." I squeeze her fingers. "With words and, apparently, every other medium you try your hand at."

She gives a little huff, but I know she's pleased.

"Why don't you invite Jasper to the harvest? Is he still in Rome? He could easily get here by tomorrow."

She turns her phone over, setting it face down on the table. "It's almost noon, and you know what we haven't done yet?"

"Irresponsibly imbibed more alcohol?"

"Well, yes, that and..." She raises her eyebrows, waiting for me.

"Solved the mystery of a missing girl's murder?" I hedge.

Tibi stands. "Close enough. Time we remedy both."

She goes to the kitchen, exchanging our caffeine and water for red wine. I retrieve *Antigone* from the bookshelf and pull out the telegram stuffed between the pages of the foreword. We sit beside each other at the table, Tibi translating the telegrams out loud, one after another.

They focus primarily on Orfeo—minor updates about his life: Orfeo rode a bike. Orfeo joined a class. Orfeo ate ice cream.

The messages are vague and lacking qualifiers. It's never Orfeo rode a bike for the first time; Orfeo joined a spin class; Orfeo was lactose intolerant and is now cured.

But as hazy as the picture is that the words paint about Orfeo, there's nothing about Diche, nothing in the text to substantiate her as a person, no proof that she exists outside of the salutation at the bottom of the page. Diche is a specter, as formless and unseeable as Eurydice in the myth of Orpheus.

When we finish reading, we've learned nothing new. We know nothing more than when we started.

Tibi twists the ends of her hair. "The only reason I'm even a little bit convinced these telegrams are important is because they are so damn boring no one would go to the trouble of sending them unless they had a significant reason to do so, something they needed to communicate."

"What if," I say, tapping a finger against my lips, "it's not just the names that are coded, but the whole thing? Like, 'O. saw the sea' means that drugs were dropped, or stowed, or whatever people do with drugs. Maybe it's some sort of secret language, and Claudio was involved in something dangerous—"

She pops her chin into her hand. "Besides the cult?"

"Maybe," I press on, "the cult was the mafia or a crime ring, and Claudio got in trouble. And Emma paid the price."

Tibi leans back in her chair. "Small town Ancient Greek professor finds himself in over his head as he tries to make his mark in the criminal underbelly of Umbria."

"Big Italian Breaking Bad energy," I say, more defeated than amused.

"I don't hate it." Tibi shrugs. "And at this point, it's not like we have any other winning theories."

I flip through *Antigone,* all the telegrams lodged back between the pages. "Now what?"

"Now," she says, standing up and shaking out her arms. "I'm going to shower and see if the mirror has any ideas. Then, I'm going to steal something cute out of your closet, and we are going to eat a proper dinner and get an excellent night's rest so that tomorrow, we are ready for the harvest and the seance..." She gestures at my face. "And so, when my mom sees you, she doesn't panic."

"This is just my face now," I argue. "It doesn't get better."

Tibi ignores me. I sit at the table and stare at *Antigone,* wondering if any of this means anything. And if it does, does it *all* mean something?

Why would Claudio hide the telegrams in a copy of *Antigone?* He owns hundreds of books and many much bigger ones that would have been far better at concealing the envelopes. Is the story somehow important?

I've read it twice now, maybe three times. Is Antigone herself a hint, something about her strength and defiance, the way she stands up to the king? Is there some parallel between the way

Antigone fights to lay her loved one to rest and the fact that there has been no resolution in the case of Emma's murder?

Or is the story a warning? Antigone is a woman whose defiance of a powerful man leads to her demise. In the story, she dies. Her sister, Ismene, does not. Her sister Ismene is submissive to the king and allowed to live. Am I putting Tibi in danger by dragging her into this?

"Fuck," Tibi yells from upstairs. "There's something wrong with you."

I jog up the stairs. "Me?" I ask, popping my head into the bathroom. She's in the shower. The steam in the room is already dissipating.

"Yes, you. Do you not have nerve endings, Tori?" She presses her hands to the glass, the skin of her palms flattened and pink. "How did you stand here with the water running at maximum hotness."

I lean against the door frame. "I've used up all the feeling in my body. I simply exist now."

"Lucky for you, who really needs a shower—" her voice is muffled as she turns around "—there will be plenty of hot water left when I'm done so you can sacrifice your flesh for the cause."

I accept, find her a towel, and wait my turn.

As Tibi gets ready in the other room, I study my reflection in the mirror for a minute before getting into the shower. I've lost weight, the hollows of my cheekbones deeper than they should be. I always tend toward thin, but now I look angular, weak, and breakable. I don't like it. If I fall completely apart, I'll be useless to Emma.

"I'll do better," I tell her, staring into my own bloodshot eyes.

The shower water is even hotter than usual. Whatever repair Claudio and Matteo made has caused the temperature to surge, and even I gasp at the sensation of the scalding water on my skin.

As I shampoo my hair, I decide that after tomorrow, after the seance, I'll somehow untangle Tibi from all of this. I was wrong yesterday. I thought that the boars were more dangerous than a ghost, but that is only true if there is no one who wants to keep the ghost silent, no one who wants to make sure that their secrets remain buried.

I step out of the shower and grasp at the hook for my towel. The bathroom is filled with such a dense fog that I can barely see my hands. I find my way to the mirror and wait.

The writing materializes in the moisture, THE appearing quickly, the DEAD following shortly after.

And then more, a faint line that becomes clearer as I hold my breath. An *L*.

Emma has more to say, and I need to make sure she gets a chance to say it.

26

"Tibi," I call, keeping my voice steady and calm like I might scare the letters in the mirror away if I'm too loud, too excited. She doesn't respond. I peek out the door, opening it just enough to pop my head out so I don't let the steam escape or let the fresh air in to ruin the appreciable results of my scalding hot shower. "Tibi?"

No response.

I slip out of the bathroom, shutting the door behind me, trapping whatever moisture I can in the small space. The door to the teddy bear room is open, and for a second, I'm worried she's gone into the room and seen the messed-up bed, the piglet, evidence of what might be actual lunacy, and decided I've gone too far, become too obsessed, and run to get help. To call my mom maybe, or to have her mom or Matteo do her dirty work. I push the door wider. She's not there.

She's not in the big room either, but I discover her on the patio when I look out the window. Tibi's massive magic bag is open on the table, and a collection of wooden-handled tools is strewn before her. She's bent over a gray block, her body twisted in her chair, one foot resting on the seat, as she chisels away pieces of linoleum.

I get dressed and bring her a glass of water.

"For you," I say, setting it by her elbow.

She drags her eyes to me and then to the glass. "That's not wine."

"What are you working on?" I ask, sitting down across from her. I pick up one of the cutters and press the pad of my finger into the sharpened metal.

"Careful," she says. She raises her own hands in front of her, blood dripping from at least four different places.

I wince. "Jesus, Tib."

"Hazard of the job. Wait—" She glances up at the bathroom window "—did I miss it?"

"There was nothing," I lie, shaking my head. "Emma must not like you."

She harumphs. "That Emma Mancini always did have questionable taste."

Tibi works a little longer, and I watch as she exhaustively carves a rendering of the palazzo across the small street from mine, even capturing the texture of the tufo. When she's done, we head to dinner. I don't bring up Emma at all. It's another great night, and hours later, as I listen to Tibi's soft breathing in bed, I feel content, knowing that I'm protecting her.

I'm not sure what from. Not yet. But it doesn't matter. I couldn't keep Alex safe, but I can shield Tibi from unnecessary risks.

Once I'm sure she's sleeping soundly, I sneak out of bed and leave the apartment. I wander the ring path, the moonlight spotlighting the trail between trees. Finding the sounder in the dark takes me a while, but eventually, I come upon the boars rooting around near the necropolis. Something spooks them, and we all turn our heads at once. The matriarch grunts, and the sounder falls into line. I follow them down a well-trodden track and into a forest so dense I'm nearly blind in the darkness.

When I get back home, Tibi is just as I left her. I snuggle up against her back, her warmth palpable through my pajamas, her ribs expanding against mine. I fall asleep quickly.

In the morning, Tibi drags me from the covers. She flicks my chest with her finger as I sit up. "How many of these did you take?" she demands, two of her floating in front of my unfocused eyes. "Tori? How many?"

She shoves the pill bottle into my face. "None?" I guess.

"None?" Tibi might roll her eyes, but it's hard for me to make out details. I blink at her. "There were twenty-two and a half when I got here yesterday, and now there are seventeen."

Tibi counted my pills?

"How many did *you* take?" I fire back.

"None. Without a question mark."

I try to stand up, dropping back onto the edge of the bed when my head swims. "What time is it?"

"We need to be at the house in an hour and a half." She crouches in front of me. "But before we go anywhere, please just be honest with me. Are you okay, Tori? I mean, I know you're not okay, but are you okay enough? Are you..." Her lip quivers, and she stops talking.

I place my hands on her shoulders, hoping the gesture feels reassuring and not like I'm trying to steady myself. "I'm doing better every day. I'm not abusing the medicine. I don't know where the pills are, but I didn't take them," I promise. I don't know if it's a lie.

She takes a deep breath, her chest and shoulders rising. "You'd tell me if you needed help, right, Tori? You'd tell me this time?"

"Of course I would," I say, squeezing her shoulders. This time, I know I'm lying.

Tibi brings me an espresso as I get dressed, then stretches out on her belly at the bottom of the bed, the pills seemingly already forgotten. She studies her nails, a small smile toying at her lips. "So, I did a thing."

"Should I be nervous?" I ask over my shoulder as I slip on a black turtleneck.

She flips onto her back, her hair dangling over the edge of the bed. "I invited Jasper."

I grab her hands, pulling her up to face me. "Is he coming?"

"We'll see," she answers, picking a strand of hair off my shirt. "Could you imagine, both of us bringing our boyfriends home to Mom on the same day?"

I smirk. "Your boyfriend, huh?"

"I pronounced it boy-space-friend," she says, pushing me away.

"Pretty sure you didn't." I walk into the bathroom and come back with the hairbrush. "And Edo can't make it today."

Tibi's brow furrows. "Like, he's not coming at all?"

"He's overloaded with work stuff because of some deal he's working on and can't get away from the office." She purses her lips but doesn't say anything. "What are you not saying?" I ask when she is silent a touch too long.

"That Matteo will be far more pleasant at the harvest than I'd anticipated. Almost takes the fun out of having Jasper there."

She's also aware, then, of the weird tension between Matteo and Edo, which has evolved from a sort of brotherly rivalry into something much less trivial. I can't say when it started because I've been away for so long, but something must have happened. Neither of them is antagonistic by nature, and in the decade that they've been friends, I've never seen them like this.

"You don't have a car," Tibi says, sitting suddenly upright. "How will we get to the house?"

"Are you in a rush to see someone?" I grab both phones off their chargers by the windowsill and walk downstairs. Tibi follows.

She yanks her coat off the rack and heaves her bag over her shoulder. "That's between me and God, *impicciona.*"

"I already asked Mirësi and Tony if I could hitch a ride with them," I say, double-checking that I have the keys and turning off the light as I open the door. "Depending on what you just called me, you can find your own ride."

"I called you a meddler, Tori." Tibi walks out onto the sunny patio and turns back to me. "You're a meddler."

I can't take issue with that. She's right, and I've only shared a fraction of my meddling with her. I am a full-blown interloper.

Mirësi and Tony are waiting at the corner. As we approach, Tibi and Mirësi size each other up. Tony reads the newspaper.

"Tiberia Graziano," Tibi says, sticking her hand out. "And you must be the witch."

"And you...—" Mirësi takes Tibi's hand and turns its face up, studying her palm "—must be the artist. Mirësi Demiri. It's a pleasure, darling."

It's love at first sight. Though I don't know if the insight Mirësi garnered from the investigation of Tibi's palm had as much to do with her reading the lines etched there by genetics as it did with the dried ink stains under Tibi's fingernails and the wounds from her lino cutters.

I kiss Mirësi's cheeks. "If it is all right with you both, Tibi could use a ride to the harvest."

Tony tucks his paper under his arm and glances up at Tibi over the rim of his glasses. "Graziano, you said? Any relation to the producer?"

"Indeed," Tibi responds, grinning as she shakes Tony's hand. "I'm Matteo's much younger and more talented sister."

Tony asks her questions as we make our way to the small car park in Piazza San Giovenale. Mirësi walks by my side. I think about how relieved she was when I told her Matteo was not my boyfriend. I wonder if she'll feel differently when she meets him—if maybe the coffee grounds got confused.

Not that I want her to think Matteo and I belong together, but I do want her to like him.

My circle is small, it always has been, but if the people in it are close, there is power there, security. I want to draw all these people together and hold them tight. I crave the comfort of that intimacy. I have since I was sixteen, when I lost Alex and then watched my relationship with my mom and dad die, too.

And yet, I am so bad at accepting that kind of love and support from Edo.

Tibi directs Tony from the backseat as he drives. I stare at the Paglia out the window.

When we arrive at the Graziano house, the table on the porch is covered with food. Matteo has a selection of bottles lined up at one end, a dozen long-stemmed glasses beside them. The sun refracts through the glass, casting shimmering starbursts across the blue wood.

June rushes first to me, her eyes scanning, though she tries to hide it. Castor follows shortly behind from his post near the beautiful home Matteo has fashioned for himself from the old stable. The dog's ears fly behind him as he runs. They reach me at the same time, with almost equal amounts of enthusiasm.

"You look good, sweet girl," June says, squeezing my face in her hands.

I smile. "I feel pretty good."

"Has the medicine been helping?" She asks in a whisper as she wraps me in a hug.

I nod against her shoulder.

"Have you told your mom? She's been so—"

"June," I interrupt, grabbing her hand when she pulls back, "let's not go there." I lead her to Tony and Mirësi. Castor sticks close to my side. Matteo is already speaking to them, and I study Mirësi as he introduces himself. She laughs at something he says—I've never seen her laugh, not like that. I could swear her eyes sparkle.

Edo once told me he'd learned about charisma from Matteo, seeing him in action their senior year. It was hard for me to believe that Edo hadn't always been so naturally, unthinkingly charming, but by all accounts, he'd been much quieter when he first arrived in Orvieto. Matteo helped bring it out in him. Or forced it out.

Edo was gorgeous, but to compete with Matteo, he needed to channel a comparable, yet not identical, magnetism, which is why, by the end of the year, they had become such a dangerous pair.

I introduce June to Tony and Mirësi.

Matteo leans closer while they get acquainted. "Edo?" he asks.

"Can't make it," I say. "Work stuff."

His jaw tenses, pulses, but then his shoulders relax, the two unconscious reactions seemingly at odds.

"Too bad," he says. The way he's forcing his lips from turning up suggests he feels otherwise.

"Too bad," I agree, pressing my lips together. I glance back at Mirësi, who is studying me just as I'd been studying her. She raises an eyebrow, a black curl falling into her lashes.

I wonder if my traitorous eyes are sparkling, too.

Luckily, just then, Jasper arrives on a full-size tour bus, and I have time to blink away whatever might be there.

27

TIBI STOMPS AWAY FROM us without a word, looking for all the world like she intends to walk right up to Jasper and slap him in the face. The bus makes a tight turn and disappears down the driveway, leaving Jasper standing alone with his hands in his pockets.

Tony whispers into the silence that is our halted conversation, "Who is that?"

"Jasper," I say. June makes a slight gasping sound.

Tibi stands in front of him with her hands on her hips. We can't hear what they are saying, but Jasper grins, reaches for her, pulls her close, and dips her. His lips meet hers, and she wraps her arms around his neck.

Tony applauds. Matteo and I share a look. I guess they are on again.

Francesco Graziano grunts before flicking open the blade on the corkscrew he's holding and heading to the table. He uncorks two bottles of vino novello, filling the glasses with the pale-yellow wine.

The rest of us follow, Tibi and Jasper arriving last. She doesn't introduce him, so we just nod, wave, and pretend this is all perfectly normal. June insists we sit and eat something before heading out into the fields, and Matteo uses the time to give a little lesson about the late harvest.

"What you are drinking now," Matteo says, raising a bottle so the sunlight strikes the straw-colored liquid, "is the early ferment of the grapes we harvested in August."

He passes around a photo of the grapes on his phone, bunches of Trebbiano and Grechetto in soft greens and golds with hints of rose. I sip the wine while he talks, smiling at the way his hands move and how animated his features become.

Matteo catches my eye and smiles back. "Today's grapes are going to look a little different. Today, we are picking the grapes we left to mold. These grapes will make the sweetest wine."

June passes me a plate of focaccia and another of charcuterie. I make a show of eating it while Matteo teaches us about botrytis cinerea, also known as muffa nobile or noble rot.

It would all sound horrific if Matteo were less enthusiastic about the topic. The noble rot is a fungus that infects ripe grapes, penetrating the skin and feeding off their insides. The numerous but microscopic traumas the fungus inflicts on the skin cause the moisture within the grape to evaporate, the desiccation leading to a high concentration of sugar and flavor.

"Like a raisin?" Tony asks.

"Ah," Matteo says, his face lighting up. "Though any grape can shrivel in the sun, only the noble rot can change their chemistry, work in harmony with the essence of the grape to create a new physiology. The rot converts the acids. It takes a normal grape and turns it into something magical, something other. The process is not something we can control or perform by design. The botrytis is a spell cast by nature, a balance between cool, humid mornings and warm, dry afternoons."

Mirësi raises a finger into the air, and Matteo nods at her.

"Does the spell ever go wrong?" she asks.

Matteo brings his hands together, his expression serious. "Indeed. Sometimes, the rot gets too deep, growing too fast and powerfully. The grapes decay. They start to disintegrate. It's a delicate equilibrium, an easily broken symbiosis." He looks at me and then back at Mirësi. "Sometimes the grape is overwhelmed by the rot, especially if it has already been weakened by other factors. Instead of transforming into something exceptional, it spoils."

I frown. Did Matteo just imply that I am the human equivalent of an ailing, fungus-beset grape?

Tony rests his elbows on the table. "Truly fascinating stuff."

"It is," Matteo confirms. He picks up his glass of wine, swirls it, and chugs it. "And now for the most important part. Finish your drinks, and let's go pick some grapes."

Before Matteo frees us into the depths of his vineyard, he guides us through the rows of vines, showing us examples of grapes that are ready to be harvested. The infested grapes are not pretty—wrinkly but still fleshy, covered in a dusting of greenish fuzz. When he pops one between his fingers, it takes everything in me not to gag. He tells us that sometimes, on an entire bunch, there may only be a few that are ripe enough with rot to collect.

"This isn't a contest," Matteo says, eyeing Tibi. "Take your time with the grapes. What you pick today will determine the sweetness and caliber of the vintage. Your choices create the wine."

We break into groups of two, Matteo supplying baskets, gloves, and clippers. Each pair is assigned a quadrant.

I end up with Matteo.

"That speech you gave about noble rot was very poetic. I didn't realize it ran in the family," I tease as we head deeper into the trellises east of the house. My pulse is quicker than it should be, and my breathing is more shallow. I don't know if I feel guilty or nervous. Things didn't end well the last time I was alone with Matteo. And yet, I haven't been able to stop thinking about it.

He tilts his head. "I generally save that side of myself for grapes and..."

"And what?" I ask, shifting the big red bin I'm carrying onto my hip.

Matteo shrugs. "Other things."

I shiver and force a laugh. He indicates for me to set the bin down, pulling a baseball cap out of the butt pocket of his jeans. He runs a hand through his hair and places the hat on his head. I've never seen Matteo in a hat before.

He's really cute.

We collect grapes for hours. When I'm not sure about a particular bunch, he stands close, shoulder to shoulder, and we investigate the fruit together. By the time our bins are full, I don't find the noble rot disgusting. It is something alive and, yeah, like Matteo said, a little magical.

The sun sets as we carry the first bins back, the air teetering toward cold. Mirësi, Tony, June, and Francesco are already at the table when we appear, finishing bowls of steaming lentil soup that June and Francesco prepared. Tibi and Jasper are nowhere to be seen, possibly tangled up together somewhere in the vines or, more likely, in her bedroom.

The red bins by the building that houses the winepress are overflowing with grapes. Matteo sighs, satisfied, his cheeks flush from the cool air. He thanks the others for their hard work.

Tony yawns and pats his belly. "And thank you, Maestro Graziano, for the thrilling experience. What happens next?"

"Next," Matteo says, grabbing a piece of bread off the table. "I crush the grapes and fill the tanks." He takes a bite and passes the rest to me.

"Do you need a hand with that?" Tony asks hopefully, though he looks exhausted.

"No, I've got it. We had a big day already. You should head home." He lays a hand on Tony's shoulder. "But what I will need a hand with is sampling the product. Would you like to return to the vineyard for the first taste in thirty days?"

"Gladly, son," Tony says, looking thrilled. "Have Victoria give you my information."

Tony stands, offering a hand to Mirësi. They say their goodbyes to June and Francesco. "Coming, Victoria?" Mirësi asks. I completely forgot about our plans for the seance tonight.

"Actually..." I hesitate, glancing at Matteo. "We still have a bunch of bins to carry up. I'll stay to help with that and catch another ride."

Mirësi's smile, the curve of her red lips, is almost wicked. I feel my chest heat. But Matteo doesn't protest or tell me it's better if I go. So I stay where I am, fisting the piece of bread he gave me.

When we return to our bins, Matteo grabs a bottle of wine. "Eat that," he says, gesturing to the piece of bread. He takes a swig from the bottle, waits for me to finish chewing, and passes it to me.

We finish the bottle on our fourth trip back into the vines. He grabs another. There is only one bin left to carry in, but instead of lifting the last of the grapes and officially closing out the harvest, Matteo sits down next to it. I lower myself beside him, hugging my knees against the cold. The moon rises between rows of grapes, low on the horizon, as we gaze down from the slope of the hill.

I nudge Matteo with my shoulder. "That was a really fun day."

He leans back into me, and the warmth of his arm makes my skin tingle. I can feel his chest rise and fall as he breathes. "It was," he says.

And his response is somehow disappointing. I rest my head on his shoulder. "It was?" I repeat. "That's all?"

"What do you want me to say, Tor?"

"That I'm the best wine harvester you've ever met, and," I consider, "without me, today would not have been nearly as enjoyable. That would be a good start."

He chuckles. "It's like you want me to slip."

I lift my head and turn to him. Our eyes lock. "Slip?"

He drops his head, the muscles in his arms flexing. "Nevermind," he says, leaning back on his hands.

"Okay," I whisper, snatching the bottle of wine from between his legs.

"Remember that last summer in Newport Beach, the one you brought up the other day when you were here?"

I smile. "Of course."

"Want to know a secret?" he asks, his voice low, his mouth surprisingly close to my ear. If I turned right now and raised my chin...

"Sure," I answer, biting my lip.

He tugs his hat off and sets it on the ground. With his sweat-dampened curls falling across his forehead, he looks younger, his smile sheepish in the moonlight. "It wasn't cat piss."

I laugh. "What do you mean?"

"The sheets." His finger brushes against mine, where I'm gripping the neck of the bottle. "I wasn't washing them because of the cat."

"Why were you?" I ask, my brows drawing together.

He looks at me then, his eyes lingering on my mouth. "You kept wearing those little tank tops around the house without a bra. Those baby-blue shorts." I feel my eyes widen; my mouth goes dry. I remember those tanks, those shorts. I was sure he didn't notice them, but he was the entire reason I owned them. "In other words," he concludes, "I was washing them because of, what did you call them? Abnormally excessive nocturnal emissions."

"Because of me?" I all but whimper.

His eyes darken, his lip sliding between his teeth. "Because of you, Victoria."

Heat tears through me, so feverish and heavy that it's hard to breathe. I feel myself leaning closer to him. His hand moves to my thigh, his thumb rubbing circles as I study the subtle part of his lips, mine opening in response as I imagine the taste of him. My eyes close.

And then, like the sun has risen, everything is illuminated. I turn toward the source of the light, shading my eyes with my hand. A car has pulled up. "Expecting someone?" I ask Matteo, my voice raspy, breathless.

Matteo stands, offering a hand to help me up. I lift his hat off the dirt and use it to shield my face as we walk over. The headlights go out when we are about twenty feet away, and the sudden darkness makes it hard to make out the person standing next to the car, but my gut must know it's Edo because it sinks before he even speaks.

28

I DON'T KNOW WHAT he saw, what he could see. Looking over my shoulder to where Matteo and I had been sitting, I try to discern how much of what happened was visible, but with the memory of the headlights still blazing in my retinas, it's hard to say.

"Hey, baby," I say, walking faster to distance myself from Matteo. I've never called Edo 'baby' before in my life. "What are you doing here?"

The moonlight brushes his features in silver, highlighting the sheen in his eyes. The sadness there makes me want to run away, to hide until this moment and I are nothing but dust.

His gaze finds mine, then drifts over my shoulder to Matteo. "I wanted to surprise you." He takes a step back. "I tried to call."

I reach for his hand, and my heart cracks when his fingers tense in mine. "Edo," I say, trying to block his view of the rest of the world, trying to consume his entire field of vision so he can forget anything else exists. "Want to drive me home?"

He hesitates, his eyes searching mine. My breathing is shaky, and so is the hand I place over his heart. He doesn't flinch away, so I move closer and tuck myself into his chest. His head drops, his lips brushing against my hair as he inhales.

"Yes," he says. "Let's go home." We turn without another glance at Matteo. I don't want to remind Edo, or myself, of what was happening when he pulled up. I grab my bag and jacket off a chair, and Edo opens the passenger door for me. I slide in, only looking up when he presses the ignition and the headlights turn back on, spotlighting Matteo's back, where he's bending to retrieve the last bin of grapes.

I know then that Edo saw it all.

He's silent as he drives. I press my trembling hands between my legs. Do I say something? Deny what he witnessed with his own eyes? Is this it? Are we over? I start to feel like I'm suffocating in the car, suffocating in the withheld expectation of his anger, of his disappointment. I crack the window open, gasping when the cold air hits my face.

"You'll catch a chill," he says softly, rolling it back up.

I drop my head into my hands and force myself to speak against the tightness in my throat. "Edo—"

"I'm sorry, Victoria," he interrupts. He reaches over and twines his fingers through mine, turning to face me as we pass under the Porta Romana and into Orvieto. "I'm so sorry."

I gape at him, blinking. "You have *nothing* to be sorry for."

"I do." A look of guilt—similar, I imagine, to the one I wear—passes over his profile, and a prickle of unease passes across my skin with it.

Edo pulls his hand away to park the car in a small lot at the edge of the cliff, around the corner from my apartment. The lamplight doesn't reach us, and when he sighs, I'm mad that I can't see his face better.

He clears his throat, but his voice is still raw and agonized when he speaks. "I haven't been a good boyfriend, *amore.* I messed up. I know you don't deserve this. I know—"

"What did you do, Edo?" I ask, my heart constricting as I think of all the possibilities, acknowledging that no matter what he tells me, I have no right to be upset because it could have just as easily been me confessing my sins tonight.

He brushes the hair back from my temple, his fingers lingering in my hair. "I haven't been here for you when you needed someone the most. I failed you."

I swallow a sob, this admission more painful than any I could have dreamed up. "You didn't fail me," I argue, tears rolling down my cheeks. "You've been busy with your deal. I love how hard you work. I love how much you care about what you do."

"None of that changes the fact that I wasn't where I should have been." He leans his forehead against mine. "I see now what a mistake that was."

"You're here now," I whisper, tracing his jaw.

He tilts his face so his lips brush against mine. "If I promise to do better, can you forgive me?"

I kiss him, deep and slow. I kiss him like I'm begging for his forgiveness, because I am. Because he has things all wrong. "Can you come up?" I ask against his mouth. He smiles, and the relief I feel is monstrous, the lightening of someone who has gotten away with something.

I hate myself for it.

Edo collects my jacket from the back seat and hands me my purse. He wraps an arm around my shoulders, holding me close as we walk, and I breathe in the scent of him, the warmth of his skin.

He's sweet with me that night, delicate almost. We take our time, rediscovering each other and savoring our favorite parts. He shifts my body so I'm straddling him, his back against the headboard. I place my hands on either side of his head, his hands coming behind my shoulders to pull our bodies closer where they meet.

"Vita mia," he breathes against my breasts as he comes inside me. "I love you."

Edo was right about one thing tonight: I don't deserve this.

When I wake up, Edo isn't beside me in bed. It's just past seven, but it's possible he had to run back to work early. I wouldn't hold it against him. What he doesn't understand about me is that I don't want a babysitter. I don't want to feel like someone is taking care of me. But I know when he's around, he can't help himself.

I roll out of bed, slipping on dirty socks before relatching the shutters against the cold outside. Edo and I will figure it out. We can make this work.

A sound floats up from downstairs, a chair being pulled over tile. "Good morning, handsome," I call down the stairs. He doesn't reply, probably tucked away in the kitchen where he can't hear me. I splash water on my face in the bathroom and brush my teeth before shuffling down the steps, freezing as I step into the living room.

Edo is standing at the table, and unlike last night when he looked dejected and heartbroken, this morning, he looks furious. His face is so enraged that he reminds me of a cartoon. The only thing missing is the steam coming out of his ears. I've never been privy to a genuinely pissed-off Edo, and between his clenched fists and red face, I can see him exactly as he must have looked as a little boy during a tantrum.

It's kind of adorable, and I struggle not to smile at the scene, opening my mouth to ask what's wrong instead.

He puts a hand up to stop me. "Before you say anything, I want you to know I'm not mad at you."

"Okay," I murmur, coming closer.

"Victoria." His voice cracks. "I need you to tell me if you think I'm an...I need you to tell me if I'm being an idiot."

"Of course not, Edo," I say, standing across the table from him. "Why would you think that?" I hate the question because I can imagine why he might worry after what he saw last night.

He runs a hand through his hair and then reaches into his back pocket, pulling something out and setting it on the table. "What is this?"

"A phone," I respond meekly.

"Why, Victoria, do you have a second phone?"

"Because..."

"Because?" he urges, his voice full of hope, like he still believes I'm capable of being the woman he thinks I am.

I crumple into the chair, my eyes desperate when I look at him. "Because Matteo gave it to me."

His whole body goes rigid.

"Edo," I plead, "whatever you're thinking..." I don't finish, because he saw us last night. Whatever he's thinking is probably close enough to the truth to make me a liar if I contradict it.

He takes a deep breath, the anger transforming into something closer to anguish when he exhales. "Listen," he says, pulling out the chair beside me. He leans close, clasping my hands in his. "You need to be careful, Victoria."

I stay silent, adrenaline sweeping its way through my body. I'm not sure if he means with our relationship or if he's discovered something else: my obsession with Emma, my attempts at contacting his mother, the boars.

"I can't risk you," he says. "We still don't know, not everything, and if something ever happened to you..." He shakes his head as if to clear the thought. "You know people can put trackers in these things, apps that can pinpoint your location?

He could read your messages. He'd always know where you were. He'd make it so easy—"

"Matteo?" I scoff, unbelieving.

He looks at me, confused, as if he doesn't understand why I wouldn't be concerned that one of my oldest friends is stalking me.

I extract my hands from his and push away from the table. "This is insane. I get why you might be upset, but Matteo is not *following* me. He's not a fucking creep." I stand up, gripping the back of the chair. "And he would never, ever hurt me."

"Have you checked the phone?" he asks quietly, pushing it across the wood.

I cross my arms, my heart beating against them. "I don't need to."

"*Amore,* I know this is distressing and awful, but can you believe me when I say I just want the best for you?" He looks close to tears, consumed by worry.

But what he's saying is crazy.

"Are you jealous?" I ask, my posture softening. "Is this about what you saw last night? Nothing happened. *Nothing.*"

"Am I jealous?" He rises from the chair and stands before me, taking my elbows in his hands. "Of course I'm jealous. Matteo has been your friend since you were little. He knows you better than almost anyone else. I have years of catching up to do, decades. And I will." He drops his hands to my waist. "But that's not why I'm concerned right now."

I wrap my arms around his neck. "I'm going to need you to spell it out for me."

"It's just—" he nuzzles his face into my neck "—after what happened with Emma."

I pull back, startled by her name, the sound of it in this conversation where it doesn't belong. "What does Emma have to do with any of this?"

Edo's face pales. "You don't know?"

My legs turn heavy; my insides are overcome with a familiar unease. Because I don't know this thing that has made Edo so fearful. Something important and big that the Grazianos have kept from me.

I shake my head, and Edo presses his lips together.

"It's all right," I promise. I don't want him to bear the guilt of sharing ugly things with me. This isn't his fault. "You can tell me."

His eyes fill with regret, but he holds my gaze, his arms tightening around my middle like he knows I will need the support once I hear what he's about to say.

"Matteo," he says slowly, "was the second suspect in Emma's murder investigation."

29

I collapse into Edo, my fingers digging into his arms as my lungs constrict, my blood singeing my veins. The betrayal is so enormous that it consumes me and threatens to burn me up from within.

The people I held closest didn't trust me. They have kept me locked out of significant parts of their lives, on the periphery of their reality, only letting me in as much as they think is safe while still protecting me. And as much as the thought of Matteo possibly hurting Emma breaks my heart, it's the knowledge that the Grazianos have relegated me to being an outsider that breaks *me*.

Edo holds me, stroking my hair. I don't cry. The fiery shame parches me, desiccating the tears—shame that so many people I love have so little faith in me, that all they see is the same shattered girl I was ten years ago.

"Fuck them," I mutter, my fists trembling against Edo's chest.

He bends, sweeping me into his arms, and carries me to the couch like a child, sitting down so I'm resting across his lap.

"Don't be mad at the Grazianos. I don't know why Matteo never told you, but I'm sure they have good reasons."

I raise my eyebrows. "Not good enough."

"Cara mia, I'm sorry." Edo leans, raising my head to plant a kiss on my temple. "It was a long time ago, and maybe it was selfish of me to say anything, but it is all so similar to what happened with Emma that..." He presses his eyes closed like he's seeing something he doesn't want to see.

"Edo," I say, scooting off his lap and sitting beside him with all the calmness I can muster. I fold my hands in my lap. "I need you to tell me everything that happened."

He winces. "Victoria, I don't think that's—"

"Please." I sit up straighter and square my shoulders. "Please don't treat me like everyone else does. I can handle it. You know I can." Right now, it seems like he's the only one who has ever known. He's undoubtedly the only one left living who does—the only person who doesn't keep things from me in the name of protecting me.

He nods, his shoulders slumping in resignation. It shouldn't be his job to do this. "Our last year of high school, Matteo and Emma dated for a while," he begins. I think of the photo I found, Matteo's arm slung over her shoulder. The gesture suddenly looks possessive. "A few weeks before the end of school, she broke up with him. And—" he sucks in a breath and looks at me, a little self-conscious "—And we started seeing each other."

"Was it serious?" I ask, cuddling closer.

Edo shrugs. "No. We were friends first and foremost, but then Matteo found out. He'd show up wherever we were, and at first, it seemed like a coincidence, but then Emma talked about him coming by her house and leaving messages for her in her locker. She enjoyed it a little, knowing our relationship made him jealous. But it made me uncomfortable. For her."

I know how charming Matteo can be, how a young girl might easily get swept up in that. I realize how much power he could wield over someone naive and vulnerable. *Jesus.* I was swept up in it all just last night. I was inches away from risking it all for one kiss. At seventeen, it sounds like Emma had better self-restraint than I do.

"She didn't go back to him, did she?" The one thing that makes someone accustomed to getting their way irrationally angry is when they don't. I know because I grew up with Meg Lancaster.

"No, but I wish she had. I wish we'd just ended things because then...maybe..."

Chills run down my spine at what he's implying, but I'm not ready to face it yet. I cup Edo's face in my hands. "Whatever happened wasn't your fault, Edo."

His expression is strained. "What if it was?"

"You are kind and generous, and you love to take care of people, and I love that about you, but you can't always be responsible for everybody. You can't take everything on."

"I can try," he murmurs, bowing his head.

I know he's thinking about his mom and probably about me. How much of his time is spent worrying about both of us? Looking out for me. I'm embarrassed by how hard I've been making that for him to do.

"Did something happen between Matteo and Emma before she disappeared?" I ask, steering the conversation back, creeping closer to the part I don't want—but need—to hear.

He chews his cheek. "Not that I know of."

"Then why was he part of the investigation?" I press. "Why did they think he was involved?"

"He was there," Edo says.

I narrow my eyes. "At the river?"

"There were witnesses who saw him, a couple walking their dog. He was parked not far from where the police found Emma's bag and her pink towel still on the rock."

My stomach churns. Is Matteo capable of murder? Would he have killed a seventeen-year-old girl out of jealousy? It should seem impossible—I *wish* it seemed impossible—but there are so many little things that, all together, paint a picture almost as horrible as the one by Caterina on the landing.

"How did he—" I stop myself, shocked by the words about to leave my mouth. *How did he get away with it?* "Why did they let him go?"

"Not enough evidence." He raises his hands. "No clear motive."

"But—"

"I know, Victoria. But he was my friend. And I couldn't accept that he might have hurt her. Now, though, with you, I don't want to take any chances."

The tension that's been boiling between Matteo and Edo has been simmering there for a decade—Edo's doubts and misgivings always hiding just below the surface. I understand Matteo's need for control, to keep the conversation safe, to keep me unseeing. Why wouldn't he just offer to help me get my phone fixed instead of getting me a new one? Why was he so desperate for me to take those pills, to drink his wine, to create space between me and my reality?

Matteo was worried that without my senses dulled, I might notice something I shouldn't.

I remember Tibi's joke about Emma being murdered and am astonished by the callousness of her comment. I remember Matteo's reaction, the outburst that seemed so out of character. The whole time, they both knew that the plot was so much deeper.

It's all so obvious now.

Matteo hid everything in plain sight, surrounding me with Emma: her story, her things, her father.

His secrets.

Edo runs his hand up my leg. "Are you going to be all right?"

"I always am." *Eventually.*

He stands, reaching down to pull me up. "I hate to do this, but I have to be back in Florence before noon for a meeting. Tomorrow, I will talk to the head of International. I'm going to tell him that after this deal is closed, I need some time off to spend with my girlfriend. If that's okay with you."

"That sounds wonderful," I say, smiling. Part of me wants to beg him to stay. The thought of being alone in the house makes my skin crawl. But I also want to show him I'm okay—that I can be an equal partner and not just another weight on his shoulders.

I make myself a coffee while he showers, and I try not to think about the letters appearing in the mirror, about him stepping out to find the words cut into the steam. He doesn't mention them when he comes downstairs. Maybe that means they won't haunt me when I shower, and in time, I can pretend I never read them.

"See you soon?" I ask as he collects his keys.

"Very soon, *amore.*" He grins, his dimples erupting in his cheeks as he pulls back. "And in the meantime, start thinking of what you want to do with that time off. Greece? Africa?"

I wrap my arms around his neck. "We are going on a trip, huh?"

"I think it would be good to get away from here for a while," he says, his voice gentle.

"I think you're right." I step back, letting my hands fall. "And Edo, thank you for being honest with me."

He tilts his head. "You don't need to thank me."

But I do, because if he wasn't around to remind me I'm not broken, I might start believing I am.

I kiss him, standing in the doorway as he disappears down the stairs. I wait for the click of the gate, the sound of his footsteps fading down the street, and then I grab the phone Matteo gave me off the table—ignoring the missed calls and messages—and scroll through the apps.

Nothing looks strange, but I don't know how these things work. I'll try to get to the phone store later and see if they can figure out what's going on with my old phone so I can start using it again. If Matteo did install a tracking device, I'd rather not know.

I return to messages, deleting one from Tibi asking if I want to meet her and Jasper for an aperitivo. I delete the one from Matteo asking if I made it home safe. I reply to Lucia, who says the girls feel better and would love to see me. I let her know I'll be there and that she can use the old phone number if she needs to reach me.

On the way upstairs, I set the phone beside the painting on the landing, where it can slowly die as the battery runs down.

As I shower, I try to think of nothing but the hot water scorching away Matteo's touch, scorching away the knot of feelings and questions tangled in my mind.

When I get out, my eyes drift automatically to the mirror. The words are traced in the moisture: THE DEAD followed by an L, and then an I.

"I'm done, Emma," I shout, tucking my head in my hands. "I don't want to know. I don't want to know. Please," I beg, "I don't want to know."

I'm lying.

I do want to know. As painful and ugly as the truth is, I want to hold it and breathe it in and seal it in my box of tragedies, trap it inside my heart where I can appraise it when I feel alone.

But I'm not sure I can handle *this* truth. Because the woman I'm trying to convince Edo I am doesn't exist. I *am* weak and unstable. I *am* dangerous.

I can't let him find out I'm crazy.

Something falls, crashing to the ground downstairs. I wrap a towel around myself and rush down the steps, slipping as I reach the bottom. My feet go out from under me, the marble racking my back as I jounce down the last three steps.

The smell of sweet almonds floats in the air. I grimace as I walk toward the mantle, my muscles and bones already aching, stiffening further when I see the glass, fractured in a thousand tiny pieces across the floor, a galaxy of transparent splinters in a puddle of Disaronno. Emma's photo is face down on the mantle.

I glance at my red bracelet, which sticks to the wet skin of my wrist. I'm almost surprised to discover it's still there.

You don't tell the dead what to do, Victoria, Grandma Miriam chuckles in my ear. *But be careful that you don't let them tell you, either.*

30

OUTSIDE OF MY APARTMENT, the world feels different, weighted. The awareness that so much of my lived experience has been curated and cropped by others has created a screen between me and everything else.

The sky is blanketed in clouds that imprison the light, casting a shadowless glow over the tufo walls lining the street, hiding the sun, and holding the evidence of time's passage hostage.

My mother would call it derealization—a stress response that causes dissociation from surroundings and detachment from reality.

But it feels more like stepping into a new truth, being forced to accept a new reality. What if before, I'd just been floating, and this heaviness is the feeling of finding my feet planted firmly below me for the first time in a decade?

I see faces: in the corroding plaster on the buildings, in the carved stone of the church I pass.

I ignore them.

Lucia buzzes me up, and I ascend the stairs slowly, sore from my fall. When I pass Caterina's door, I drag my fingers along the wood, and I think I can see her face, too, on the other side.

My ears ring as Lucia talks to me. My replies are automatic. I wince when she shows me the small bruise on Ada's lip from her fall at the Duomo. She tells me it's nothing.

When I head out with the girls, it is still too cold to play outside, so I strap them into the stroller and head to the medieval quarter, to San Giovenale. The church is quiet during the days, and I figure that if it has withstood a thousand years of human use unharmed, it can hold up against a set of two-year-old twins.

Ada and Ileana crawl over the pews while I wander the perimeter, studying the 12th and 13th-century frescos, feeling like I'm constantly looking for something that will make everything make sense again, like it did when I was a child, before Alex got sick, long before I lost her.

That thing, I think, does not exist, but my mind can't accept that.

The girls start fussing, hungry and bored. When we leave the church, the sun casts spotlights over the valley. We go down to the little park beside the church. Someone once told me it used to be a cemetery. I like the idea that the grass and trees that overwhelm it now are born from ancient bones. I like the idea that death begets life.

I think about Emma and how her body was never found. I wonder what her life begot.

I try not to, but I think about Matteo. My heart pumps sideways in my ribs, compressing my lungs, and I rub a hand over my chest.

There's so much of Emma's story that doesn't check out and that I can't line up in my thoughts. But it's too scrambled to work through. My mind is too compromised to set it straight and figure out where all the pieces go.

Edo told me the truth. It would be too wild a lie, too easily disproved. Matteo was there. Matteo was a suspect.

But there is more. There are things Edo doesn't know—about Claudio and his mother. About Claudio and Matteo? The two are friends; their relationship is close and tender, almost familial. A man does not befriend the person he believes murdered his daughter.

Which means that either Claudio has some reason to believe Matteo is innocent, or I was wrong, and he is somehow guilty, too.

One of the girls starts to scream, and I whip my head around, remembering where I am and what I am supposed to be doing. My stomach sinks when I see Ileana gripping her hand, tears springing to Ada's eyes beside her. I stand too quickly, and my back spasms. I choke on a groan of pain that upsets the girls further, and both begin to cry in earnest.

I pull Ileana's fist into my hand, but she won't open it. The girls are standing near a patch of stinging nettle, and I assume that it's the cause of her distress. I sweep both girls into my arms, abandoning the stroller and their bag, and hobble down the street and around the corner to my apartment.

As I struggle to unlock the gate, the hairs on the back of my neck rise, and I glance back up the street before twisting the key and pushing the metal bars open, Ileana still balanced on my hip, Ada clinging to my pant leg.

I prop them both on the kitchen counter, rinsing Ileana's hand with soap and plying them with cookies to stop the crying before moving the girls to the couch. As I prepare a cool compress, I watch from the corner of my eye, the Disaronno and glass shards still littering the floor just feet away.

When the doorbell rings, I drop the towel and run to lock the door. The twins shouldn't be here. They are too precious, too fragile, and this home is all sharp edges—disjointed echoes of lost children and unseemly affairs and cults, the names of Greek heroes typed in telegrams, hinting at the demons who trail them.

And me.

We are all trapped in this nightmare.

I pick up the intercom, holding my hand over the receiver, listening.

"I can hear you breathing, weirdo," Tibi says, her staticky voice shocking in the quiet of the apartment.

"Tibi," I respond coldly. My love for her, the way the sound of her voice makes joy flare in my chest, is all suffocated by the knowledge that she lied to me. She's been lying to me for a decade.

"I brought you something. Buzz me up."

I glance at the girls and place my finger over my mouth for them to be quiet. "Now's not a good time."

"It'll be quick." I can hear her shaking the bars of the gate. "Hurry up. Jasper's waiting."

I can almost feel her despondency when I don't respond, like an ache in my belly. Tibi has been my best friend since before I formed my own consciousness. Cutting her out is like cutting off a part of myself, but once you lose one piece, the rest are easier to say goodbye to. I can't dwell on the Grazianos. I can't allow myself to feel their betrayal too deeply or mourn the loss of what was. It's easier this way.

"Seriously?" Tibi says. She's hurt. She's always worn her heart on her sleeve. "What the fuck."

I startle when the phone on the landing rings. I don't check it. I know it's her.

Tibi's exhale fills the apartment. "You can't hide from me, Tori."

Her footsteps resound through the intercom. I check Ileana's hand, swipe some cream on the blisters, and wait five more minutes before bringing the girls out onto the patio, peeking over the side of the wall to make sure Tibi's not in the street waiting to ambush me.

We get back to the Riccis' thirty minutes late. Lucia, luckily, seems to have enjoyed the extra peace. When I mention the stinging nettle, she tells me to stop worrying; toddlers are magnets for these kinds of accidents.

Maybe she's right, but our track record—between Ada's fall and Ileana's swollen palm—isn't great.

"Same time tomorrow?" I ask after getting the girls changed and ready for their naps.

"Yes, please." She hangs Ada's sweater on the back of a chair. "And this weekend, in the courtyard downstairs, we have our annual pig feast. I know," she says, laughing when my brows furrow, "sounds delightful."

"Pig feast?"

"Carlo's family has a small farm, and traditionally, when they harvest the first pig, they host a little party to share it with friends and family. I told Matteo to invite you, but in case he forgot, you have to—"

"I have plans," I say, my voice flat.

Lucia's face changes, taking on a hint of desperation. "If they change, I could really use some help with the girls. I'll pay you, of course. But honestly, the pressure of trying to look like a decent mother, wife, and housekeeper at these things means I've sort of come to hate them."

"I'll see what I can do," I lie, smiling.

She hugs me and tells me I'm a savior.

When she shuts the door, I amble down the hall and to the stairs. I stop in front of Caterina's door, cupping my hands over my mouth before I press them to the wood.

"I know you're there," I say.

And we will talk soon, because the skeletons in Caterina's closet know something about the skeletons in mine.

When I get home, a small package is jammed in my gate, a postcard-sized box tied with butcher string. I grab it as I enter, slamming the gate shut behind me, and hurry up and away from the dark space beside the stairs. The phone on the landing rings as soon as I'm inside the apartment, and the phone in my pocket follows immediately after.

I dump the box on the table before jogging up the steps to silence the phone from Matteo, placing it face down before answering the other call.

"Hi," I say.

"Principessa," Edo responds. "How are you doing?"

"I just got home from the Riccis'. The girls are good. We played at the park most of the morning." I leave out the part about that park being an ancient cemetery, Ileana's injury, and holding the twins captive in my apartment so I didn't have to see Tibi.

His murmur is deep and lands right in my belly. "Victoria, when you talk about kids, it makes me want to move you up here so I can run home between meetings and—"

"And what? Make babies?" That seems like the absolute last thing I should be allowed to do right now.

"Maybe one day?" he hedges.

My cheeks warm as I smile. "Yeah, maybe. Will you make it back to Orvieto tonight?"

"Not tonight, Victoria."

I glance around the apartment. "No worries," I lie.

When we hang up, I check the other phone. Tibi hasn't texted, but she's called a lot, which means she's serious. There's one text and it's from Matteo.

I'm sorry.

I block both of their numbers before pouring a glass of Matteo's wine. I eye the package from the kitchen, swallowing half my glass before opening it.

The string is knotted, and I work at it before being able to loosen it enough to shimmy it off the box. When I lift the lid, I see a stack of paper, each printed in black ink with the same image. It is the stamp that Tibi made on my patio, her linocut of the palazzo in front of mine. I study it, going through copy after copy, my blood running colder with each reproduction.

There's a person in the window, someone watching.

Clutching a print, I look out my door at the tufo wall, so innocuous on the other side of the street. I see it, the window in Tibi's image, my eyes widening as the curtain seems to shift. A shadow? The wind?

My eyes dart to the table on the patio, one of Tibi's tools having fallen beneath a chair. I race onto the patio and grab it, gripping it like a weapon before locking myself in the house. I have no one left to call. I have nowhere to go.

In the kitchen, I grab the pills, swallowing one with the last sip of my Orvieto Classico.

I'm tired of knowing things.

I'm tired.

I just want to disappear like Emma.

31

THE NIGHTSTAND SQUEALS AS I drag it across the floor of the teddy bear room, pushing it against the door. As far as security, the small wooden table doesn't offer much, but if someone tries to enter, at least the scraping of its legs will wake me and buy me time.

Rain spits against the window when I curl up in the sheets, and I listen to the sound of it, like waves rolling against the glass. The shutters are open. I didn't bother to latch them, and besides, if I need a quick exit, the window is my only option.

The fall from the window scares me less than the horror I've created in my imagination, the thing waiting for me on the other side of the door, in the window across the street.

For hours, I lie there, too aware to be asleep but also not fully awake. I am trapped in the falling space, the crossroads of dreams and wakefulness, my body too exhausted to jerk me back into consciousness. My limbs are stretched out straight, still, as my mind cycles through images like Alex and I used to with our vintage red View-Masters.

Click, a duck drowning in a lake.

Click, a hand pushing through the wall.

Click, Caterina's painting; the face no longer black, but bloody.

Click, my body splayed like a star at the bottom of the hill.

Hypnogogic hallucinations, my mother tells me, her voice unnaturally reassuring.

Click. Click. Click.

They continue, and I am forced to bear witness to the horrific things my mind invents, the things it hides in daylight. The things I hoped to have forgotten.

Click, Alex, choking on her tongue.

Click, Grandma Miriam's body, forgotten and wasted and stinking.

I feel the moment I slip back into my body like the whoosh at the end of a playground slide, the hollow-tummy feeling of driving too fast over a dip in the road. Relief. I don't move, not wanting to tempt the paralysis, the little sleep demon who visits to squash my lungs.

Mokthi, Mirësi had called him.

He doesn't come. My eyes wander to Matteo's hat hanging on the handle of Emma's armoire ever since I accidentally brought it home after the harvest. Maybe even Mokthi is afraid of murderers.

I scoot the bedside table away from the door, wincing when it grates on the tile, and slide out when the space is wide enough for me to pass. The phone on the landing lights up when I run a finger over the screen to check the time; it's just past three in the morning. I set the other phone beside it.

My jacket and shoes are at the table, and I keep the lights out while I put them on before twisting the door handle so slowly I startle when I hear the latch click open.

The rain has stopped, and the streets are muted and damp as I make my way out of town and to the ring path. Once in the trees, I scent the air, tilting my chin to the sky. Hints of sweet musk linger in the humidity, trapped in the orbs of moisture, and I track them like breadcrumbs, sniffing as I go.

I follow a game path into the woods, and the matriarch grunts in greeting when I come upon the boars. I fall in with the others, wandering with them while the moon sets.

When the sky is darkest, I return to the apartment, mud covering my sneakers and caked deep into the spaces underneath my fingernails. I make coffee and flip through *Antigone* until it's time for me to watch the twins. I don't shower. Emma needs to know I'm in charge.

Carlo buzzes me up when I ring the Riccis' bell.

"Rough night," he says as he lets me in. At first, I'm unsure if he's asking or telling, but the messy kitchen and screaming toddlers soon make it clear. "Lucia is still in bed," he adds quietly, as if his whispering can counteract the shrieking of the children.

I smile, but inside, I feel a shock of resentment. I wish someone could babysit my worries so I could be free of them.

Instead, I'm bundling someone else's into my arms, offering to carry a weight I'm barely capable of shouldering.

Ada leans into my shoulder, and I soften.

"I've got it from here," I tell him.

He steps hesitatingly backward out of the room. "Thank you," he mouths, his eyes drifting to the girls and then back to me.

I wonder if Lucia told him about Ada's fall and the stinging nettle. I wonder if he trusts me with his children or if he's just as desperate as his wife. Maybe desperate for her.

The girls and I hold hands as we descend the stairs. As we pass Caterina's door, Ileana gasps.

"What's wrong?" I ask her, but of course she can't answer me, much less explain to me in English what frightened her. I grip their hands tighter in mine until we are out of the building, strapping them in their stroller and heading down the main road for the fortress—with walls too tall for them to climb and nothing but grass to play in.

I stand guard while they run around, the sun hot in the wet air. We weave pieces of grass together and watch the clouds.

No one gets hurt, and when I return the girls to their mother, Lucia looks reassured.

On the way down the stairs, I drop Ileana's dirty diaper outside Caterina's door—a warning not to frighten them. A warning to leave my twins alone. And then I go home the long way, shimmy my way back into the teddy bear room, and nap.

The sky outside is dark when I wake up, though it's barely early evening, according to my phone. I know that in Europe, daylight saving time ends earlier. Is it possible I missed it? Or have I not been paying any attention to the quickening changing of the season? Paul screams, and I go to the window, looking over Mirësi's garden. The gold of the leaves captures the gold of the streetlamp, all the trees radiating a gentle glow in spite of nightfall's imminent arrival.

My attention snags on a silver thread rising from the corner of the garden, a wisp of smoke curling from Mirësi's clandestine cigarette. Our eyes meet. She's staring at me. Mirësi exhales, a burst of metallic blue charging from her mouth like flames as she holds my gaze, and I inch sideways, pressing myself into the wall, hiding in the room's shadows.

When my breathing calms, I go downstairs, get myself a glass of wine and a cookie, and sit at the table, opening *The Orphic Hymns*. It is too early to go back out; I'd be too visible. So I read, from the beginning, as the stars come out.

The glass trembles in my hand when I turn the page and see the dedication of the following poem.

To Dike.

I leave the book open, setting my glass in the crease to hold the page, and grab the Greek mythology guide I picked up at the bookstore, thumbing through the index and flipping to the page listed.

Dike, pronounced Dee-kay, also spelled Dice or Diche.

I read the meaning of the name, and my hand goes to my mouth, my lips curving. It was never Eurydice I was looking for. It was her.

It was *Justice*.

I'm here for justice.

A draft whistles through the room, a shutter slamming upstairs, and I know the house is pleased, and so are the ghosts who live in it.

As I read the poem, I whisper the words out loud.

TO DIKE

The Fumigation from Frankincense

The piercing eye of Justice bright I sing,
Plac'd by the sacred throne of Jove the king
Perceiving thence, with vision unconfin'd,
The life and conduct of the human kind.
To thee revenge and punishment belong,
Chastising ev'ry deed unjust and wrong
Whose pow'r alone dissimilars can join,
And from th' equality of truth combine:
For all the ill persuasion can inspire,
When urging bad designs with counsel dire,
'Tis thine alone to punish; with the race
Of lawless passions and incentives base;
For thou art ever to the good inclin'd,
And hostile to the men of evil mind.
Come, all propitious, and thy suppliant hear,
Till fates' predestine'd fatal hour draws near.

"For thou art ever to the good inclin'd/and hostile to the men of evil mind," I repeat louder. I say the words as I put on another sweater and tie my shoes. I recite them in my mind as I walk out of the apartment, a ward against the chilling sense of eyes pursuing me onto the cobblestone.

The line becomes a prayer, a promise.

I quote it for the boars when I find them, and they quiet their grunting to listen.

When I get home, I chug a glass of water and then dump all but two pills down the drain, turning on the faucet to rinse them away. I hide the others. My stomach rumbles, the sound feeble but demanding, and I realize I can't remember the last time I ate a meal. I prepare pasta with butter. I slice chunks of Parmigiano on top. I finish two bowls.

"Come, all propitious, and thy suppliant hear/Till fates' predestine'd fatal hour draws near," I sing under my breath as I go upstairs to get ready for bed. I study myself in the bathroom mirror—I've gotten too thin, too weak, almost wasted.

I'll need strength.

In bed, I snuggle the piglet, the nightstand back where it belongs, and I sleep well, peacefully, for the first time in months, finally understanding what I must do.

The next morning, I ring Caterina's buzzer instead of the Riccis' when I arrive at their building. I have twenty minutes until I'm due to watch the twins. It's not enough time, but it's a start. The entryway pops open, and I jog up to her door.

As I raise my hand to knock, it opens.

My breath catches in my throat.

"Signor Mazza," I stammer.

"What a pleasant surprise, Victoria," Edo's father says, taking my hand and pulling me inside. Goosebumps erupt along my skin. "I didn't know we were expecting you today."

I glance around before meeting his eyes—there's no sign of Caterina—and keep one hand clasped on the door frame so he can't close me in. "I'm so sorry to bother you. I didn't…I came to…" I trail off, realizing it's better to leave my thoughts unsaid. *I didn't know you were here. I came to speak with your wife.*

His wife, who, presumably, he believes is bedridden.

"Don't be silly." The elder Edoardo runs his hands through his hair, black as Edo's, with glints of silver at the temples, his eyes scanning my face. "I've been hoping I'd run into you."

I clench my teeth against my shudder. "When did you get in?" I ask, hating how his eyes drop down my body as I speak.

"Late last night." He leans against the wall and crosses his feet as he slips his hands into his pockets. "Way too late for lovely young ladies like yourself to be out alone."

But I was out, and something in the lilt of his voice implies he knows so, or at least suspects. I retreat a step back through the door, reversing into the hall. "Well, I don't want to keep you. I just stopped by to see if someone might have found a small shoe—" I indicate the size of a toddler shoe with my fingers "—in the hall."

"No shoe." Edoardo raises his eyebrows. "But the maid did mention a misplaced diaper," he says, smiling like my lie is a joke we're sharing. Like he is perfectly aware that I'm the lunatic who left it on their doorstep. "But I'm guessing you don't want that back."

"All yours." I laugh, gripping the door handle and preparing to shut it in his face. "Goodbye, Mr. Mazza. Have a nice day."

"See you soon, Victoria. And please, call me Edo."

I shut the door, pressing my back against the wood and slouching down so he can't see me through the peephole.

How the fuck is that creep Edo's father?

32

THE TWINS AND I leave for the morning and return four hours later without another glimpse of Edoardo Mazza. The absence of him makes me almost as uncomfortable as the shock of finding him in Caterina's home. He seems too big, something about him too loud, to slip in and out of my world unseen, unobserved.

But he did, and I can't shake the way his sudden appearance left me with a heavy feeling in my gut.

On my way home from the Riccis', I call Edo to ask, in much less direct terms, why the hell he didn't tell me his father was going to be in town and when he's going to leave. As long as Edoardo is in Caterina's home, I have no chance of speaking to her.

"My father was there?" Edo asks, his voice tight. "In the apartment?"

"Yes," I respond. "You didn't know?"

He's silent for a moment. "Did he say why?"

"Did he tell *me* why he was there?" I repeat. Edo and his dad are much closer than my parents and I. It's laughable to suggest that his father would confide something in me that he didn't share first with Edo.

"That's what I asked, Victoria," he shoots back.

I cringe at my insensitivity—and also a little at his shitty reaction. "Sorry. No, he didn't say why he'd come."

"Right, well, unfortunately, I won't make it down there this evening. If you...If you see him again, I'd appreciate you letting me know."

"Should I have him call you? Is everything all right with your—"

"I have to go," he says, and the line goes dead.

It seems their relationship isn't so perfect after all. I'm surprised by the sudden urge to call my mother and tell her about it. *Look, Mom! My boyfriend's family dynamics might be almost as questionable as ours!*

I chuckle, wondering if she'd remember who I was when she picked up the phone. By now, she's probably forgotten that she ever had two daughters. Or she probably wishes she could forget after hearing from the Grazianos about what a mess I am.

Having a child who likely needs psychiatric care doesn't engender a lot of confidence in Meg Lancaster's head-doctoring abilities. With me out of the picture, I'm not a liability to her self-image or her reputation.

You're welcome, Mom.

I stop at the little market in Piazza della Repubblica and buy myself cheese, prosciutto, and fresh bread. I even pick out a few shiny apples and a bunch of carrots, the greens braided together and tied with string.

At home, I unlock the gate and pause, staring at the iron door set into the wall. Setting my groceries on the second step, I pull out my phone and try to persuade the flashlight to turn on, but I am relegated instead to the faint glow the screen produces. I press the phone and my face to the small, barred opening at the top of the door, the metal cold against my cheekbones.

The light lands flatly, illuminating only the closest objects in a thrum of lifeless blue—stacks of file boxes, some padlocked. Most likely, they are stuffed with old papers and whatever teachers acquire over decades in a classroom. However, I don't know why you'd need to protect those things with hardened steel when they are already being kept in what is—for all intents and purposes—a literal dungeon.

I try the two keys on my set from Claudio on the lock. Neither fits. A noise comes from inside, probably a mouse or a rat scurrying across the stone, but I lift my mouth to the bars anyway.

"Emma?" There's no reply, because Emma, at least a living version of her, hasn't just been hanging out in the dank storage space all these years—not the part of it that's visible anyway.

I carry up my groceries, pour myself a glass of wine, and make myself a sandwich that I eat on the patio, my eyes fixed on the window across the street. The glass on one side is swung open, brown shutters locked on either side of the frame, heavy iron latches holding them against the stone wall, the tufo a patchwork of irregular shapes and sizes.

Tibi captured the scene perfectly in her print. I wish I could talk to her and tell her how amazing she is without it feeling like double-crossing my own well-being. I slide my hand into my jacket pocket and grip the handle of the tool she left behind. I've carried it with me ever since I found it under the table—a reminder or a weapon, I'm not sure.

Paul screams on the other side of the wall, mocking me for thinking I could do anything more than scratch someone with the tool in my pocket. Still, he is my only company, so I let it go.

I sit there until the sun goes down.

But even after dusk has fallen, I don't leave the house; instead, I walk room to room to close the shutters. I'm not as brave at night. When I get to the window in the teddy bear room, Mirësi is outside again, standing there, staring up at me. The fingers of her left hand dance in the air, empty, craving the weight of a Marlboro Line Gold.

I swing the glass open. "Why not just smoke?" I call to her.

"I don't smoke," she responds, lifting her chin.

I squint at her. "I saw you yesterday."

"Darling, I saw *you* yesterday," she repeats back to me. "And since I've lived through and survived my fair share of dark times, I know it's not ideal for a young woman to spend her evenings alone in a house full of ghosts stalking around without the lights on."

I nod before closing the shutters, flipping the ceiling light on as I leave the room to sit in the dark downstairs.

Finally, it comes: a text from Edo.

My father was there to check up on a security issue at the house. He left for Genoa a little while ago. I'm sorry I was short with you.

When I don't immediately respond, he adds: *Forgive me? Please.*

Of course:) I type between tying my shoes. *By the way, what kind of car is your dad driving these days?*

Why?

Because he makes my skin crawl, and I don't want him to be able to sneak up on me again. *I didn't see the Mercedes at your mom's building this morning.*

He probably parked by the barracks.

...

And he isn't driving the Mercedes anymore. He's in an Audi Black Edition now, like mine.

My mind immediately goes to the day I met Mirësi, standing in the street at the corner and waving at someone I thought was Edo—someone in the same car Edo drives.

I think of Edoardo's comment about being out last night, the figure in the window of Tibi's print, and the feeling of being watched—which all beg the question, why would Edoardo Mazza be keeping such close tabs on me?

I walk for hours that night, deep in the woods where there are no human witnesses. I recline amongst the boars while they wallow near the river, mud clinging to their wiry hair.

A piglet presses its side against mine. A sow nearby bares her teeth at me in warning. I bare mine back.

She grunts, a sound so low I feel it in my bones.

They've accepted me.

Only with them do I know I am truly safe.

Back home, I shower with the lights off, my filthy clothes in a heap in the corner. The scent of boar sloughs off my skin and churns in the steam—soil and game and green things.

When I get to the Riccis' building in the morning, I scan the entranceway, halls, and especially the area around Caterina's door for cameras—any evidence that Edoardo is monitoring Caterina's apartment, or maybe even the whole building.

I don't see anything, but still, I don't knock on Caterina's door.

We both know she's lying to her family, but she's the only one who knows why. If I have any chance of finding out, it will require me to be a lot sneakier than leaving chocolate croissants on the doorstep and telling lies about missing shoes.

I must find a way to get her out of the apartment or get me in. A quiet way. A secret way.

Because I'm pretty sure Edoardo Mazza is keeping as close an eye on her activities as he is on mine.

Instead of taking the twins out right away, we admire the view from the hall windows overlooking the courtyard.

"Red," I tell them, pointing at the Fiat 500 parked inside the arches. I count the terra cotta flowerpots lined up on the gray stone below us.

"One, two, three," the girls repeat, their sweet voices mimicking mine.

I survey the windows across the way, the rickety, half-sized doors at ground level that probably lead to small storage spaces. Behind a locked gate in the corner across from the main entrance, I can make out the contrasting strokes—light, dark, light—of what I think is another set of stairs.

We play hide and seek on the third floor, while from the corner of my eye, I watch the barista from the cafe on the ground floor of the palazzo as he carries a case of Illy coffee to the gate, unlocks it, and disappears upstairs before reappearing in a window a floor above.

The Mazza's apartment wraps around nearly the entire second floor.

This building used to be a single home, an elaborate mansion built for one of the wealthiest families in town. Fifteen hundred years later, their names are still inscribed in the stone of the vestibule. Historically, the rooms and all three stories of the building were connected internally by servants' halls and hidden staircases, which were mostly torn down or converted when the palazzo was divided into apartments.

But if one still exists, there's a chance it can get me where I need to go.

Lucia is washing dishes when I return to the Riccis' with the girls. I gently nudge her out of the way and start rinsing sippy cups, curdled milk crowding the straws.

"It's so strange," she says, sitting at the table and pulling Ileana onto her lap. "I have no sense of the last two years passing. You haven't even been coming to help for two weeks, and already, I can't remember what our days used to look like. What did I do with the twins for these four hours every morning? I have no idea."

My mother once told me that when you are stressed or anxious, your brain doesn't process memories the same way; the chemicals and hormones your body produces prevent you from encoding new information, the increased cortisol wreaking havoc on the hippocampus.

Only the very worst things stick, which is why my memories from the time I was six onward are essentially a Rolodex of horror and trauma.

Some of the best things make it, too, but my best things were Alex, Tibi, Matteo, visits to the Grazianos' house, and summers in Newport Beach at Grandma Miriam's. They've all had to be refiled.

"I think that's normal," I tell her. I've found that being a nurse, people like to hear this from me.

She laughs and walks me to the door after I dry my hands. "I hope so."

"Oh, and Lucia," I say after hugging the girls. "I'll be here for the pig feast. At least long enough to get Ada and Ileana to bed so you can enjoy yourself."

She grins, placing a hand on her chest.

I'm glad she doesn't thank me because I'm not doing it for her or the girls.

The next day, I put on makeup and a cute top. Or, a top that was once cute, but now hangs on me in a way that is almost worrisome. I pull my hair into something other than a messy bun. By the time I'm done with myself, I look pretty.

I stare for longer than I should. I haven't seen this Victoria for a long time. Or have I? Maybe it's like Lucia said: I've been in Italy less than three weeks, but already I can't remember anything else beyond Emma, beyond the secrets and the obsession and the boars at night and the words on the mirror and Paul's screaming and the chill on the back of my neck.

I was always only these things.

The girls and I go out for breakfast at the cafe on the ground floor of the palazzo, where I make fast friends with the flirty bartender, who is more than happy to tell me all about the storage space they use on the second floor.

"The original frescoes?" I ask, widening my eyes after he tells me about the painted walls and cloistered ceilings.

He leans across the bar. "If you want to see, I can take you up."

"Yes!" I draw in a breath and bite my lip as my eyes drift to the girls. "But I can't right now."

"Maybe another time?" he asks, his finger playing with the handle of my espresso cup.

I pretend to think for a second. "Are you working Saturday night?"

33

I arrive at the Riccis' early to watch the girls while Carlo and Lucia set up for the feast downstairs. They are in and out of the apartment, where in the kitchen, Carlo's parents are preparing their newly slaughtered pig in every way possible that doesn't involve curing: a ragu for pasta, ribs baking in the oven with potatoes, a pork loin *arrosto morto* simmering on the stove.

The Riccis' pig is also in two other apartments on this floor. Its dismembered parts are being heated, boiled, and sliced into pieces before they will all be reunited—no longer recognizable as the animal it was—on the long table in the courtyard.

Eventually, the apartment becomes chaotic—too many people coming in to say hello and check on the progress of their meal, the spaces too small for sizzling oil and small children and socializing. Lucia introduces me to a beautiful woman named Renata as I try to squeeze out the door with the twins. The same Renata, I surmise, that Matteo was dating before I arrived in Orvieto. She knows who I am and asks kind questions in broken English. Ada pulls my hand, and I excuse myself. The girls need to run around a bit before dinner.

When Matteo arrives, I'm sitting on the ground in the corner of the courtyard, Ada in my lap while Ileana uses my knee as a trampoline for her wooden doll. The toy's arms and legs are poseable, and she has them stretched out as wide as possible.

Matteo doesn't see me. I'm not even sure if he knew I would be here. I scoot back further into the shadows, watching him.

The string lights shine off the arcs of his curls, glint off his glasses, and shadow the dip of his lip. His shirt sleeves are stretched tight against his arms, which strain under the weight of the wine case he's carrying. Lucia comes down the stairs. He sets the wine down and waves, his whole face brightening when he smiles.

I'm not the only one who notices. Renata sits up a little straighter in her seat at the long banquet table.

I wonder if she knows he might have hurt Emma.

If she does, I wonder if she cares. Someone could overlook a lot for a man like Matteo. Maybe even murder?

Carlo calls us to the table, and I take the girls' hands, finding my spot between their booster seats. I feel the moment Matteo sees me; his gaze is a ribbon of heat along my neck and down my arms. It pulls, and even though I shouldn't, even though I don't want to, I turn my head and raise my eyes to his.

We stare at each other.

My pulse quickens, the sensation of his gaze now a fever on my skin, and I think of a thousand words I want to shout across the table. But only one falls to my lips. It lingers before my mouth forms the soundless, selfish word: *Why?*

Not why did you do it, why did you hurt Emma, but why did you lie to *me?* Why didn't you tell me what was going on?

My vision starts to blur, and I tear my eyes away, focusing on the girls and the blood-red pasta sauce already dripping down the front of their pretty dresses. I pick at my food, moving the chunks of pig around my plate as they finish. I drink two glasses of Matteo's wine.

When Ada and Ileana start to rub their eyes, I unbuckle them from their seats and carry them upstairs, giving them baths and putting them in their pajamas. We read and cuddle, and when the twins are finally asleep in their beds, I double-check the baby monitor and text Lucia that I'm heading out. I wave at the camera in the corner of the room when she says she's got the feed pulled up.

I slip into the Riccis' bedroom before leaving, fixing my hair in the mirror over their dresser and swiping on some of Lucia's lipstick. My muscles tighten as I pass Caterina's door on my way downstairs. "Be there soon," I whisper, patting my pocket to ensure the cigarette and lighter I stole off the table at dinner are still there.

It's easy to get out of the building unseen, sticking to the darkness along the wall of the entranceway. Everyone is too busy stuffing their faces with pork and having a good time to care about what's happening outside their little bubble anyway. I don't bother looking back—especially not at Matteo.

Couples, teenagers, and families loiter on the cobblestones, laughing and kissing and arguing with their hands. I skirt the exterior of the building, first, the facade that lines one main street and then right along the other until I reach the bar.

When I walk in, Alessio, the bartender, grins at me from behind the glass-top counter. The tight space smells like perfume and lust. People crowd the bar, waiting to order fun, bright-colored cocktails or occasionally a shot of something stronger. People who are probably my age, I realize. But they are young. I don't know that I've ever been young.

"Ready for your tour?" Alessio calls as I push my way closer.

I point toward the restroom. "Give me just a minute," I say before making my way up the three stone steps that lead to the bathroom and the tiny supply locker inside it. The space is made entirely of tufo and concrete. The door is frosted glass. The bar has two exits.

I repeat these words to myself as I pull the cigarette from my pocket, light it, and stuff it into the stack of toilet paper rolls.

As soon as I see a thread of steady smoke, I walk out.

Alessio comes around the end of the bar and takes my hand, leading me out the exit into the courtyard. I keep my head down as he works the key into the gate lock, standing closer to him than I should be, knowing that Lucia, Carlo, and Matteo are barely twenty feet away.

When the gate finally swings open, the sharp sound of the hinges swallowed by music and laughter, I let out a huge breath and slide past Alessio into the dark stairwell.

The steps here are tiled, terracotta, not carved stone like the main set. They are also much narrower. Alessio shines the light from his phone a few stairs ahead, placing a hand on the small of my back to steer me right when we reach the top. Pigeons flap above us when his light illuminates the large room. I gasp. The walls are plastered and covered in fading frescos, the floor a dusty, cracked mosaic, spackled in bird shit. Broken glass from the massive arched windows is scattered atop the broken tiles. And it is still beautiful.

"This is incredible," I say, spinning in a circle to take in the space, searching for another door, another hall, to follow when he leaves. "Why wasn't it renovated with the rest of the building?"

"Rumor is it's haunted. Every time the workers started doing something, a piece of the ceiling would cave in, or a lighting fixture would blow. They say there was a ghost."

I chuckle softly. *What's one more ghost?* When I turn to him, the light casts shadows under his eyes. "Have you ever seen anything?"

"Honestly? I've never seen anything, but I try not to come up here at night alone." He shrugs, his smile flirty and teasing.

Alessio is sweet, but I need his phone to hurry up and ring.

I reach for his wrist, shifting his hand so the light hits the far wall. "What's back there?"

"I haven't been back there," he admits, drawing the phone closer to his face as it vibrates in his hand. "There aren't any windows."

He answers his phone, the glow from the screen highlighting the widening of his eyes and the hinge of his jaw. *"Porca miseria,"* he swears into the receiver, then to me, "I have to go. There's a fire in the bar."

I press my fingers to my mouth in feigned surprise before pushing him back toward the stairs. "Run. Hurry," I say. "I'll be right there."

He nods and flees down the steps, the light of his phone swinging back and forth against the walls as he goes. I hear the gate shut and pull out my phone, hammering my fingers against the screen.

Nothing.

I stand still, waiting for my eyes to adjust. A beam creaks above me. A pigeon squawks, and it sounds like it's being strangled. Slowly, I make my way to the dark space in the back of the room. My hands feel stone, not plaster, and I drag them along as I walk into the blackness, broken pieces of flooring skittering at my feet as I stumble along. The corridor turns abruptly, and I know I'm getting closer to the Mazzas' apartment.

Something gleams faintly on the tile about thirty feet ahead, and as I get closer, I realize the light is coming from under a door. I grip the handle and twist when I reach it, but the door is locked.

Of course, it's locked. Why would you have a door in your home open to this black hole of a hallway? But I'm so close to Caterina.

So close that I am willing to force my way into my boyfriend's mom's house to speak with her.

I slam my shoulder against the wood. My body and unsubstantial bones aren't strong enough to do anything. It's useless, but I try again anyway. My breathing becomes heavy as I throw myself against the door again and again before crumpling to the floor.

The light hits my face. I throw my hands over my eyes, blinded by the sudden brightness as bony hands pull me up to my feet. I glimpse the apartment through my fingers while my sight returns to normal.

When I finally look at Caterina, hugging my arms as I face her, I'm struck by the similarities. She is my height. She has the same brown eyes, the same brown hair, and the same breakable frame—things I didn't have the time to acknowledge in our first brief meeting.

"You shouldn't have come," she says.

"I know," I whisper.

"*Allora,* it seems we agree. I'll prepare some coffee." She shuffles out of the room before I can respond.

I follow. In the kitchen, she gestures for me to sit down. She prepares a Moka and sets it on the stovetop. She is delicate but definitely capable.

"Why do they think you're bedridden?" I ask.

She raises an eyebrow. Her features are gaunt, swallowed by something internal. She looks nothing like Edo. "They think what I want them to think."

"But—"

"I have my reasons, and they are valid." She turns her back on me and checks the coffee.

"Why did you paint a star that day? Is it related to Claudio Mancini's cult?" I observe her closely to see if she reacts to Claudio's name.

Her shoulders rise with a gentle laugh. "You get straight to the point, don't you girl?"

"You're hard to get in touch with. If I don't ask now, I might never have a chance. As it is, I had to break in to have this conversation."

"I let you in," she corrects. "And Claudio Mancini was never in a cult. Unless you consider a book club a cult?"

I shake my head.

"They called themselves the *Scuola di Pitagora,* the School of Pythagoras. They were a bunch of Classicists who read and translated Ancient Greek works for fun. And like the Pythagoreans, they identified each other by a coin with a pentagram on it—the symbol of the perfect human microcosm. Sugar?"

"No, thank you. Were you in the book club?"

"My sister was," she answers, setting down our coffees and sitting across from me.

Her dead sister. "But you knew Claudio. He taught you English."

"He did," she confirms, narrowing her eyes at me. "My sister introduced us."

"Your English is excellent. He must be a very good teacher. Did you spend a lot of time together?"

She stiffens. "It wasn't me who wrote those letters." Her voice breaks. "Claudio and I never—"

"Who was it then?" I interrupt.

Caterina's eyes drop. "It was her."

"Your sister?" I ask, leaning forward.

Her voice drops. "It's not what you think. Their relationship was never romantic. But they were close. Too close. She couldn't let it go."

"Let what go? And what about Emma?"

Caterina straightens. "All men make mistakes, but a good man yields when he knows his course is wrong and repairs the evil."

"*Antigone*," I murmur.

"Sabrina, my sister, she knew things she shouldn't. She dug too deep. Not all men are good." Caterina holds my eyes, a warning there. "I couldn't protect her. He...he..." She trails off, her eyes darting to the window.

"Who?" I press.

"Listen, Victoria. A parent will do anything to protect their child. *Anything.*"

I blink at her, a tickle of dread awakening in my belly. "What happened?" I demand.

She stands, the coffee cups trembling against their saucers as she pushes away from the table. "You shouldn't be here," she says, suddenly breathless. "It's not safe. I'm sorry, Victoria."

She tugs me from the chair, dragging me back toward the hall. "I'm sorry."

I don't resist; everything in my body tells me to run, to get away. But then we both freeze, the house filling with the sound of banging. Someone is at the door.

"I know you're in there, Tori. Open the door."

Matteo.

34

"What do I do?" I ask Caterina, sweat beading on my forehead as I cling to her arm, as thin and powerless to protect us as my own.

She huffs, her dark eye pinning me. "You answer the door, Victoria." It's an order, and I find myself scurrying to obey. As my fingers twist around the handle, she says, her voice lower, "And when you leave, you close it firmly behind you and never come back into this home again."

As I gape at her, she turns and disappears down the hall. Matteo knocks again, calling my name, his voice so close that I jump.

"How did you know I was here?" I say through the door, pressing my hand to the wood. My tone is accusing and unkind.

"I saw you go up the service steps with that kid from the bar. You never came back down. Open the door, Tori." There's a tremor in his voice. "We have to go."

Cautiously, I tug the handle down, pulling the door toward me. "Go where?"

"It's Tibi," he says, his eyes pleading. "She was in an accident. She's in the hospital in Rome."

The world threatens to swallow me, darkness and cold smothering my senses. *Not Tibi. I can't lose Tibi.*

Matteo catches me as I lurch forward, throwing my arm around his shoulders and hauling my body away from the door, his fingers tightening around my waist. "Shut it," I manage to say. "Please." He lets go of my side just long enough to slam the door, every window on the floor shaking as the latch clicks into place.

By the time we are at the bottom of the stairs, my head has stopped spinning and now I'm tugging him out of the building, asking where his car is. We run to the parking lot, and I'm yanking at the handle of his Alfa Romeo before he can hit unlock.

"What happened?" I ask, sliding into the passenger's seat. "How bad is it?"

"I don't know," he says, looking over his shoulder as he backs out of the spot. "I don't know. Jasper called, and he was too upset to say much, but he texted me the name of the hospital."

"Fuck," I murmur. "Fuck, Matteo. What if..." I start to cry, a deluge of tears streaming down my face.

He shakes his head and reaches for my hand. I pull it away. His jaw tightens. "She's going to be okay, Tor."

"Give me your phone," I say, wiping my eyes with the back of my arm. "I'm calling Jasper."

"He's on Tibi's phone." He blasts through a roundabout, honking at someone who tries to pull out in front of him. "You can call hers."

I swallow. "My phone doesn't work."

His eyes are sad when they meet mine, maybe even disappointed, but he doesn't say anything about the phone he bought me. "Here," he says, digging his phone out of his back pocket and setting it in my hand.

We pull up to the ticket machine for the autostrada, and I call Tibi's number. When I call the second time after no answer, Matteo is already tearing through Umbria at nearly twice the legal speed limit.

I touch his arm as Jasper picks up. Killing us won't do any good. He eases off the gas.

"It's Tori," I say, putting the call on speaker. "How is she? What's going on?"

Jasper clears his throat. "The doctors just came out. They said she has a few bruised ribs and a broken wrist."

"Thank god," I murmur. Matteo squeezes my free hand, and I don't pull away this time. "What happened to her?"

"Tibi told me that if I tell anyone what happened, she'd kill me," he says. "And since I'm inclined to believe her, and since she's going to live, you'll just have to pry it out of her yourselves."

Matteo and I look at each other, a small smile tugging at his lips. "Tibi," he mouths.

"Tibi," I agree. "We'll be there in an hour, Jasper. Take good care of her in the meantime."

I close the call and lean back into my seat, my heartbeat slowing, the sudden exodus of adrenaline from my system leaving my muscles twitchy and unsettled. We are silent as hill towns fly by the windows, lit up like little galaxies as we pass, floating by in the inky landscape.

Matteo exhales, and I turn to him, his profile dark against the window.

"She's not as strong as you, Tori," he says. "She can't just keep standing the way you do."

"Tibi?" I ask in disbelief. Tibi, my wildest, most self-assured, creative friend. Tibi, who is so delightfully, perfectly, always Tibi.

"She's sensitive and" —His grip tightens on the steering wheel— "And when you ignore her, cut her off, she doesn't understand. She thinks she did something wrong, and it breaks her."

My mouth falls open. He's mad at me. He's mad at me for how I've been treating Tibi. But I'm the one who is supposed to be angry.

"It's not that simple," I argue, needing to defend myself.

He glances at me, then back at the road. "She adores you, *patatina.* What's not simple about that?"

I bite into my lip, fighting the heartache. "I have reasons, Matteo, and you know it. You know better than anyone."

"Because I'm an idiot, you're going to stop talking to Tibi?"

"You weren't just an idiot, you were..." I throw my head back, trying to think of the right word to express the sense of betrayal, the way I've been sinking ever since finding out.

Matteo's shoulders fall. "Do you think I don't realize how stupid I was?"

"Why didn't you just tell me?" I almost shout. "Why didn't anyone say anything?"

He scoffs. "How embarrassing would that be? My family telling you that after years, I still hope that, maybe, you feel the same way I do? I can't believe I said that crap when we were at the vineyard. That I tried to kiss you? I was a dick, I know that. But Tibi didn't do anything, Tori. It's not fair of you to punish her when it was me who fucked everything up."

Something pulls tight right through my center. "What?" I whisper.

His chest heaves when he breathes. "You know what, though? I'm not sorry. Edo doesn't deserve you, Tori. I don't know if anyone does, but it's not that lying piece of shit."

I feel my eyes widen. And before I can say anything, before I'm even close to getting my bearings in this conversation, Matteo goes on.

"Did he ever tell you?" he asks. "He fucking swore he would. He told me to leave it alone, said he'd do the right thing." Matteo pushes a hand through his hair. "Did he?"

"Tell me what?" My voice is small, and Matteo winces when he hears it. I watch as he softens, his brows drawing in. "Tell me what, Matteo?" I ask again, more forcefully.

Matteo looks like he'd like to leap out of the car. I stare at him, but he refuses to meet my eyes. "I'm sorry, Tori. I shouldn't have said anything. Or you know what, fuck that, maybe I should have said something sooner." He licks his lips, squeezing his eyes shut long enough to make me worry that he's driving. "Edo is cheating on you," he says, finally turning to me, his entire face collapsing. "Or he was. I don't know if it's still going on."

I take a wheezy breath before a laugh roars through me. "Edo's cheating on me?"

"He was," Matteo says, his gaze flicking between me and the road. "Like I said, I'm not sure if he ended things. But you have a right to know."

I cross my arms. "Why should I believe anything you say?"

"I've never lied to you. I know how it looks, like I'm trying to push my way in, but I wouldn't ever hurt you, Tor."

"You lied to me about Emma," I say, my voice flat. "That people thought you murdered her."

"I didn't hurt Emma," he says through clenched teeth.

"You were a suspect in the case!" I cry. "None of you told me."

He frowns, the lines creasing his face. "I was questioned for potentially murdering one of my best friends. It was terrible. The police never released any information from our interviews. My parents and I didn't tell anyone. Not even Tibi."

That doesn't make sense. Edo knew. Did he tell Edo? "But you were at the river," I insist. "Why were you there, Matteo?"

"Because Edo asked me to go," he says, slamming his hand on the steering wheel. "His dad had a campaign party in Genoa, and Edo was up there with him. He said Emma had called and that she was upset. He asked me to go check on her." His eyes gleam in the streetlights dotting the side of the road as we enter the outskirts of Rome. "But I was too late, Tori. I was too late, and by the time I got there, she was gone. I got there too late to save her."

A tear streaks down his cheek. He doesn't wipe it away.

I don't know what to say. But I understand. I was always too late. I'll always know I was too late. That wound will never heal. I lean over and kiss Matteo's shoulder, shifting in my seat to rest my head against his arm to let him know I'm not angry. To let him know I carry that weight too, that I'll carry his with me.

I don't think about Edo. There's no room for Edo in this moment, in this car.

"Tori," Matteo whispers, pushing his fingers through my hair. "We're here."

I wipe the back of my hand over my mouth and check his shirt sleeve for drool. "I fell asleep?" I ask, looking up at him.

"Just for a while." He smiles at me. "You okay?"

"I'm good," I say.

He nods. "Good."

"Good." I laugh softly.

"Let's go get Tibi," he says, unbuckling my seat belt.

I stretch my arms. “But she’s not allowed to get in the car unless she tells us what happened.”

“Deal.”

I reach for Matteo’s hand as we walk into the hospital. He twines his fingers through mine.

“Good,” I say again under my breath, and I want to believe it, but something in me is deathly afraid of what this means and all the ways I’ll find to ruin it.

35

Tibi is exhausted and barely speaks the entire car ride. She's mad at me, and rightfully so. Tomorrow, I will apologize, but for now, we are all quiet so she can rest. I steal glances at Matteo in the rearview mirror as he drives. He does the same, smiling every time our eyes meet.

June and Francesco run out of the house as soon as the headlights hit the windows. Tibi winces as June wraps her in a hug. I almost do the same when she hugs me, but more from guilt than discomfort.

"Thank you," June says, rocking me in her arms—like I had anything at all to do with the fact that Tibi is mostly okay after her mysterious accident.

All I've done to her daughter recently is hurt her.

I catch myself crying against her shoulder. "I'm sorry, June," I say. I can feel her head shake, slow and firm, her chin brushing against my hair.

"You stop that immediately, Victoria Jacobs. Do you hear me? We love you. We are family. We are in this together."

Unsurprisingly, I cry harder, sniffling and pulling back only when Tibi groans in pain as she tries to take the small step up into the house. Matteo helps her, her arm slung over his shoulders, his around her waist, the same way he helped me down the stairs when we left Caterina's—more or less. His fingers don't splay on Tibi's ribs. He doesn't tuck her in quite as close.

Because she's injured, I tell myself. And she's his sister.

But I know now that it's more than that.

I collect her bag and jacket from the passenger seat footwell and carry them in as the others get Tibi settled in her room. I study the coat in the light under the sink, my mouth going dry. It looks like it got run over by a semi-truck. Rubber marks mar the sleeves, and street dirt soils the printed flowers on the fabric.

Part of me wants to throw it away, the jacket a chilling relic of what happened to Tibi—or a remonstrance of what could have happened, how much worse it could have been. But I think that is what she'll appreciate about it: *This* happened to her floral pleated jacket, and she's still standing.

I stretch it over the back of a chair and sit beside it while I wait.

Matteo enters the room, pulling off his glasses to rub his eyes. "She's asleep," he says.

"Did she tell your parents how she ended up in the hospital?" I ask, standing.

"She did not. But Mom will get it out of her." He slides his glasses back on. "How are you?"

"I'm fine. It was just a...." I drop my eyes to the ground as I trail off.

"Strange night," he offers.

"Big strange," I confirm, looking up at him. I shrug. "But not necessarily bad."

Matteo's eyes search mine. "You're probably tired. Let me go make sure my parents have everything covered, and I'll drive you home."

"Yeah, sure. Sounds good," I murmur.

He hesitates, our eyes locked, then shakes his head. "Be right back." His arm grazes mine as he walks past, and tingles range up the bare skin beneath my sweater.

My pulse quickens, and I reach for his hand, tugging his fingers toward me as I swallow. "Actually, no."

"No?" he asks, tilting his head.

"That doesn't sound good," I clarify. "I don't want to be alone tonight. Do you think...Would it be all right if I stay here?"

"Of course, Tor." He chuckles. "Mom set up my old room for you before you even arrived in Italy."

I press my lips together and inhale a deep breath through my nose. "Could I stay with you?"

Matteo stills. "If...I mean...yes. I...Tori, I don't want you to feel like you have to—"

"I want to stay with you tonight," I insist. "If that's okay with you."

The struggle plays out in his eyes, and I watch as all the countless reasons he should say no evaporate one by one. "That's okay with me."

He disappears upstairs and reappears with a set of Tibi's pajamas.

"What did you tell June?" I ask, following him out of the house and across the gravel path to his home.

He unlocks the door. "Nothing."

"Do you often steal your sister's pajamas?" I ask, following him inside. The fluttering in my belly makes the words come out warbled, breathy.

"No," he says, handing me the pajamas. "You can change wherever you want. I'll go find an extra toothbrush."

"Anywhere?" I ask as he grabs two glasses from the cabinet, filling them with water.

"Any—" he glances at me over his shoulder as I pull my sweater over my head and slip my shoes off before unbuttoning my jeans.

"Tori," he says, his voice tight.

I wiggle out of my pants. "Matty G."

He grimaces, and it looks like he's in actual agony. "We can't."

"Why not?" I ask, standing up straighter.

His eyes dip down my body, his hands flexing as he shoves them into his pockets and stands before me. "Because I'm fucking terrified you'll regret it."

"I won't," I say, reaching out for the top button of his shirt.

He clears his throat. "Because I'm worried that you're only interested because of what I told you about Edo."

"You're wrong," I promise, unbuttoning the second button.

His fingers brush my cheekbone, my jaw, his thumb lingering on my lip. I moan at the pressure of his touch. "Because I care about you and don't want to screw this up," he whispers.

I graze my teeth against his thumb. "Then don't."

His hand slips to the back of my head, his fingers digging into my hair as he pulls me toward him, our mouths colliding. His other hand presses into my back, drawing us together, and I can already feel his want, the length of him against my hip.

I wrap my legs around his waist as he lifts me, setting me on the table. I work my hands between us to undo his shirt and pull it off his shoulders. He nuzzles into my neck, nibbling the skin behind my ear. The feel of Matteo under my fingertips sets me on fire, wishing I could explore every dip and ridge of his chest and abdomen with my tongue.

His lips drag across my collarbone and the top of my breasts, and when he takes my nipple in his mouth, I plunge my hand into his pants. We moan against each other's tongues, and he lifts me again, falling on top of me on his bed.

I grin as I watch him step out of his pants and his briefs, and I kneel at the end of the mattress, reaching for him and taking him in my mouth. "Tori," he moans, his head falling back as I drag my tongue along his length, tasting him for the first time. I grip his base and pump, watching with an almost feral pleasure as his cock jerks in my hand. He bares his teeth and pulls away out of my grasp, leaving me pouting as he pushes me back onto the sheets. I feel his hot breath meet my center, his bite against the sheer fabric of my panties, like he wants to eat me whole. Like he's as hungry for me as I am for him.

I tilt my hips, begging, and he pulls the material to the side, pressing his face against my core, licking and sucking. He's ravenous. Insatiable. I rock against his mouth, his hair clasped in my hands. I scream as I come, and when he reaches up to cover my mouth, I suck his fingers into the back of my throat.

Matteo growls as he rises over me, his eyes black, his mouth gleaming with my come. I squirm beneath him, and in a flash, he flips me over, skimming his lips along my back, his hands working into my thighs.

"Get on your knees," he orders, and I reach out for the headboard, curling my fingers around the wood. When he thrusts into me, I cry out, my center convulsing, and his hands splay over my ribs, holding me tighter as he slams himself against my ass, our bodies as loud as we are. My muscles seize as he speeds up, tightening around him, holding him as we both find our pleasure.

He flips me back to face him, resting my head on a pillow, his fingers surveying the mess of us between my legs. I twitch and moan as his touch wanders, slow strokes drawing out small gasps. "Fuck," I whimper.

He bends his head, kissing me deeply, still full of want. I feel him grow hard against my thigh and buck into his fingers. "Finally," he says before stretching my hands over my head, pinning my wrists together as he pushes back into me.

In the pocket of my jeans, somewhere in a heap on the floor, my phone vibrates. Again and again and again.

We fall asleep, wrapped in each other, our bodies damp with sweat and sex. The smell of Matteo still on me makes me feel heady when I wake up. He's lying beside me, his head propped on his elbow.

Matteo grins. "Good morning, *patatina.*"

I reach up and trace a finger over his lips before kissing him. A warm slant of sunlight falls across us from a gap in the curtains. I feel like I've been plucked out of one timeline and dropped into another.

Like I've been dropped into the right one—where I know I have a family that loves me just across the gravel path. A timeline where Alex and Grandma Miriam are more than just voices in my head, where they are alive in memories I share with people who adored them as much as I did.

A timeline with a better view of a future for myself.

I change back into my clothes, and we walk into the main house together. Matteo loosens his hold on my hand only when we reach the door. I know he does it for me, giving me an easy out.

I squeeze his fingers tighter in mine.

As he opens the door, he's gazing at me with so much tenderness on his face that my knees almost give out.

My head swings around when I hear the distinct ting of silverware being dropped on tile.

"Holy fucking shit," Tibi barks.

June's mouth hangs open, her hand hovering in front of it.

Francesco glances up from his newspaper. "About time," he mumbles, reaching for his espresso.

"Hi," I say, my lips tugging up at the corner.

Yep. It's definitely the best timeline.

We all turn our heads at the sound of tires on the drive outside, staring silently as a black Audi pulls up to the house. Edo gets out, looking around, and Matteo pulls his hand from mine. I can hear June's quick intake of air and Tibi's quiet swears.

Edo's eyes lock on mine through the glass of the French doors, and I see it. The moment the timelines collide. The moment Edo's heart breaks.

36

EDO DRIVES ME HOME. In the car, the heat mixes with the smell of me, intensifying the evidence of what I've done, sex that isn't ours heavy in the air.

His nostrils flare.

"Matteo told me about your affair," I say, my voice calm, matter-of-fact. It feels like a poor justification for my actions, but I like the thought of leveling the playing field a little. I don't feel bad enough to feign the kind of guilt that the passing of our two-year relationship deserves. This will be easier if we just skip straight to righteous indignation.

"Of course he did." Edo sighs. "Did he also tell you that it didn't mean anything?"

"Maybe it means that this—" I lean over to rest a hand on his heart and a hand on mine "—isn't the right fit."

He covers my hand in his, his chin trembling. "You're willing to give up on us so easily? Just end it like that?"

My chest tightens. "You're so busy, Edo. I've barely seen you since I got to Italy." He tries to argue, but I keep going, "And

I don't blame you. It is an important time in your career, and you need to focus on that."

I wonder then if he ever ended things with the other woman. And if so, is it really work that's been keeping him so busy, keeping him away? Or is there someone else, possibly someone new?

Does it even matter?

He parks the car. "Victoria, I love you. It was just a difficult time. You were so distant after Miriam's death," he says, cupping my face. "And even after you got here, it was hard to see you so fragile and not know how to help. It was like watching my mother fall apart all over again."

I choose not to take offense at that. He thinks I was losing my mind *before* I got here, and he doesn't even know half of what's happened since. He doesn't know that only last night, I broke into his mother's home and had coffee with the woman he thinks is incapacitated. If Caterina doesn't share my secrets, I won't share hers.

"I am so grateful for everything." I grab his wrist and kiss his palm.

He runs his thumb along my lip. "I'll miss you, *tesoro.*"

And that's it. The universe readjusts, the transition complete. "Goodbye, Edo," I say, slipping out of the car.

I take a deep breath of jasmine as I walk past Mirësi's. All things tilt toward rightness, finding their place, and I'm unsurprised when her gate opens just after I pass.

"Victoria," Mirësi calls, and I turn back. "Will you join us for dinner this evening?"

"What time?" I ask.

Mirësi smiles. "Be here at eight."

When I get home, I grab the phone Matteo got me off the landing and set it on the charger, placing my old phone in its place. I clean up the spill of Disaronno in front of the fireplace, slicing my index finger just once on a sliver of glass. I pop Emma's picture back up on the mantle before going upstairs to shower.

My center clenches as the hot water beats down on my skin, the scent of sex that seemed so vulgar in Edo's Audi now filling me with memories of last night with Matteo and thoughts of more of them in the future. I run my hands over my breasts. God, it feels good to be so awake again, to feel so alive. I turn my face up, letting the running water fill my mouth, the sound of the spray like being underwater, the thunderous tossing of waves rolling through my body.

When I get out, my legs wobble as I walk to the mirror, sore from my night with Matteo. I grab my brush to work out the tangles Matteo put there—it tumbles out of my hand, hitting the ground just before I almost do, my hands grasping for the counter when I see the words.

I forget to breathe as I trace them with my finger, contemplating the unholy explicitness of them on the glass.

The writing on the mirror is clear, even if the intention isn't. Even if the message is particularly ironic for a ghost, almost mocking.

But there is no denying what Emma wanted to say:

THE DEAD LIVE

"Okay," I tell her, leaning forward on the counter. "Then prove it."

I talk to Matteo, and then Tibi is on Matteo's phone as I get ready. Tibi still refuses to tell anyone what happened to her. She doesn't mention what she saw this morning or ask about what happened after I left, but she does tell me she's looking forward to more overnights.

"How are your ribs?" I ask.

Tibi snorts, then takes a sharp breath, like the sound hurt her. "Delicious."

"Just like the lunch I'm making for everyone tomorrow," June shouts in the background.

"I'll be there," I confirm before a last goodbye to Matteo. I can't believe I ever doubted that these were my people. My family.

Mirësi opens the gate for me when I arrive. Paul struts behind her, screaming as we walk across the garden to the door, arm in arm. "I see the lights are back on in the apartment," she says, glancing up at the window of the teddy bear room. "Things are better?"

"Things are good." I smile.

"Tony will be so glad to hear it. He's been asking when we can have that wine fellow over since last weekend."

"Oh," I say. "How did you..."

Mirësi smirks, leading me through their front room. "The coffee never lies, Victoria."

"You never mentioned that the coffee had something to say about Matteo."

"It wasn't quite that," she says, averting her gaze. She doesn't offer more of an explanation. "How do you feel about cheeseburgers? Tony has had an itch for them recently. He thought he'd enjoy eating them more with a fellow American who could commiserate."

"So I'm here because Tony had a craving for McDonald's?"

"That's one reason." She pulls out a chair for me at the table and offers wine.

"Just water, thank you."

Tony turns from where he's flipping burgers at the grill on the stove. "Happy to hear it. I'm running low on my Graziano Classico and not inclined to share." He winks. "How much longer until the tasting, Victoria?"

"I'll double-check, but I'm sure either way that Matteo would love to hear from you before then."

"Remind me," he says, "is Matteo the boyfriend?"

I feel my cheeks flush and make a face at Mirësi. "Something like that."

"It's new," she explains to Tony. "Victoria just got out of another relationship."

I furrow my brows as I regard her. "The coffee sure had a lot to say."

Tony sets a bunch of fixings on the table: lettuce, onion, slices of tomato the color of Mirësi's lips. "Young love," he says before bending down to kiss Mirësi's cheek.

Mirësi brushes her hand along Tony's gray stubble. "What was his name, Victoria? The other boy?"

"Edo," I say. "Edo Mazza."

Tony turns back to the burgers, plating them and returning to the table. "Interesting," he murmurs, setting the burgers in front of me and Mirësi. I want to cackle at the thought of Mirësi eating a cheeseburger. She looks at me like she knows it.

"His mother lives here," I say, shifting toward Tony to avoid Mirësi's glare. "Caterina Mazza."

"I don't know Caterina, but an Edoardo Mazza contacted me when we first moved here. It was Edoardo, wasn't it, dear?" he asks Mirësi.

She rests an elbow on the table, eyeing me before turning back to Tony. "Yes, darling. Edoardo Mazza was his name."

"You see," Tony says, sitting and piling his burger with onions, mustard, and mayo, "I was well-known in D.C. circles for my work. Word got around when I moved to Italy, and Mr. Mazza reached out. He was looking to hire some private counsel."

I smother my burger in ketchup and pickles from a jar that reads Burger Gherkins. "I don't doubt that Edoardo has a handful of lawyers on retainer to keep everything in their world moving smoothly. They are some sort of Italian royalty and are involved in politics and banking. Edoardo is a powerful man."

Mirësi takes a doubtful nibble of her undressed burger and sets it down. "Tony was a contract attorney before he retired."

"What kind of contracts?" I ask, wiping a smear of ketchup off my mouth.

Tony sips his wine—Matteo's, I'm guessing—and hums. "NDAs. Are you familiar?"

"Non-disclosure agreements?" I ask.

"Exactly," Tony responds brightly. "Here they have some other colorful names, my favorite being *accordo di segrezza*. Agreement of Secrecy. Feels appropriately sordid, at least based on many of the contracts I wrote."

"Who did you work for?" I ask.

"His clients were very high profile," Mirësi offers. "Politicians, celebrities, occasionally other lawyers."

Tony leans back in his chair, somehow already finished with his burger. "The work itself was a bit demoralizing. Almost entirely relationships of one sort or another that needed to be kept quiet. Humans can be quite dishonest."

"That many people have affairs?" I ask, my chest a little hot at the acknowledgment that my outrage is hypocritical.

"Çdo pyll ka derra," Mirësi says, translating when we both stare at her. "Every forest has its pigs."

Did Edoardo Mazza want to work with Tony because he has a prenup with Caterina and was having extramarital relations that he needed to keep quiet? Women he needed to silence? Maybe Caterina found out, and that's why she's so miserable.

I wonder if, with Edo, it would have turned into a case of like father, like son. If I didn't get out now, would my future be curtained with NDAs, keeping me constantly in the dark? But Edo is a good guy, even if he cheated. He's sensitive and caring and just wanted to take care of me.

He can't help that his father is a massive asshole.

We finish the burgers and when Mirësi offers to make us Turkish coffee, I tell her it's probably time for me to turn in.

"Can I take a rain check?" I ask. "I'd love to come back soon and hear what new things the coffee has to say."

Mirësi agrees, insisting on walking me to the gate, but before we leave, Tony wraps me in a hug. "When you come back, bring the Graziano boy," he says. "And no offense, but I much prefer him to that Edoardo Mazza."

I laugh, even though the thought makes me a little nauseous. "I was dating Edoardo's son," I correct.

"Yes," Tony replies. "I know. He's the one who came to see me."

37

When I open the door to the apartment, my phone is ringing—the phone Matteo gave me. The call ends and starts again, the incessant droning breaking me out of the agitated headspace I fell into after Tony told me it was Edo who'd come to see him.

My Edo, looking for someone to write him Agreements of Secrecy. For what? For who? He never asked me to sign anything. He's a young, unmarried Italian man; it's not like the world is going to hold a few paramours against him.

He wasn't my Edo then, though. And he's not my Edo now.

The phone rings a third time, and I pick it up. The call comes up as private, but only a handful of people have my number.

"Hello," I answer, tucking the phone under my ear as I hang up my coat. I drop my keys into the pocket and feel the sharp stab of Tibi's carving tool against my palm. I'll return it the next time I see her.

"Hello?" I repeat, picking up on the faint sound of breathing from the receiver. "Someone there?"

"Mai!" a voice screeches, high and pained and manic. *"Mai, mai, mai, mai, m—"*

I hang up, my fingers shaking as I close the call, and stare at the screen, crouching at the base of the stairs.

Mai.

Never. Never, never, never, never.

Maybe they dialed the wrong number. They don't call back, so it must have been a mistake, a wrong number. I shiver, feeling bad for whoever the call was intended for. My mind is too full of other things to worry about it.

I get ready for bed and curl up in the teddy bear room. Matteo's hat is now on the bedside table to keep Mokthi at bay. I sleep, and the time is filled with dreams—the abstract kinds that are more sensation than story, that words can never do justice, but I feel rested even though it's still hours from dawn when I wake.

The boars aren't far from the road when I find them, and I imagine someone, maybe a farmer, driving into town before daybreak, their headlights hitting a sounder of boars and seeing a woman's eyes reflected back.

In this case, I am the scary thing, the nightmare. The thought makes me smile.

I'm home before dawn. There are five missed calls on my phone—all from a private number—and one text message from three hours ago, just around the time I left the house.

I see you.

I block the number and walk into the bathroom, staring at my reflection in the mirror. Leaves are tangled in my hair, dirt dry on my hands. "Till fates' predestined fatal hour draws near," I whisper, the sense of time closing in on me almost suffocating, the caving in of then and now. I couldn't help Alex or Grandma Miriam. But maybe I can make up for what I couldn't do for them; perhaps I'm being given another chance.

Mirësi said I was here for justice; the coffee doesn't lie.

#

When I get to the Riccis', the twins are happy to see me, and we play at the park all morning. Lucia lets us in when I bring them home, leading us to the kitchen where Matteo is helping her prepare the twins' lunches while he waits to drive me to our own midday meal at the Graziano house.

He wipes his hands on his jeans when he sees me and walks straight over, brushing my hair back before kissing me right there in the middle of the kitchen. I kiss him back, and when he pulls away, we grin at each other.

My heart constricts at the look on his face. I hope that the thing I have to do won't hurt him. I hope that he'll forgive me if it does, if it goes wrong. I hope that he'll understand why I had to do it.

Lunch with the Grazianos is like coming home. Jasper is there, keeping Tibi's glass full and heating compresses for her to press against her bruised side. She still won't tell us what happened, and something about the way Jasper shifts when we ask, his chin dropping, makes the scene a little sinister. He looks guilty, and I wonder if Tibi is protecting him.

I wonder if he is capable of hurting her.

Castor rests his head in Jasper's lap, but I don't trust the dog's judgment. He hasn't sensed the monster in me yet, either.

Matteo and I do the dishes after lunch. While I'm drying the salad bowl, he stands behind me and wraps his arms around my waist, his lips brushing against my ear. "Do you need to get back to town, or can you stay for a *sonnellino?" A little sleep.*

"I'll be right there," I tell him, turning in his arms. "I just need to talk to Tibi real fast."

I find her alone upstairs in her bedroom. I shut and lock the door behind me when I enter. "Tibs," I say quickly, "Are you safe? Is Jasper hurting you?"

Her eyes widen and then start to gleam. I'm worried she's about to burst into tears when a rolling laugh explodes from her mouth before she breaks down in a fit of hysterical giggles that have her writhing in pain.

"Stop it," I order. "Your poor ribs."

She takes a shaky breath. "Fuck, they hurt."

"I'll get ice. After you answer my question." Although, I think the laughter was her answer.

She narrows her eyes at me. "You ignore me for days, sleep with my brother, accuse my boyfriend of doing this to me," she says, gesturing at herself with the hand wrapped in a blue cast. "Lock yourself in my bedroom, and don't even think to tell me about how absolutely gorgeous those linocut prints I gave you were? Tori, it's like you don't even love me."

I sit at the side of her bed and wrap her in the gentlest hug. "No linocut print will ever compare. You're the best carving artist who ever was and ever will be."

"Better," she says, softening in my embrace.

"But I do have a question. Was there actually a figure in the window, or were you taking creative liberties with my mental well-being?"

Tibi cocks her head. "You mean the woman in the window."

"A woman?"

"You haven't seen her?" Tibi asks, and she's dead serious.

I'm shaking my head, my heart pounding, when Jasper knocks on the door. I get up and let him in.

"Isn't she incredible?" he asks me, pulling a chair out at Tibi's desk. "I still can't believe she—"

"Jasper," Tibi warns, and he chews his lip contritely.

I flick her knee through the sheets. "One day," I tell her, "you will tell me what happened."

"Never," she fires back.

Chills still bloom along my spine when I curl up beside Matteo in his bed.

Never, never, never.

He drives me home and walks me to my place before heading to a meeting with a new wine distributor in the center of town. There's an envelope on the first step when I open the gate. Inside is a handwritten note: *Stai zitta o te ne penterai.*

Stay silent, or you'll regret it.

This is ridiculous. The phone calls, threatening letters, being watched. I glance up at the window in the tufo, the one from Tibi's print. I walk to the door beneath it and ring the bell. It's so loud I can hear it in the street, blaring out the open window, bouncing off the stone walls. I press it until static comes over the intercom.

She doesn't speak, but I can hear her breathing, just like with the phone call.

"Either leave me alone," I say, leaning close, "or open this door right now and talk to me."

The door clicks open, and on the other side is a young woman wearing a flowy dress and oversized cardigan, probably in her early 20s. She looks familiar. Maybe she's one of the pretty girls I saw taking shots in the bar the night of the pig feast. Maybe I've passed her in the street a hundred times and never noticed that she's stalking me.

"What do you want?" I ask, crossing my arms.

She peeks over my shoulder, up and down the street. "Not here," she says, the watcher afraid of being watched herself. "Will you—" She eyes me nervously "—will you come in?"

I walk past her into a small living space, and she gestures for me to have a seat. I sit at the very edge of the cushion while she paces. "I promise," she says, "I'm not as pathetic as I look."

"You don't look pathetic," I contest. "You look insane." *Trust me,* I want to tell her, *I would know.* "Why are you watching me?"

She pauses. "I wasn't intending to watch *you*. I was trying to keep an eye on Edo. I want to know why you were watching *me?* Do you..Do you know?"

"Do I know what?" I blink at her. What are the chances that Edo was having an affair with the girl who lives across the street from my new apartment? "Did he know you were here?"

"Of course not." She rears back. "I haven't spoken to him in months." My head reels. Does that mean there were other women? "But I saw him on your patio. I thought maybe he'd found me."

Cold fear burrows into my skin. "Why would he be looking for you?"

"Because," she says, pressing her hands against the fabric of her dress, "I'm worried he found out about this."

Her belly isn't huge, but it's evident by how it curves that she's pregnant. Probably about four months, if I had to guess.

"Jesus Christ," I murmur. "You're pregnant with Edo's baby?"

She nods, her eyes welling.

I press my trembling fingers to my mouth. "Have you told him?"

Panic flares in her eyes. "No," she rasps. "And you have to swear you won't say anything. He can't know."

"Why?" I ask, startled. Edo could help with costs; he could support her and the child. He's a cheating piece of shit, but he isn't evil.

"You know why," she practically hisses at me.

I put my hands up. "I don't."

"The contract?" she articulates the word like a question, rhetorically, like I should know. And part of me is starting to worry I do.

"We didn't have a contract," I say gently. It feels like I'm slapping her in the face with lace gloves on.

She scoffs. "You're the only one."

"How many were there?"

"Does it matter? If he finds out about the baby, he'll make me get rid of it."

"He can't do that," I insist. "He has no control over your body."

"I signed the contract, don't you understand? I signed away the baby's life. They are the Mazzas. They can do anything they want."

38

The woman's name is Giorgia, and she's twenty-three. She tells me how she and Edo met. She tells me everything.

"Fuck the NDA," she says, wiping tears away. "I've been so afraid he will find me that I've barely left the house. I haven't been to the doctor in case he somehow has access to their files. I'm going to have to go eventually. What happens when I do? If he finds out when it's no longer possible to get rid of the baby legally? What will he do then?"

What she's saying sounds completely crazy. But she's upset and hormonal and afraid. Otherwise, she wouldn't be confiding in me, a stranger, a recent ex of the man who impregnated her. I'm drawn to her instability. I want to help her.

"I know someone who can look at the contract and see if it's even enforceable." I can't imagine it is.

"Do you trust them?"

"I do."

She consents.

"Do you want to text me a photo? Email a copy?"

"To *your* phone?" she asks, her tone incredulous. "No. I'll figure something out."

Giorgia watches out the window before giving me the go-ahead to leave her home. I've never been happier to walk into mine. I fall onto the couch, rubbing my temples.

Part of me wants to justify Edo's actions. It's possible his relationship with his mother fucked him up somehow. Or their lack of relationship. And there is whatever weird game Caterina is playing, even if it's starting to look like she might have a decent motive for her performance. I glance up at the mantel.

And then, there's Emma. Was she the catalyst for whatever broke in Edo? Has that loss shadowed his relationships since? I wish I could ask her. If she wasn't pushed, what happened? If she didn't fall, why would she jump into the river? What could have made her that desperate?

I tug my phone out of my pocket and pull up Tibi's number.

Are you still up for that seance?

Tell me when to be there. I'll have Jasper start preparing sage bundles RIGHT NOW.

We plan for Friday night. The next day, on my way to the Riccis', I stop at Mirësi's to invite her and Tony as well. The more the merrier when invoking the dead, right?

I'm hesitant to invite Matteo, not because I'm worried he'll think I'm crazy—that ship has sailed—but because he and Emma were close, and he still carries wounds from that time.

But he already knows, of course, because Tibi hasn't stopped talking about it.

I understand why they never told her Matteo was a suspect and why they never told me. There was no need to add more hurt.

Friday morning, he asks if it's okay for him to come.

"If you want to," I say. "I don't want you to feel like you have to be there. I know Tony would be glad to see you, though. I don't think he's the seance type."

"What can I bring?" he asks. I smile at the eagerness in his voice.

By Friday evening, the event feels much more like a dinner party than an attempt to communicate with spirits.

The table is covered in food and wine, and we all spill out onto the patio, laughing together as the sun goes down. Jasper eventually summons us back inside, refocusing our energy on what we're here for: Emma.

"Is this the only photo we have?" he asks, lifting the portrait on the mantel.

I point to the drawer where I found it. "There are more in there," I say, flicking Matteo's shoulder when he starts chuckling at my blatant admittance of snooping.

Tony sits back in his chair, watching me as I push the coffee table off the rug. "Victoria, if you'd indulge an old man, I'd love to hear what additional evidence you've accumulated of paranormal activity in your residence."

"Mirësi, help," Tibi calls. "Your husband is lawyering Tori."

"It's purely curiosity," Tony assures. "Despite having spent the last fifteen years with Mirësi, I've no personal experience with the other side."

Matteo hands Tony a glass of wine and sits down in the chair beside him. "I'm curious, too, actually. So far, I've been spared the details."

I hesitate. What do I tell them that can't be explained away? The nightmares are only a confirmation of my troubled mental state. The windows and shutters and even the crawl space opening after it was nailed shut could be rationalized by a strong draft, the age of the house, and the fixtures. The creepy art wasn't put up by ghosts, and they didn't store the baby clothes.

"The mirror," I say. "There's writing on the mirror."

Tony and Matteo's eyebrows rise over their eyeglasses. It's kind of adorable.

Tony leans forward. "And what does the writing say?"

I glance at Tibi and Mirësi. I haven't told anyone the rest of Emma's message. Everyone stands still, waiting for me to speak.

"It says: The dead live."

Tibi gasps.

"Show me?" Matteo asks quietly.

I go into the bathroom and turn on the hot water while the others wait downstairs, then I slip out and wait with them for the steam to fill the room. Ten minutes later, we all go up to check.

Everyone sees it. Mirësi takes a step back. Tibi clings to Jasper's side. Tony crosses his arms.

Matteo steps forward, studying the words, a smile spreading over his face. "No way," he says with a laugh.

"What?" I ask, confused by his reaction. He looks too happy for someone reading a dead girl's message on a haunted mirror.

He must realize because he clears his throat before turning to the rest of us. "Someone discovered in high school that if you use soap to write a message on the glass, it will reappear when the mirror is steamy."

Tibi interjects, "I remember a penis appearing on ours one morning."

My heart aches a little at the thought that Emma's words are nothing more than a prank, something someone put there to be funny.

"But why," Mirësi says, "would someone write *this*."

She's right. Why would they?

Matteo doesn't have an answer.

We all gather in front of the mantel, where Jasper has set up all three photos of Emma: the one just of her, the one with her parents, and the one where she's with her friends. When I inspect it now, it's clear she's not looking up at Matteo but past him, his arm around her shoulder more brotherly than possessive.

Her eyes are locked on Edo.

"How do we begin?" Tony asks, drawing my attention back. He sits beside Mirësi on the rug.

Mirësi's skirt puddles on the ground around her. "Matteo, why don't you tell us about Emma? The more connected we all feel to her, the easier it will be for her to connect with us."

Matteo chews his lip, and then he starts to speak. He talks about Emma's laugh, friends, and distaste for pizza. He talks about her family and her favorite animal—pigs. I wonder if he's ever had a chance to talk about Emma like this, to miss and remember her openly and all at once. Tibi cries when Matteo's eyes well up as he recounts that day at the river. I squeeze his hand in mine.

"It never made sense that she'd hurt herself on purpose and less sense that someone would want to do her harm," he says, tucking me under his arm. "In the end, I think it was just a shitty accident."

A breeze sends the shutters slamming against the window frame and we all startle, even Tony.

"Or not," Jasper amends. "Not an accident?"

We sit silently, waiting for another sign like the wind before was sent to refute Matteo, and now Jasper is trying to give the dead a chance to set the record straight. Nothing happens.

"Sometimes," Mirësi says, looking directly at me, "the dead just want to be acknowledged. Victoria has done a good job listening. Maybe when Emma's ready—or when Tori's ready—Emma will share more."

It's an anticlimactic end to the seance, but everyone wordlessly accepts that Mirësi has decided we are done for now. We clean up and move the furniture back. Mirësi and Tony leave.

Jasper opens the drawer to return the photographs and pulls out the two newspapers I'd seen when I'd ferreted through its contents, copies of *Il Secolo XIX.*

Jasper opens one up and starts reading. "Strange that these are here."

"That's a Genovese paper, isn't it?" Tibi asks, reading over his shoulder.

Jasper nods. "I had to study these cases as part of a socio-psychological anthropology class," he says, pointing at the paper. "They didn't get much coverage, according to my professor. It was over a decade ago, but he was convinced someone was trying to keep them quiet."

"What cases?" I ask, coming around to see the page.

Matteo joins us, translating the headline out loud, "Pregnant sixteen-year-old from Genoa dies from anaphylaxis alone at home." He picks up the other paper and flips through the pages. "Pregnant fifteen-year-old from Genoa dies alone in home fire."

"Two different girls," Jasper says, "two tragic deaths, five months apart. There were never any investigations."

"Did people suspect foul play?" I ask, looking at the girls' photos—their happy, smiling faces.

"Of course, but the police shut down any discussion. The stories were in and out of the newspaper, never picked up by any media outside of Genoa."

"What's the month," I ask, "on the more recent one?"

"August," Matteo answers.

Nine months before Emma went missing.

Matteo stays over, and when he goes to bed, I take his laptop out of his briefcase and tip-toe downstairs. I feel exposed by the blue light of the screen spotlighting my face, unable to hide from the horrible things I'm thinking.

I start with the girls, googling their names. Not much comes up, but I use a website to translate the articles into English. One of them mentions the name of a school, and my stomach hardens. But it is not enough.

I search for similar cases. No results come up in Genoa, but there is a hit from a little town on the outskirts of Orvieto: pregnant eighteen-year-old dies after falling asleep at the wheel and driving off bridge.

Then, I google Edo's aunt, Caterina's sister.

I'd always assumed she'd been sick, that it was cancer or something chronic that had killed her. I was wrong. Caterina's sister broke her neck, falling down a flight of stairs in a hotel while visiting family in Florence. It happened in the middle of the night. No one found her until morning.

My lungs tighten, my breath squeezing, barely a wheeze when it leaves my mouth.

I see Grandma Miriam's face. How it was, and then, how I found it.

If someone had found Caterina's sister sooner, would she still be alive today?

If I had gotten to Grandma Miriam sooner, would she?

Before sneaking back into bed, I plug in my old phone. When it turns on, I type out a message. *I can't live like this.*

I send it to Alex's old number.

39

OVER THE NEXT WEEK, I text Alex every day—multiple times a day. I carry the old phone with me when I visit the boars.

I tell her all the things I've felt for years and never shared out loud.

I should have been there.

I'm so sorry.

You should have been the one who lived.

I know she can't respond. I don't need her to. I just need the messages to exist.

On Monday, I sit down with Tibi on my patio, and she shows me everything she's been working on. I tell her how proud I am of her and how much I admire her vulnerability.

"How did you get hurt?" I ask as she takes a sip of red.

She eyes me over the glass. "Swear you won't tell?"

"On my life."

Tibi tosses her head back, talking to the sky. "I rented a scooter."

"And," I press on.

"And it turns out I am very bad at steering scooters."

I lean over and hug her. "You can't have it all, I guess."

"I'm going to try again," she says, defiant.

I kiss her head. "Please don't."

Mom doesn't love me.

I don't want to be here without you.

The nightmares are back.

On Tuesday, Giorgia brings me a copy of the contract she had signed. I deliver it to Tony, who is appalled that a contract lawyer would put something like that together—Giorgia's in good hands. I hope by next week, she won't need to worry about the future of her baby.

I sit down with Mirësi, and we share a coffee. She sucks in a breath when she sees the grounds. I tell her it's better if she doesn't share what they mean.

"Don't worry," I say, the pressed silk of her top soft against my hands as I hug her goodbye. "I'm not afraid."

She pulls me closer and whispers, "Be careful."

I don't know who I am without you.

You were the strong one.

On Wednesday, Matteo and I have lunch with June and Francesco at a small trattoria with a beautiful view of Orvieto, the high cliffs pink, rose, and coral in the glow of the southerly sun.

June laughs, her cheeks the same shade as the cliffs. I rest my head on her shoulder, and she reaches her hand up to hold my face.

I haven't been okay since I lost you.

It's my fault Grandma Miriam died.

It's my fault you died.

I can't sleep.

Thursday, I call my mom. She doesn't answer. I try my dad. Their phones both go straight to voicemail. They're probably flying somewhere on the way to a conference or a talk show. At least I tried.

I miss you.

I wish I could see you.

On Friday, I take the twins back to the Duomo, and we lay in the grass watching the clouds. I catch the girls as they roll across the small lawn. We trace the mosaic stars together, and I tickle them whenever I catch up.

I don't know what to do.

The test was positive.

Saturday, I spend the whole day with Matteo. We sample the wine he made from the grapes we harvested together, the sweetness of the muffa nobile rich in our mouths. We walk Castor through the vineyard, now little more than twining bases and dried leaves.

Matteo makes me umbrichelli al tartufo for dinner, per my request.

And it's still true: this is the last thing I'd like to taste before I die.

He brings his stuff to stay over at the apartment. He has a headache, which I pretend to feel bad about. I bring him a glass of water and two pink pills from the kitchen. My pills.

When he's asleep, I send a text from my new phone, entering the number manually: *Edo, we need to talk.*

Is everything okay? He types back not even a minute after I press send.

I want to see you.

I'm in Florence, he responds. *I could come down on Monday.*

Monday works.

Victoria?

Yes?

You'd tell me if you weren't okay, wouldn't you? Should I be worried?

Yes. *No. Everything's fine. I'll see you Monday.*

On the old phone, I send one last message to Alex: *I don't think I can do this any longer.*

Then, I wait. Sometime past midnight, I put on my shoes. An hour later, my jacket. I flip through the pages of the books on the table while I sit there, the stars cutting a short path outside the window. When the sky is darkest, I go back upstairs, crouching beside Matteo in the bed. I check his breathing. I kiss his forehead.

"It was always you," I whisper. I tuck my old phone in my pocket and walk out of the apartment and off the hill.

I've barely made it to the ring path when I hear footsteps. I walk faster, trying to listen over the pounding of my heart in my ears. If he stops me here, I have no chance. Luckily, I know the path well, and he won't risk using a light, so I have the advantage. Still, I can practically smell my fear, viscous and cloying, on my skin.

I know they'll be able to smell it, too. I'm betting on it. I just have to pray that it plays out to my advantage.

Past the turn for the necropolis, I divert off the path and into the trees, keeping my steps loud enough for him to hear. The brush grows denser before clearing, and the cliff rises before us like a wall. I turn my back to it and face him.

My breath is heavy, panicked. Behind him, on the horizon, the moon starts to rise, thin and slicing. No more than a boar's tusk breaking through the black sky.

"What's wrong, Victoria?" Edo asks, his lips turning up. "Worried it's another nightmare?"

"What are you doing here?" I ask, my voice tight.

He takes long steps, his blue eyes locked on my face as he circles me. "It didn't have to be like this, you know."

"Like what?" I whimper as I back closer to the cliff face.

He pauses, rage burning on his face in the starlight. "I picked you—*you!*—Victoria, to be my broken thing. I would have kept you as my perfect pet, my perfect cover: a man who loves and cares for his demented, useless wife. If you'd just been more like her, if you'd just fucking given up, none of this would be happening. That's all I was looking for—"

"Your mother?"

His grin is chilling. "Someone weak. Someone sad and twisted. Which you are, of course."

"I am," I agree, tears springing to my eyes.

"Which will make this part so much easier to get away with." He stalks toward me, his shoulders rounding with power.

"Wait," I shout, stumbling sideways as I grip my spread hands over my belly. "I'm—"

Edo snarls before his features go disturbingly still. He reaches out and grabs my hair, tugging my head back. His breath meets my neck, and I shudder, crying out.

"I hope you understand, Victoria, why I have to get rid of both of you."

"No," I gasp, pushing at his chest. "Edo, please. This isn't you. You don't have to do anything."

He sighs, his grip tightening as my neck crooks unnaturally backward. "One after the other, and never even an inkling. How were you all so disappointingly stupid?"

My hand reaches into my coat pocket. "Fuck you," I rasp, barely able to find the breath for words, Edo's chest crushing into mine.

"What was that?" he asks, smirking, consuming all my space as my spine grates against the cliff. "I can't hear you."

"I said," I try again, my voice like rocks as my fingers tighten around the tool. I slide it out of my pocket, raising it to his side. "Fuck you, Edo."

He howls when I slam the carver into his flank, just below his ribs. He pulls it out, touches the wound, then rears back and slaps me across the face. My head spins, but I charge out from under his arm while his other hand is busy holding the wound on his side. Blood drips through his fingers.

Not much, but enough.

I scramble through the forest, and he stalks behind me. "You can't get away."

"I know." I gasp, glancing at him over my shoulder as I crawl over a fallen tree.

"Up the stairs," he orders, "by the garden."

"You're going to push me off the cliff," I accuse, shouting backward into the dark.

Edo hums. "Accidents are preferable to suicide, cleaner, less strings to tie up. But with you, I'm not worried. The messages to Alex, the desperation, the trauma. Even your mother knows how damaged you are. A leap off the cliff will surprise no one. You even told me once. Do you remember, Victoria? How you'd dreamed of that fall."

And I chose life, asshole.

"All it will take is a little push," he adds, clutching my jacket in a bloody hand.

I close my eyes, a smell catching my attention. A grunt in the distance. "Just like you pushed Emma?" I yell as he pulls me up to standing.

"Exactly," he says, sounding almost gleeful. "And my aunt. She fought, of course, because she knew. That's what broke my mother. She knows, too, but killing her would be too obvious.

Instead, I made sure she'd be too scared to tell. I took away the thing she loved most."

"Did your dad put you up to it?" I demand. I can feel them closer. I can feel their eyes on us.

"My father? He's horrified by all of it, but his ego conveniently keeps him from doing the right thing. He has all of Genoa in his pocket and does what he needs to protect the family name, but mostly to protect himself. He's the one who insisted on the NDAs. You know about those, don't you? I'll visit Giorgia when I leave here."

I stop walking and stand up straighter, his words making me nauseous. "You won't get away with this forever. You can't just keep getting rid of women when they become inconvenient."

"Can't I?" He shrugs. "You know too much, *principessa.* Who else knows?"

"No one," I say, my muscles tightening. "No one, I swear."

"Not even your beloved Tibi?"

I clench my fists. "If you touch Tibi, I'll kill you. I swear to god, Edo, if you hurt her—"

"That would be a neat trick," he says, cocking his head. "When you're dead."

I scream, and the noise is terrifying, full of sorrow and regret and pain.

Edo's eyes light up at the sound. "No one can hear you, but please continue. I do love the sound of hopelessness."

My gaze dips to the drop of blood at the tip of his finger. I watch it fall in slow motion, the small thud echoing through the trees before there is nothing but silence.

And then, a growl so low it shakes my bones. A scream that isn't human. The boars pick it up like a chorus. The young squeal. The sounds are haunting and monstrous, made even more horrific by the eyes gleaming in the low brush around us.

The matriarch steps forward, her fur bristling, ears erect. She swings her face from mine to Edo's, and I hold my breath. She huffs, the sound hollow, and turns her snout up to the air. Edo's hand clamps to his side, to the blood slowly blossoming on his shirt.

He looks at me, his pupils blown. "You bitch," he says, and I hardly hear him as he topples to the ground, surrounded. I cover my ears against the shrieking, his and theirs, retching into the grass when he goes silent. It takes longer than I'd anticipated, and each pop and crunch of bone and tendon draws another wave of sobs.

I stand as the boars start to drift away, back to the warren. The sun will be rising soon. Their work was clean; hardly anything remains but torn clothes and shoes, a chunk of hair and another of jawbone. His car keys are missing. I smash his cell phone to pieces with a rock before wrapping it in my jacket with his wallet and what's left of him, and I walk home.

The space is still dark, Matteo's soft snores filling the upstairs. In the teddy bear room, I strip out of my clothes, smeared in Edo's blood, then stand there staring out the window in my bra and panties, tremors racking my body. Paul screams, and I look down. Mirësi is smoking in the garden, staring up at me.

I push the window open. "Mirësi," I start, not sure what to say. The cold air slaps my bare skin.

She drops the cigarette and grinds it under her heel. "Throw them down," she says, her voice gentle. "I'll take care of it."

I gape at her. "B-but," I stutter, "I—"

"This isn't my first war, darling. But it is yours. Let me help you."

I nod, my arms shaking as I lift my blood-stained clothes, the jacket with the phone and wallet, to the window and push them out. "Thank you," I say through tears.

She collects the pile and heads into the trees, turning to wink. "For what?"

After a quick shower, I slip back into bed beside Matteo. The medicine will wear off in a couple of hours, but I can still get some rest.

Eventually, the trembling stops and the exhaustion takes over. I sleep, and it is deep and dreamless and perfect.

In the morning, Matteo and I decide to visit the lake. "Go get the car," I tell him. "I'll meet you on the street."

Once he's gone, I tear the poem to Justice out of *The Orphic Hymns* and write a message at the bottom for Claudio before sealing it into an envelope and leaving it in the mailbox on my way out, my heart feeling both weightless and settled.

Emma can come home now.

Nine Months Later

I HELP JUNE CARRY the dishes to the table and pull a chair beside Tibi. Matteo bends to kiss my temple when he walks past, holding a soccer ball. He drops it, kicking the ball to Orfeo before Castor can steal it.

Emma's son turned nine in March. They took the teddy bears off his room's walls, covering them instead with posters of his favorite sports teams. He's sweet and funny. He has his dad's dimples but nothing else of Edo. The only other thing they share is proximity to Mirësi's garden. The safest view of Edo is the one of him buried.

Or the few parts that remained.

When Edo went missing, Tony had a couple of weeks to get everything he could together to create a case against Edoardo Mazza. Someone called in an anonymous tip to the state police. Someone also reached out to some big-name international journalists.

Men like the Mazzas smooth things over at the expense of others, and many people in their periphery were more than happy to throw them under the bus. Including Caterina, who testified against her husband and her son before leaving the country.

I only saw her once more, about a month after Edo went missing. As I turned onto Via del Corso to meet Tibi for a coffee, my gaze wandered to Caterina's windows out of habit. She was there, framed in the glass as if waiting for me, the curtain clutched in her bony fist. Our eyes locked, and I stood still on the cobblestone as she inclined her head. I bowed mine to her. When I looked back up, the curtain had already fallen. She was gone the next day.

Around the same time, Silvia, Emma, and Orfeo appeared in Orvieto.

A miracle.

But really, it was a well-planned, incredibly carefully orchestrated ploy to keep Emma safe. Caterina's sister had post-dated letters, creating false evidence of an affair and providing an excuse for Silvia to leave for Spain with Emma.

Emma, who now sits smiling between Mirësi and Tony across from me, survived the plunge into the roiling Paglia. Emma, who had known that as long as Edo was free, she wouldn't be safe. They couldn't compete with the weight and resources of the Mazzas, so they waited.

Claudio existed in limbo, in a hell of knowing his daughter lived but having to constantly subsist on grief. The grief was real. He lost his family. He missed watching his grandchild grow up—the first time he rode a bike, went to school, ate ice cream.

But it turned out that while he waited, he collected evidence, a whole dungeon-full. Anything he could find that might come back to the Mazzas, from murders to bad business deals, was stashed in the room at the bottom of the outdoor stairs. The lawyers were thrilled. The case was ironclad when it went to court.

Not in that evidence? Any mention of the tracking apps Edo had installed on my phone, the ones he used to follow me. The ones he used to read the messages I sent to Alex.

Our little game of chase was best kept private.

About a month after Edo disappeared, someone reported a smear of blood on the cliff face. After that, the remnants of his clothing were discovered, and soon, the police pieced it all together. A tragic accident, they called it. At first, residents demanded the boars be hunted, but as the press began picking up stories about the Mazzas, people started to wonder if the boars had smelled it on him—the evil. They never hurt anyone else, after all. The animals must have known.

They called what happened Justice.

I turn my head when I hear my mom calling to Orfeo to pass her the ball.

Meg Lancaster—Mom—helped me find a psychiatrist I could talk to online and followed up with me about medication. She'd been helping before that, too, when I called her late at night, forgetting by morning. Meg Lancaster hasn't always been a perfect mother, but damn if she isn't trying.

My dad is on the other side of the drive, by Matteo's house—our house—plucking a ripe apricot off the sagging tree that shades the front windows and tossing it once into the air on his way to join Jasper and Francesco where they are playing cards, *le piacentine,* at the other end of the table.

Tibi touches my belly. "How are you feeling?" She's the only person Matteo and I have told.

I'm actually pregnant this time, barely two months along. Giorgia knew before I did. My glowing skin, she said, rocking her perfect baby in her arms when I stopped by. She thanks me every time I see her. I don't know what she thinks I did.

"Good," I tell Tibi.

She eyes my dirty fingernails. "Are you sleeping well?"

"Better than I have in a decade."

And it's true. Because I know now that I'm more powerful than my nightmares.

Acknowledgments

This part always makes my heart want to burst a little bit.

Thank you to Caitlin for her thoughtful feedback and for making me pause to enjoy the beauty of a word (unison) or question the sense of one (ingenious) along the way. I'm so grateful I get to lean into whatever this is with you and use your art as inspiration for cool characters, too. To Rebecca and Danielle, would these words exist without you? Would they have ever multiplied into whole scenes and then chapters? Maybe. But they certainly wouldn't have been as much fun to write. I am so lucky to know you both, and my stories are absolutely the better for it. (Coincidentally, I'm the better for getting to enjoy yours.) Thanks, Gia, for capturing the rotting heart of this novel on the cover and still making it beautiful. Huge shout-out to all my early readers. I appreciate you taking the time to make it through before the proofreading, and apologize for the flair-ing nostrils, brown-shuddered windows, and general lack of apostrophes. I also appreciate your enthusiasm, without which I wouldn't be enjoying this process nearly as much (because it turns out I really care a whole lot bout what you think).

To anyone who reads this: sharing stories with people, connecting with readers, and being part of this space with so many cool humans is a big part of what I love about storytelling. Thank you for being here.

And though not based on a true TRUE story, this novel does incorporate some lived experiences. To the Fall '07 study abroad crew: what the hell was that?! Thanks to everyone who helped pour the grappa and light the candles, and who remembers—or maybe hopes to forget—THE DEAD LIVE.

And thanks to Alba and Claudio for putting up with us.

Photo by Gisella Prencipe

BONNIE CALLAHAN was born in Tucson, where she went on to study Classics and Italian at the University of Arizona. After seven years in Italy, she is back in the Sonoran Desert, where she lives with her Italian study abroad sweetheart, their two kids, and a few bilingual pets.

CONNECT ONLINE

bonniecallahanbooks.com

authorbonniecallahan

Made in the USA
Coppell, TX
24 February 2026

72321111R00206